VACANT SPACES

BY

MARK ANDREW WARE

© 2002 by Mark Andrew Ware. All rights reserved.

No part of this book may be reproduced, stored in a retrieval system, or transmitted by any means, electronic, mechanical, photocopying, recording, or otherwise, without written permission from the author.

ISBN: 1-4033-7887-8 (e-book)
ISBN: 1-4033-7888-6 (Paperback)

This book is printed on acid free paper.

PROLOGUE

Her eyes fluttered open to a terrific pain between her legs. A burning, piercing heat that sent sharp stabs of agony throughout her abdomen. There was hot breath at her neck and ears, wet with the sounds of pleasure. That was when she first realized that there was someone on top of her, pressing down on her. She tried to move and could not. Her fingers wiggled but her hands were held above her head. Rope cut into her wrist as she struggled. A voice inside her head laughed. "Don't fight it," it said. It sounded old and familiar and tainted with evil. Now heavy, throaty grunts of hot breath came quicker from the attacker on top of her and the pain worsened. She was held down by the person's weight, sweaty skin sticking to her own. She wanted to scream but could not. Her head shook violently. Objects began to come into focus. She could make out shapes in the room as her eyes adjusted to the darkness and she realized then that she was in her own bedroom, in her own home. Somewhere in the house she heard the faint voices of her mother and father drift down the hallway. My God, did they not know what was going on! Could they not hear their own daughter being brutally raped right under their noses? This must be a dream, she kept repeating in her head. It must be a terrible nightmare. But the sharp pangs that now seized her body assured her that it was indeed real. The voice inside her head laughed in unison with the sickly sweet moans of the intruder and as she tried to scream one last time she made the most horrifying discovery of all. She was smiling herself. Her own lips were twisted into an evil grin of pleasure. And then the darkness wrapped itself around her in a cold embrace and took her.

PART ONE

DELIVERANCE

Mark Andrew Ware

CHAPTER ONE

The brown manila envelope protruded out of the mailbox, dotted with specks of June rain. Forbidding clouds had gathered in the east and were now pressing down hard on the city of Atlanta. Ashley Malone grabbed the mail, holding the manila envelope over her head with one hand and her pink terry-cloth robe closed with the other just as a gust of wind lashed out at her, whipping the ends of her robe up revealing white cotton panties speckled with little yellow flowers. As she took the steps up to her front porch two at a time she made a self-conscious glance behind her, to the looming Catholic Church that jutted from the sodden moist earth like a living entity. The gray stoned face creeped with ivy and its stained glassed eyes seemed to be watching her, disapprovingly. The aged and historic structure sat just across a tree lined, two-lane street, lurching upward from a perfectly manicured lawn. On the days when the sun was shining it would cast a great shadow over her tiny, red brick house, and the huge concrete cross that crowned it would eclipse the sun and hang there with a dark faced silhouette watching over her home as if enveloping her and her young son in its safety. Ashley liked the feeling. It was in fact why she had rented the small house from the Church nearly five years ago, when her son was only four. And the Church had had no qualms about taking an unwed twenty four year old mother in. She smiled to herself as she entered the house; wonder what they would think now if they just saw her flash the entire neighborhood?

She lay the mail down on the foyer table as she shook out her long brown hair. Damp from the drizzle it clung limply to her face, contrasting with the paleness of her cream colored skin.

From here she could see her son, Austin, in the living room. He sat cross-legged on the floor in front of the cold, unused fireplace. Sprawled before him over the beige carpet was a one thousand-piece puzzle only just beginning. Austin worked meticulously and unhurried. He would stay like this for hours sometimes if left alone, working steadily, one piece of the puzzle at a time, until all the pieces fit. Thinking of this made Ashley smile a sad smile. Perhaps that is what Austin was doing on a higher level too, trying to make all the pieces fit. He was born autistic; never speaking a word, withdrawn into a world of his own. Ashley used to go to a support group for mothers of autistic children, until at one of the meetings when one of the mothers had said; "You want to know what's most frightening? It's not when they bang their heads or make awful noises, it's the fact that they're a body with no soul. Like a robot." Soulless, that was the word the woman used. Ashley couldn't fathom anyone saying that about his or her own child, and so she never went back.

As she looked at her son now, a normal looking nine year old boy, his brown hair disheveled atop his head, she knew there was a soul in him. There was a look in his eye, a knowing look. Maybe everyone else

Vacant Spaces

was just on a lower level and Austin was waiting for them to catch up.

The shrill ring of the phone in the quiet house snapped Ashley out of her thoughts. Austin didn't seem to even hear it. She picked up the receiver on the second ring to hear hoarse coughing on the other end of the line.

"Hello," she spoke into the mouthpiece when the coughing had finally subsided.

"Miss Malone?"

"Yes this is Ashley Malone," she pushed a stray strand of hair behind her ear.

"I'm so sorry to bother you so early in the morning like this…" a kindly old woman's voice said. "…this is Sister Margaret with the church."

"Oh yes Sister, how are you?"

"Have a bit of the flu I'm afraid dear," and then, as if on cue the coughing started again. This time it came in long wheezes. Ashley waited patiently until she heard Sister Margaret clear her throat. "Excuse me for that dear. Anyway, the reason I was calling you is because Father Malley would like to speak with you today, say around two. Is that possible Miss Malone?"

Ashley's mind immediately thought of the 'panties' incident and had to stifle a giggle at how silly she was to be so paranoid. "Yes Sister, two will be fine. I'll see you then." She expected to hear a goodbye, but instead got another earful of crackling, wheezing coughs. She cradled the receiver and went back to the mail on the foyer table. There lay a sales paper, a telephone bill and the manila envelope.

She picked up the manila envelope and turned it over. It was very light. There was no return address in the corner and her own name and address was rather crudely typed with what must have been a very old typewriter. She noticed that the type-set looked odd and all the "A's" had there tops cut off, as if that particular key of the typewriter had been overused for many years. Just as she was about to open the mysterious package, she got a forbidding feeling that she was not alone, a feeling that someone was watching her. She saw movement out of the corner of her eye, Austin. He was standing in the entryway of the foyer looking intently at her. His dark and monastic eyes pierced her like a thousand needles.

"Oh Honey," she said, pushing his hair across his forehead and out of his eyes, "you must be starving. Lets go into the kitchen and fix some breakfast." She kissed him lightly on the head and as if on command he followed her out of the tiny foyer. The envelope was left lying on the table, forgotten for the moment.

As the aroma of bacon frying and coffee brewing filled the kitchen Ashley's mind kept wandering to her two o'clock meeting with Father Malley. With the church itself being her landlord, Father Malley was like the superintendent, and not once in the years she had lived there had he called to have a meeting with her. In fact it was always the other way around. For one reason or another she seemed to always find herself calling on the priest. The toilet is broken or there's a leak. Then there was the time a poor squirrel had died under the house and the smell had become unbearable. Usually Father Malley would simply send the caretaker of the church grounds to solve these minor annoyances, but sometimes he would take care of them in person, and this led Ashley to stop and consider her motives for calling for things she could probably fix herself. Her intentions were completely wholesome mind you, this she knew. Even if the good Father wasn't a man of the cloth he was not in the least her type. No, she believed her neediness stemmed from lack of conversation. Being in a house with a nine year old who doesn't speak, and working from home as a medical billing agent, she longed for that closeness of human contact. God, she thought to herself, he probably thinks I'm a loon. Then she realized she had not thought it to herself at all but had said it out loud. She looked at Austin who was shoveling a forkful of scrambled eggs into his mouth. Had he heard her he showed no signs of it. "Maybe I am a loon," she said aloud on purpose this time.

The front entrance to ST. Andrews Catholic Church was dead bolted shut, so Ashley wandered around to the side of the awesome mid nineteenth century structure. There she knew she would find the church's office annex. It was a more recent addition to the building, within the last fifty years or so, and Ashley was glad that it was hidden from sight from the main road because it jutted out like a cancerous tumor on an otherwise flawless body.

Inside the annex she was met with an impeccable silence. A narrow carpeted hallway revealed a row of doors to her right and left. She walked softly as if she might disturb the peacefulness; interrupt the mode of tranquillity the church had established. The first door on her left boar a small gold plate marked "Office". She entered.

"Hello Miss Malone, so nice to see you again." Sister Margaret stood greeting her while spraying disinfectant into the air. She sprayed so much in fact, that the room began to cloud with the aerosol, and Ashley inhaled a lungful before she realized it. She stifled a cough as she tasted the disinfectant in her mouth.

"Right on time." the Sister said sitting down at her desk and looking at the wall clock. "Two o'clock on the dot."

Ashley tried to smile as the nun took a tissue from a box on her desk and blew her nose. Talk about disturbing the peace. She watched as Sister Margaret tossed the used tissue into the already overflowing trash can beside her desk. The tissue rolled off the top and toppled to the floor.

"You know they say they have lotion in them, but I can't tell." The nun picked up the box and examined it through her reading glasses.

"Is Father Malley in his office?" Ashley questioned.

"Yes, go right on in."

Ashley smiled at the Sister as she headed toward the office door. She said, "I hope you feel better soon."

"God bless you child." Sister Margaret replied.

Inside the office she found Father Malley sitting behind a heavy cherry-wood desk riddled with papers and the largest bible Ashley had ever seen. He greeted her, shook her hand lightly and motioned for her to have a seat. The priest was a short man, about five-five. Reddish blonde hair topped his head but it was thinning, which actually suited his small, thin frame.

He looked at her for a long moment as if trying to find the right words to start. Ashley sat uncomfortably in the squeaky leather wingback chair.

Finally he said, "Miss Malone in all the years of the church I don't believe we have ever had a better tenant living in our rental house than you."

Ashley smiled, almost thanked him for the compliment when she realized it was a lead in for something more, something she didn't want to hear. "I don't think I like where this is going." she replied instead.

Father Malley shook his head and let out a sigh. He was avoiding eye contact with her before but now he looked her square in the face. "The church has found itself in some recent financial trouble and had to compensate by relieving itself of some of its assets. The property your living in was the first to go. I'm afraid it was sold to a private buyer who doesn't wish to lease it out."

His words hit her hard and left a ringing in her ears. She wasn't grasping what he'd said right off. She had to keep repeating it to herself. The room wavered, her stomach did flip-flops and she really thought that she was going to be sick right there on the desk, all over the big bible and everything. Her mind kept going back to Austin, right now in their tiny house snuggled in his bed, safely taking a nap. She was homeless. Well, maybe not quiet homeless, but it was the safety of the church she'd sought after when she rented the house. Safety for her son and for herself.

"Miss Malone? Are you going to be all right? Can I get you anything, some water perhaps?"

"N-NO," stuttering, she stood, then sat back down.

Now the priest looked shaken too. He hadn't expected a reaction quiet like this. A shock yes, of course, but he was afraid the poor girl may actually faint. "Of course you'll have ninety days rent free to compensate the, uh, the inconvenience," he tried to sound cheerful. "And your security deposit will be returned."

"Yes, of course. Thank you." Oh what a thing to say, she thought. Here he is kicking her out and she's thanking the man. Thanking him after putting her and her son out on the street like yesterday's trash!

He smiled and added, "Maybe the church can help you find other arrangements." At that Ashley stood and held out her hand. The Priest took it hesitantly and Ashley told him that she really must be going now because she had a million things to do and her son was all alone in the house, and oh yes, don't worry about her the least little bit. As she left the building and inhaled the fresh air that only comes after a rain, her head quit spinning. The way she rambled on and left the office so quickly she was sure that Father Malley thought her a stark raving lunatic. She didn't care though, all she knew was that she had to get out of that office, out of that building before she became ill. She walked hurriedly across the street, her feet smacking puddles along the way. She felt the need to be in the safe confines of her home, if only for a short time longer.

That night, after she put Austin to bed she sat on the sofa in silence. Only a side-table lamp was on and its conflagration caused long shadows to stretch out like fingers toward the dark paned glass of the

Vacant Spaces

windows. Beyond the night Ashley could see the faint glow of the stained glass windows of the church as if it were sleepily nodding off to dream. This made her yawn although she knew she could not sleep. Her mind was racing a hundred miles an hour. What would she do? She didn't even have the will to begin to look for a new place to live. Her hand absently went to the rosary she wore around her neck. A gift her father had gotten her from one of his business trips to New York some years ago when she was away at college. She let her finger caress the necklace, fondle the wooden beads and the movement caused her to catch her reflection in the window. She looked slovenly. The shadows did little to soften her worried expression. Maybe the best thing to do tonight was to just go to bed and start a new day tomorrow. Then her mind went to the mysterious envelope she had received this morning. With the day's events it had completely slipped her mind. She went to the foyer table and brought the package back to the sofa with her. Flopping down onto the cushions she examined the outside of the envelope one more time before tearing into it. Inside, to her surprise, was the New York Times. Well actually it was page 3b of the New York Times. Near the bottom was a small article circled in black magic marker. It read: Still no leads in the disappearance of Susan Bishop of 311 Beech St. The victim of an apparent home invasion, it is still unclear if Miss Bishop was abducted from her residence or simply never returned home since the break in. Neighbors in the building say they neither heard nor saw anything unusual the night of the break in but found the door forced open the next morning. It is still unclear as to what properties if any were taken. Miss Bishop had no relatives to contact but friends and neighbors are very concerned for her safe return. They are asking that if you have any information pertaining to this case to please call 555-6247.

Ashley let the paper fall into her lap. She was wrong when she thought this day couldn't get any worse. Susan Bishop missing. My God, poor Susie, she thought. She had to do something. Susan Bishop was her best and lifelong friend. They played together as toddlers and were inseparable all through school. In college they where roommates and even kept in close contact when Ashley had become ill right before graduation. As fate would have it, Susan went on to graduate and got a dream job in New York while Ashley had still been recuperating. Afterwards, Ashley had gone back to college and become pregnant, her father died and her mother sold the house, so any forwarding address Susan would have surely sent must have gotten lost in all the commotion, never making it to Ashley. Still, Ashley had been determined to find her old friend. Checking telephone directories for New York and asking old mutual acquaintances, but her efforts where to no avail. And now the possibility that she may never see her friend again was too much to bear.

She picked the paper up and looked in the right hand corner. May 23. It was two weeks old. Picking up the envelope she held it upside down and shook it but nothing fell out. She peered inside. Empty. Who would send her this? She knew no one in New York. Definitely knew of no one that would send her an anonymous package. Was it Susie herself perhaps?

Vacant Spaces

No. Even if Susie did want to fake her own disappearance she would never have been so cruel as to make her best friend worry like this. Could it have been from the person that abducted her then? But how would they get her address, and what would they hope to gain? She had no money, save a small insubstantial trust fund her Father had left her when he died. She read the article once more. If you have any information pertaining to this case please call 555-6247. Ashley looked at the clock on the wall. 11:05. Was it too late to call? She didn't know the time difference in New York. She went to the telephone and picked up the receiver, hesitated, and then dialed the number.

The phone rang several times and Ashley was just about to hang up when she heard a faint and muffled "Hello?"

Again she hesitated and then, "I'm sorry, I may have the wrong number. I was calling about Susan Bishop." She heard the person on the other end clear their throat suddenly.

"Yes you have the correct number, this is Mrs. Winthrop," a kindly old woman's voice said and again cleared her throat.

"I read the article in the paper and I guess I just assumed that the number I was calling was for the police station," Ashley stated to the old woman.

"We're all friends of Susan's here," Mrs. Winthrop replied. "I'm her landlord and friend, and well you know the police never do anything. Why poor Susan could meet her fate by the time they got off their asses and so we, that is, myself and other tenants in the building, offered our numbers instead. Do you have any information dear?" she probed.

Ashley sighed, "No I'm afraid not. I was actually hoping she would have turned up." She felt a sinking feeling in her stomach and found that she was trembling.

"Are you a friend of hers then?"

"Yes," Ashley said and nodded. She could feel tears tugging at her eyes, burning.

"Then you're just the person I need to talk too. I'm in quiet a predicament I'm afraid."

Ashley wiped tears that tried to escape from her eyes. "I don't understand."

"No of course you don't dear, how could you? You see poor Susan has been missing for nearly three months now and I'm only the property manager. The owner, a nice man though he is, is also very business savvy and well, do you see where I'm going with this Miss…?"

"Malone. Ashley Malone. And no, I'm afraid I don't Mrs. Winthrop."

"Well let me just lay it out on the table then. The owner didn't know Susan. To him she's just another tenant who ran out on the rent."

"Oh Susan would never do that," Ashley interjected.

Mrs. Winthrop sighed. "You and I know that Mrs. Malone-it is Mrs.-isn't it?"

"Miss," she replied.

"We know that Miss Malone but the landlord is ready to set her belongings out on the street."

Vacant Spaces

"But he can't do that!" She was suddenly furious. The nerve of some people. Treating Susan like she wasn't even a person, the same way they treat Austin.

"Oh but he can. And he will, I'm afraid." The kindly old woman continued. "That's why I thought you could help me, if you two were close, I mean."

"Lifelong friends," Ashley stated, absently staring into space, her mind reeling with scenes from the past. The two of them snow sledding…double dating. Susan's having gone into the hospital for her appendix. College, and then, Susan standing over Ashley as she lay sick in bed on a visit home from college. But when was that exactly? She couldn't quiet remember. She pushed the thought from her mind.

"Good, good," Mrs. Winthrop continued. "Then perhaps you can come by and pick up her things. I must warn you there's a lot. Some costly things too, antique furniture and the sort, not too mention all of Susan's clothing and personal belongings."

"I'm sorry," Ashley said, "I'm afraid I haven't been very clear with you, I live in Atlanta."

This seemed to catch the sweet old lady off guard. There was a moment of silence and then, "Oh, maybe I could have her things shipped to you then? It will cost a pretty penny but I will gladly pay it out of my own pocket. For Susan, you know?"

This time it was Ashley who was caught off guard. Of course she would love to store Susan's things. She would do anything for her friend, and this sweet old lady was willing to pay out of her pocket to help Susan. Ashley was sure it would cost a pretty penny indeed for the woman to ship a truck full of antiques and properties across states, but Ashley had nowhere to keep herself and her son at the moment, much less an apartment full of furnishings. But how could she explain that to this woman? This perfect stranger.

"Miss Malone, are you still there?"

"Yes," she answered back into the receiver. "But I'm afraid I can't help you, Mrs. Winthrop. You see I'm looking for a place to live too, me and my son…'

"Oh, I see," the old woman said sadly. "I guess I was just hoping Susan would come back, you know. The police didn't even look for clues. And now if she does turn up, she'll be homeless. All the things she's gathered over the years thrown out."

"Like yesterday's trash," Ashley said softly.

"Exactly, dear."

"I really am sorry, I wish there were something I could do."

"Perhaps there is dear." Mrs. Winthrop's voice sounded suddenly different, and Ashley had the strange sense of preamble, as if this conversation were a prelude to something, a beginning she was stumbling toward.

Later that night as Ashley Malone lay in bed, snuggled beneath the cocoon-like warmth of her covers, she thought about what Mrs. Winthrop had suggested she do. Ashley giggled at the sheer thought of it. It was utterly ridiculous, really. The old woman had in all seriousness suggested that Ashley move to New York and live in Susan's apartment. Ashley had to admit, though, the old lady was quiet a salesman. Ashley could live in the brownstone apartment for the same rent she paid now. Even though the landlord would be taking a loss, Mrs. Winthrop knew she could

Vacant Spaces

convince him in exchange for Ashley taking care of Susan's personal properties. In the case that Susan did return, then Ashley could move to another unit in the building that would be available soon.

It was quiet the pitch. No matter what excuse Ashley threw up Mrs. Winthrop had an answer. No, a child is not a problem at all, everyone in the building loved children and Mrs. Winthrop herself loved to baby-sit. Not to mention there is a park close by. You need the feel and safety of a Catholic Church nearby for pure psychological reasons and so your son can grow up Catholic, you're in luck! A priest lives in the apartment just under the one you would be in.

Ashley had to admit the offer was appealing and everything seemed to suggest that this was fate stepping in to help her. Her job would be no problem since she didn't work for a local branch and billed nationwide, no her job wasn't the problem at all, it was portable, it could go wherever she went. The idea of a furnished home was quite tempting seeing how the church owned all the furnishings here. She and Austin would be left with just their clothes and a few personal belongings. And last, she could not use her son's autism as an excuse. New York had some of the best specialist in the field of child psychology, she should know, she had done enough research. But maybe the most important reason of all that the move seemed so tempting was the opportunity to help Susan. Maybe she could find some clue that the police overlooked, if they looked at all. She didn't think it strange that the people in the brownstone were so concerned for Susan; rather, she would think it was strange if they were not. Susan had always been the most popular. You know the type, good at anything they do. But Susan wasn't like most—she was genuinely kind. She would do anything to help anyone, especially Ashley. And now here she was. Needing Ashley's help. There was no reason whatsoever that Ashley couldn't go-except one. She was afraid. And that was reason enough for her. She hoped Susan would understand and forgive her. It was just too big of a step all at once. She needed baby steps. Ashley's entire life after her illness in college had been sheltered. And Austin's birth and autism had only added to her reclusive life. She had never traveled, really. She never dated, never did anything daring or dangerous at all. Ashley wasn't like Susan was. Susan was adventurous and everything she touched turned to gold, as if she were charmed. But not Ashley, she was only sheltered and definitely not charmed. That is why she had told Mrs. Winthrop no. It was simply out of the question. Ashley sighed. It was too much to think about for one day. She needed sleep and knew that it would be hard to find. Reaching over, she turned on the small clock radio and tuned it to an "oldies but goodies" station. Music always helped her to drift off. She adjusted the volume and sank back into the pillows. Sleep came quicker than she thought and the dreams came even faster than that.

In her dream Ashley was in a dimly lit room. It was long and narrow and the ceilings hung low. Someone was on the other end of the room but she couldn't make out whom. "Susan, is that you?" she asked, her voice breaking. She was filled with an inexplicable fear. She listened but heard only her own breathing and the creak of a floorboard behind her.

Vacant Spaces

She spun around and instantly shielded her face with her hands as someone leapt at her, knocking her to the ground. The dark figure held her down with his weight. She couldn't move, and then she couldn't breathe as he placed his hands around her throat and began to squeeze. Her eyes began to roll back in her head and she could see who the person standing at the other end of the narrow room was. It was Austin, her son. The boy stood there as if nothing was happening. Not even this she thought, not even this will make you snap out of it? Then another dark figure appeared behind her son. Susan! The hands around Ashley's throat were squeezing tighter now. Her lungs felt as if they were on the verge of exploding. Why wouldn't Susan help her? For God's sake! She was dying and Susan wouldn't even move. Why? She would help Susan if she could…and then she woke up.

Ashley's heart was beating fast and sweat beaded her forehead. White linen bed sheets twisted around her like tentacles. She would help Susan. She would. And if it meant moving to New York to do it then she would do that too. She would phone Mrs. Winthrop first thing tomorrow. She fell back and let her head sink down into the pillow. All was calm now. A car passed by on the street outside and its headlights caused fleeting shadows to dance across the walls and ceiling. She felt sleep coming again as the bells of ST. Andrews began to toll midnight.

The radio's music was the last thing Ashley Malone heard before she was lulled off to the land of dream.

Peter, Paul and Mary were leaving on a jet plane.
They didn't know when they'd be back again.

CHAPTER TWO

"Your what? Oh you must be joking!" Loretta Malone said, leaning back uncomfortably in her chair at the kitchen table. She sipped on a cup of steaming hot coffee, grimaced, and then added more sugar. "I mean really, Ashley. What would anyone in their right minds want to move to New York for in the first place? Much less take a nine year old boy in Austin's condition?"

Ashley watched, bemused as her mother shoveled spoonful after spoonful of sugar into her coffee. Her mother always referred to Austin's autism as 'his condition.' "Honestly, Mom, if you don't like coffee why do you drink it?" She walked to the kitchen sink and grabbed a towel and began wiping up the granules of sugar her mother had left in her wake. If you ever wanted to find her mother, she thought to herself, just follow the trail of sugar. Thank God she wasn't diabetic.

"Stop trying to change the subject," Loretta didn't miss a beat. "Let's discuss this further."

Loretta Malone was a thin woman. The sharp features of her face only accented her bony structure. Her nose was narrow as was her chin. She kept her hair in a held-just-right-by-enough-hairspray-so-it-will-never-move-type of seventies fashion. Ashley wasn't sure what that type of hairstyle was called, then or now, but she thought her mother was probably once a very beautiful woman. And if you wanted to know the truth, probably she was once very kind and supportive too, just not as long as Ashley had known her.

"I'm not trying to change the subject, Mom, because there's nothing to discuss here. Austin and I are moving to New York and that's final. I am a grown woman. I've made a decision and I'm sticking by it." She talked while she poured herself a cup of coffee, sloshing it over the side of the 'I LOVE MY MOTHER' mug. She rolled her eyes and thought, Really, wasn't life just a little too ironic sometimes? "Now I didn't call you over here to discuss or argue the matter with you. I just thought you may want to spend some time with Austin before we go." Again she used the towel to clean up the mess on the table.

Her mother rose and walked to her, took her by the shoulders and looking at her said, "I just don't want you to do anything too impetuous. You haven't seen Susan Bishop in almost ten years, this just doesn't feel right." Then she hugged her daughter. Her mother rarely made these sorts of displays of affection and Ashley was taken aback at first, then fell into the embrace. God! How she had always needed this from her mother. Still, something was quite off here. The look that was on her mother's face when Ashley told her earlier that Susan Bishop was missing was nothing less than frightening. The woman had gone pale and began to stutter, almost incoherently, about why Ashley simply could not move.

Just as quickly as she had started it her mother ended it now, pulling away and straightening her clothes. She patted the air around her hair, never actually touching the hair itself. My God did she actually think it would move out of place? Ashley knew that, much like her mother's emotions, her hair was impenetrable.

"Okay, enough talk then. If I can't change your mind and you want to leave me here all alone that's fine. But mark my words young lady, three months. I give you three months in a city like that and you'll be running back. Now, where's my grandson. I've got a full day planned for us at the historian museum. They have the dinosaur's bones display this month."

"He'll like that." Ashley said softly. "He's in his room." She stood with her back to Loretta, staring out the kitchen window. She heard her mother step closer behind her, felt the heat of her hand as it hesitated just over her shoulder, thought she was going to lay it there, say something, and then felt her pull away, thinking better of it. Ashley sighed as she heard her mother walk out of the room.

Maybe her mother was right. Two nights ago in the wake of that horrible nightmare, moving to help Susie seemed like the right thing to do, but now, she just wasn't sure. Mrs. Winthrop had been delighted, on the other hand, assuring her that she was making the right decision and that she would absolutely love New York City.

"Oh the beautiful skyline and the rush of the city. It lets you know that you're alive." The old woman had said. Ashley needed that, to feel alive. She had felt dead for such a long time now, as if she may be sleeping and this everyday routine of a life she was living was just a dream-induced haze.

"And the apartment,' Mrs. Winthrop had continued, "The apartment is so, well, beautiful too. Beautiful is the only word to describe it. I just know you'll love it here with us, dear. It's as though you were meant to be here."

"It certainly seems that way." Ashley had replied. She was feeling it too. It did seem as though something great and unknown was pulling at her, tugging her in one direction and one direction only. Too many things had happened at once to consider it coincidence. First, the Church selling the house she was in, then the mysterious envelope, and finally Susan's disappearance. Well, actually all of that was backwards. It started the other way around. Susan's disappearance was first. Regardless, she felt as though she were stumbling towards something. As if by opening that envelope and making that first initial phone call to Mrs. Winthrop, she had somehow set into motion a chain of events that would ultimately lead her to her destiny—or, perhaps, her destruction.

She shook the thoughts from her head. She had to quit thinking and worrying about herself so much. It was Susie that needed her help right now. God, she prayed silently, please let her be all right, safe and alive somewhere. Poor Susie, as Mrs. Winthrop kept calling her. It was true though. For all of the popularity and success that Susan Bishop had seemed to acquire, there went along with them a lot of heartache. She had lost both of her parents right after she started college; a horrible accident that could have killed Ashley's parents instead.

It was shortly after her Father had returned from a business trip. The one were he brought her the antique rosary as a gift. He and her mother had planned a trip to Mexico, the first they would have taken together in years. Her mother was furious when her father got called away on a business emergency. Susan's mother had begged Loretta for the tickets, wanting to offer them as a surprise honeymoon to her husband, the honeymoon they had never gotten to have. How could Loretta Malone have said no to such a thing? The woman even offered to pay double. Loretta gave them the tickets for free, as a gift. They paid with their lives instead. Shortly after take off the plane crashed, killing everyone on board. Susan was devastated, as was Ashley. It was not long after that that Ashley became ill and had to return home from college. Her memory was always hazy about that time. Her mother said it was because of the stress and Ashley always thought, if anyone was under stress it was poor Susie.

 Her mind snapped back to the present as she heard a door open and close at the other end of the house. It was her mother and Austin leaving. Not even a goodbye.

The next two weeks flew by. It was as though she never had enough time now that it was limited. Ashley hadn't remembered moving ever being so hectic.

 Mrs. Winthrop had discussed everything with the landlord and he agreed on the terms and conditions. Ashley had purchased two one-way tickets in coach for her and Austin. When had it become so expensive to fly? At the utilities company she told them when they should disconnect and left her forwarding address. Boxes. She needed boxes. The people at the grocery store looked at her like she was crazy. "Sorry, we break all of our boxes down and recycle," they said. So she went instead to the "U-MOVE" office and paid for cardboard boxes. Ironically, they were broken down too. When had everything become so damn costly? She was only twenty-nine and felt like she was fifty. But then again, she thought, people who are fifty probably feel the same way.

She wrote a letter to Austin's special school (it was out for summer break) to let them know she would contact them about sending Austin's files to his new school, wherever that would be. There was just too much to do and not enough time. To top it all off, she had not realized that the two of them had accumulated so much stuff. She was trying to decide what to donate, what to throw out, and what to keep. She felt it was unorthodox to throw away anything. Shouldn't it all be donated? Couldn't people with nothing use anything at all? But she knew how snotty thrift stores and so-called help organizations had become lately; even they wanted name brands nowadays. Ashley could just visualize the fashionable and well attired poor and homeless people skirting around the streets of Atlanta, as if they were in a rejected fashion show of life, the streets and alleys their runways. And so the trash pile was growing larger and larger. By the time she had finished, the thrift store and the trash had more belongings than she did.

Thursday they had dinner at her mother's apartment. The mood was sullen but Loretta never uttered a word that would suggest they stay. She did however spread the guilt on thick.

"Thank goodness your father has passed away already…" she said, hand on heart. "…He would worry himself to death otherwise."

Friday the movers came to take her meager belongings away.

And Saturday they flew.

Ashley had a seat by the window. Austin seemed only mildly interested by the flight, although he made less noise than usual, suggesting to Ashley that something was going on inside that head of his.

"Whad'ya think kiddo? Did Mom make the right decision for us? You know you could have a say so in the matter. All you have to do is speak up." Did she sound like her mother? Is that something Loretta would say? "That's okay," she added, "I love you just the way you are." Leaning over she kissed the top of his head, smelled raspberry shampoo and smiled. Out the window she could see the skyline of New York. Mrs. Winthrop was right. It is beautiful. Breathtaking, she thought, and as she peered into the distance her mind went back to the nightmare, someone choking her as Austin and Susie watched. She quickly pushed the memory away as the plane began to descend.

She was doing this for Susie, she reminded herself. She had the best of intentions, she repeated over and over again in her head. Then a little voice slipped in "the road to hell is paved with those."

And Ashley thought about that as she fell thousands of miles an hour towards the earth.

The cab smelled like urine and the cab driver smelled worse than that. He was a plump man with a Brooklyn accent. His face was so red it looked as though he had a severe case of sunburn, Ashley thought it was probably more likely a case of high blood pressure. The man's breath came in short wheezes, as though his breathing were restricted. Ashley watched him. Austin was looking out the window, a thin layer of film and grime put a skin over the glass. He would make noises every time they would pass huge skyscrapers. Not the ordinary oohs and aahs, but grunting noises. This caused the cabbie to keep looking in the rearview mirror at the boy. He saw Ashley watching him watching, nodded, and said, "The kid all right back there?"

Ashley knew he was waiting for her to explain. "He's just fine," she said instead. Her son needed no explanation, especially to a perfect stranger. Besides, with breathing like that this man was in no position to pass judgment.

As the buildings began to get smaller they also began to get more dilapidated. Trash was piling up in street gutters. Graffiti defaced the buildings and shady looking characters stood in door and alleyways. Ashley's heart began to palpitate. She leaned forward, "Are we almost there, yet?"

"Cupplamore blocks," the cabby told her.

She sat back. The next neighborhood didn't seem quiet as bad, but still, you wouldn't want to walk down it at night. Hell, for that matter she didn't want to walk down it in the daytime.

A sudden fear gripped her heart and began to squeeze. Oh what had she done? What had she gotten Austin and herself into? She was a fool. A damned fool! Moving to a city she did not know, taking an apartment she'd never seen. What had she been thinking? Her mother was right. Except it wouldn't be three months before she came running back with her tail between her legs, no. She wouldn't even last that long.

Suddenly the cab seemed to be closing in on her. The hot, smothering smell of urine was making her nauseous. She couldn't find her breath. She tried the handle to the window. It didn't work. Austin's grunts and the cabby's wheezing seemed amplified a thousand times. She needed out of this cab! And then…

"Getting close now," the plump, red-faced man said, turning the wheel sharply, throwing Ashley and Austin into each other. The streetscape outside had changed. Lawns were well manicured. Row houses lined the streets, fresh paint masking their surfaces. Children played nearby, their laughter carried on the breeze that was blowing the branches of the trees that lined the street. The cab passed an elderly man walking a white poodle with a red collar. The neighborhood was beautiful. And just beyond, Ashley could see the beginnings of a well-developed commercial district.

Near the end of the street, the cab began to slow as a majestic, three and half story brownstone dominated the neighborhood. It was bold, perhaps eighteenth century. Great tall and narrow windows peaked upward with wrought iron window guards that were molded and curved with intricate designs and painstaking detail, their tops and bottoms ending in sharp arrow like points. In every corner, sconces and leaves were carved into gray slate above protruding bay windows and modest stone overhangs. Oval copper paned portal windows like nothing Ashley had ever seen before announced the attic. A pitched slate roof with twin towering brick chimneys on either side crowned the magnificent work of art and Ashley thought her heart would stop with the cab as it slowed and pulled up to the curb in front of the brownstone.

"Three eleven Beech Street," the cabby said, hitting a button on the meter. "That'll be sixteen fifty, tip withstanding."

He smiled a rotting teeth smile as Ashley handed him a crumpled twenty-dollar bill from her purse.

She unloaded their bags herself and she and Austin stood at the curb staring in awe at the grand structure.

"You have to be kidding me," she said, suitcase in either hand and realized she was smiling. Of course, Susie would only live in a place such as this. They walked the cobblestone-paved pathway, lined with monkey grass, up to the front stoop. Six granite steps led up to a set of heavy oak doors, stained dark and rich in mocha brown. Mounted in the center of each door, were wrought iron lion's heads with heavy rings clenched in their ferocious jaws. Ashley lifted one of the knockers. It was heavy and cold to the touch. Into the mouth of the lion she thought as she pounded at the door. No answer. She tried the oversized iron knob. It turned and the door opened slowly, creaking hinges announced their arrival as Ashley Malone and her young son stepped out of the wrath of the midday sun and across the threshold into the shadows of the unknown.

CHAPTER THREE

If the outside of the brownstone made one think of an eighteenth century artist's thoughts, then the inside of the building must surely reflect his innermost dreams. The foyer rose around Ashley and Austin Malone, swallowing them in its vast array of rich, warm woods and stone cold marble. The staircase steepled upward, trailed by an impeccable hand carved banister that twisted with deep rivets and curves. An oriental rug draped the steps that curved up and then turned the corner out of sight. Mahogany paneled walls were trimmed with heavy wooden crown moldings that lurched and jutted outward with intricate detailed leaves and vines carved into their faces. The corner moldings were cherubs, naked and beckoning from the shadows of the room. In the center, suspended from the mountain-high copper plated ceiling, was the largest and most amazing chandelier that Ashley had ever laid eyes upon. Its delicate crystal teardrops rained down with a soft amber glow, pyramiding into a thousand tiny facets of light, radiating warmth over the foyer, bathing everything in a deep, rich hue. It floated there, above their heads, like a dimly lit star that seemed to be burning with a life of its own. There were only three doors leading out of the room, all heavy, dark, wooden ones. A small one, half a door really, fixed just under the stairs, spoke of a closet. Another lay at the back wall, and the third just to

Ashley's right, this one displaying a large "A1" on its exterior. Immediately Ashley thought of the steak sauce and her belly growled on cue with threats of mutiny. The food on the plane had nauseated her before she had even had a chance to see it. The smell wafted through the stale air of the cramped coach compartment, mingled with perfumes and aftershaves. Ashley had noticed her senses were going haywire the moment they left Atlanta. Amplified to a sickening degree. Dizzy then, she had passed up lunch and barely maintained the contents of her stomach as Austin wolfed down a thick grayish-brown slice of airline meatloaf topped with ketchup and a side of peas and carrots. Now, though, standing here in the brownstone, inhaling its scents, absorbing its history, her stomach settled, and now raged with hunger. A big dinner later, she thought as she walked to the door and rapped her knuckles against its hard surface.

The door opened silently and with a slight, cool breeze that swept across their faces.

"Well hello there," a kindly old woman said from across the threshold. She was small, about five-five. The same size as Father Malley, Ashley thought. She was old, much older than Ashley had originally suspected. Her head was a puff of hair sprayed curls dyed fall leaf auburn, and her eyes, a fierce green that blazed with a fire of activity and thought behind them. Ashley could barely tear herself away from those eyes.

"You must be the Malones," the woman continued, smiling a perfect row of white teeth smile.

Ashley nodded, smiled herself, closed lipped, suddenly self-conscious of her own dull colored teeth.

"Let me see if I can get this right," she pointed a jeweled finger at them, one of many. "Ashley," she winked at Ashley and then bent down low to face the boy, "and this handsome devil must be Austin Malone. It is so very nice to meet you." The old lady stared so deep and intent into Austin's eyes it made Ashley a little uneasy. Nothing really, just that the glare was a little too long, unwavering, like the look you would give a lover, not a nine year old boy. The thought was broken as the woman straightened and the green flamed eyes were back on Ashley. "I've been rude," she said, and at first Ashley, startled, thought the old woman must have known what she was thinking, but then, "I haven't even introduced myself. I am Harriet Winthrop, and it is a pleasure, I must say, to finally be able to put such a beautiful face with a voice, Miss Malone."

Ashley blushed. She actually blushed.

"Thank you, Mrs. Winthrop, a pleasure to meet you at last too," she replied, burning face and all. Her eyes however, could not help but to wander past Mrs. Winthrop, into the dimly lit apartment beyond. It was like a library. There were books, hundreds of them everywhere, covering bookshelves and tables. Laid about on sofa and chairs, piled in high, precarious stacks that rose skyward and seemed to sway with threats of tumble.

"Quiet a mess, aye dear?" Mrs. Winthrop followed her glance and again the feeling of precognition. "It seems that since my husband passed away, years ago mind you, that reading is the only thing I've left to do. Romance novels mostly, but then, a pretty young thing

Vacant Spaces

like you probably knows all about that." She giggled as the burning returned to Ashley's face.

"No, not really." Ashley said, patting Austin's back, "This little guy is the only man in my life at the moment.

"And a heartbreaker he is too," Mrs. Winthrop said, ruffling the boy's hair. "Would the two of you like some tea, dear?"

Ashley hesitated, looked at their bags, and said, "Maybe later. We're actually really anxious to see the apartment."

The old woman rolled her eyes, "Of course you are. Silly old woman I am. After a long trip like that you'll want to get settled. Just leave the bags dear and I'll get Topples to bring them up in a few."

"Topples?" Ashley asked, puzzled.

"The Mister-fix-it of the building. His real name is Johnny, the owners' drunken brother. Always coming in and falling over everything when he's had one too many. So we call him "Topples", cause he's always toppling over, you see?" she added when she thought Ashley didn't get it. Ashley just smiled and nodded. "Now follow me." The little old lady started climbing the stairs, ancient hand on ancient banister. "I'll give you the five cent tour." And then she was off and out of sight. Ashley took Austin's hand and the two ascended, on the heels of Mrs. Winthrop.

The second landing was only a long hallway. Dim wall lamps did little good lighting the passage and the only real illumination came from a thin curtained window at the opposite end of the hall just past the stairs to the third landing.

"This is Thomas Robinson's apartment," Mrs. Winthrop said, pausing at the first door to her left, a heavy brass "2A" decorated its face. "He's a famous author. Ever heard of him, dear?" she asked.

"No, I'm afraid I haven't." Ashley replied, thinking, she couldn't remember the last time she had had time to read a book that wasn't in relation to autism in one form or the other.

"Don't worry, you will. Three books published. Nothing I read, of course, no romance. Mostly war and bombs, that kind of stuff, you know?"

Ashley didn't know.

"And apartment 2B belongs to Father Jerod our resident priest I told you about. Oh, he's rarely in though, what with the church and his charitable work and all, but I'm sure you two will meet sooner or later." Moving on rather swiftly, Mrs. Winthrop trotted up the second set of stairs. Ashley, still holding her son's hand inhaled deeply and tried to keep up. The energy Mrs. Winthrop had for such an old woman was amazing, Ashley thought, and at the top of the third floor landing she said just that.

"Where do you get your energy?"

"What was that, dear?" the woman looked at her with her head cocked to the side.

"Your energy," Ashley repeated. "I was just remarking on how much energy you have."

"Ah yes," Mrs. Winthrop said raising that jeweled finger in the air again, "comes from clean living. And the occasional good, stiff drink," she chuckled.

Ashley glanced around the landing as Austin slipped his small hand out of hers. There were three doors here and yet another stairway, this one more narrow and dark.

"Your floor, my dear," Mrs. Winthrop began. "And you share it with the Briar sisters. Elizabeth and Lily. Two spinsters. Only a year apart in age, but trying to find out who's the oldest of the two could start a world war." Mrs. Winthrop leaned in close and whispered, "Wonderful women both of them, just lovely. But—" she pointed the jeweled finger to the crack at the bottom of the door of apartment 3A, shadows moved about. "Nosy as all get out."

Ashley tried not too giggle out loud, failed and caused Mrs. Winthrop to loose composure too. The two women laughed until the landlady finally put her hand up and, with barely a straight face, said, "Let us continue with the tour. Now at the end of the hall is a small efficiency apartment. 3C. A young girl lives there. Going on about four months now. She says her name is Cross."

Ashley looked confused, "Says her name is?"

"Yes. I'm not sure if it's her real name. She's nineteen and in one of those 'let's wear black because we feel that way on the inside' stage. I mean really, black clothes, black hair, black eyeliner. I always say a nice auburn could bring out anyone's beauty." The old woman patted her hair and giggled more. "Anyway, a simply marvelous young woman, if you can deal with her rock music. Not really very loud at all."

"I'm sure it will be fine." Ashley said, then, looking around, "Where's Austin?"

"I don't know, he was here just a moment ago," Mrs. Winthrop, looking up and down the hall, replied.

A dark, sinking feeling formed in Ashley's stomach, bringing back some of the nausea she had felt on the plane. "Austin?" she called out. Her voice seemed to echo, bouncing mockingly back at her from the shiny lacquered hard wood floors and the paneled walls. No answer. No, she thought, of course he's not going to answer, he doesn't speak.

Then, there was a sound. Deep, throaty grunts coming from the narrow third floor stairway. The two women moved into action at the same time, the older of the two reaching the stairwell first.

Austin was standing there, about halfway up the flight of twelve, tiny steps, pointing into the darkness beyond. The grunting noises gurgling and rising from his throat didn't sound human at all, but more like a wild animal that has just come upon an intruder. A chill ran down Ashley's spine and Mrs. Winthrop looked at her helplessly at a loss.

"Austin," his mother said softly, almost inaudible. The noise stopped, the boy's hand dropped down to his side and he turned, looked at Ashley, no, past her, and then walked down the stairs.

She didn't know what to say, tried, "I'm sorry for that. He's autistic as I explained to you over the phone—"

Mrs. Winthrop held up a hand cutting her off, "No explanation necessary, my dear. A spirit of adventure in a boy is a good thing." The elderly woman smiled down at Austin who waited outside the door of apartment 3B. "See, already he's prepared to take on another one. Lets join him and take a look at your new home, what do you say?"

Vacant Spaces

Ashley nodded and came down the stairs. "What's up there anyway?" she asked.

"The attic," Mrs. Winthrop replied, and then, "It use to be apartment 4A but the roof has gotten bad in some places. It's been vacant for sometime now. Locked up safe and tight so you don't need to worry about your little adventurer wondering up there."

Ashley smiled, waited as Mrs. Winthrop fumbled with a large ring of keys. She found one, fitted it into the lock, it clicked and she turned the knob. The door swung inward with a creak.

"Just as Susan left it," she said. "Now it's all yours."

Ashley held her breath. Walked in.

"I'll leave you two at it, get the feel of the place, you know. Mr. Topples will be up with your things shortly." At that Mrs. Winthrop left, softly closing the door behind her. Ashley had barely heard her leave.

Susan's apartment, no, Ashley and Austin's apartment, if only temporarily, was gorgeous. One of the bay windows Ashley had noticed from the outside filled the room with radiate light; filtered only through sheer, white drapes. The lightly stained hardwood floors reflected this light, causing a hazy glow that was reminiscent of a dream. The floors looked rich and warm and smelled of lemon-scented polish.

Ashley moved further into the room, let her hand glide across cherry wood tables, brush along the fabric of the broken in camel back sofa, upholstered in earthy, rustic tones of amber browns and sandstone tans. Tiffany lamps crowned each end of the fireplace mantle. Above, in a chipped golden frame was a Monet print. At least Ashley thought it was a print.

The ceilings were high and held a smaller version of the large foyer chandelier in its center.

As Ashley moved through the arched doorways and into the slightly modernized kitchen, Austin found a half finished puzzle at a small breakfast nook table and began to work it.

The master bedroom was spotless. Bed made, digital clock radio glowed red numbers. 4:55. Ashley checked her watch. It read the same thing. She walked slowly over to the closet, feet gliding over oriental area rugs with faded designs. Inside, the large, narrow closet was filled with women's clothing. Shoes lined up against the wall, belts on hooks. Susan's clothes. Ashley could feel the stings of tears coming on. No. She mustn't cry. There was no time for that. She was here to find Susan. To discover what happened to her, and she would. With a determination that she knew was deep inside her she would find Susan Bishop. She would not fail, she could not, she needed her friend, any friend right about now.

She closed the closet door and with it the dreaded feelings seem to leave too.

Ashley moved on.

The bathroom was small but sufficient. The spare room, Austin's room, was sparsely furnished. Only a twin bed, side table with a lamp, and a small dresser decorated the room. That's okay, she thought. We'll just give it our own personal touch. It's like a blank canvass. Suddenly that made her think of Austin, a blank canvass, and she quickly pushed the thought away. Walking back to the living room she watched her son, still working the puzzle. Everything will be

Vacant Spaces

all right, she told herself. Susan would come home and they would all live happily, she thought silently.

Ever after, she added as an afterthought.

At around seven o'clock, just as Ashley was beginning to think about dinner there was a knock at the door. More than a knock, really. It was a pounding under what must be big, heavy hands. Ashley went to the door, started to turn the knob, halted, and said, "Who is it?"

Silence.

"Who's there?" She repeated and still got no reply. Inching the door open slightly she peered out into the hallway. It was empty, but in front of the door sat her and Austin's bags. Mr. Topples she thought. Must not be very social, but then again neither was she. It wasn't that she didn't want to be a part of the world; she just often felt the world didn't want any part of them. Ashley dragged the bags into the apartment. Dinner first, unpacking later.

At first glance the kitchen cupboards looked well stocked, but upon further inspection Ashley found that it was mostly filler items. Sugar, flour, spices and baking soda. No 'real' food. Looks like the big first night dinner she planned would have to be take out. Going to the end table beside the sofa she picked up the telephone. Damn, no dial tone. Austin was napping and she had no idea were the closest restaurant would be.

Minutes later she found herself knocking on the door of apartment A1.

"Well what a pleasant and unexpected surprise," was the greeting she got as Mrs. Winthrop appeared in the doorway.

"I really am sorry to bother you," Ashley started.

"Never a bother dear, an old lady loves company. Where's the boy?"

Ashley smiled and wrinkled her forehead, "That's the thing, Austin's asleep and I need to go out and pick up some things."

"Say no more. Standing in front of you is the world's greatest baby-sitter."

She made a gesture of grandeur with her hands and gave a curtsey bow, both laughed and it relieved some of the embarrassment Ashley was feeling about asking this almost perfect stranger to watch her child.

"I really hate to ask," she added.

"Think nothing of it, dear. You go. Austin will be just fine I swear it. I'll go up now. You'll not need a taxi either by the way. There's a whole street of little diners and a grocery store just two blocks away. Just past the park. Take a left when you leave the brownstone and then again at the corner, you really can't miss it," the old woman directed.

Perfect, Ashley thought and smiled. Everything seemed just perfect. And for the moment her missing friend had slipped her mind.

When she returned home she had two bags of Chinese takeout; sweet and sour chicken and fried rice. In another bag was a six-pack of colas and a candy bar for Austin. She had to sit the bags down as she opened the front door. Light poured lazily into the hallway coming from Austin's new room. He must be awake,

Vacant Spaces

Ashley thought. Good, just in time for dinner, besides, if he slept too long she would have a hard time convincing him to go to bed later. The trip had worn them both out and that combined with the lack of food was already making Ashley drowsy. Perhaps that was the explanation for what happened next, it would be the only reasonable one Ashley could think of.

As she entered the apartment and put the groceries on the breakfast nook table, she heard Mrs. Winthrop's voice. Inaudible words she couldn't make out. But then, that's when it happened, what sounded to her like the old woman asking some sort of question and then...a reply! The voice of a boy! The room seemed to be closing in toward Ashley, dizziness swept over her and she thought she might faint. She had heard it that clearly. Austin? Could it be? She forced herself to move and ran down the hallway. It seemed twice as long now, Austin's door lay partially open and she rushed in and stopped at what she saw. Austin was still asleep. His blankets pulled up to his chin. His rhythmic breathing indicated a peaceful, undisturbed sleep. Mrs. Winthrop sat at the edge of the bed and she smiled as Ashley entered the room.

"Hello dear, I didn't hear you come in."

Ashley found she was breathing hard. Austin was beginning to stir now.

"Are you okay?" the old woman asked. "You look as though you've seen a ghost."

"Or heard one," Ashley said under her breath.

If Mrs. Winthrop heard her she paid no attention. Instead she ruffled Austin's hair and said, "Look, the little man is waking up, just in time for dinner.

Ashley watched as her son stared into the woman's deep green eyes. What had just happened? My God, was she hearing voices? Stress. It was stress, she told herself. A lot has happened, imaginations play tricks. She tried to calm herself, but it was in vain.

"Well," Mrs. Winthrop said rising, "Time for me to go and let you two enjoy your food." Then looking at Ashley she said, "Are you sure you are okay, dear?"

Ashley smiled and nodded, thanked her profusely and invited her to stay for dinner because there was enough, really, and was secretly glad when the elderly lady declined.

Mrs. Winthrop said one last goodbye and then just before leaving added, "I'm so glad you're finally here." Then she was gone. The odd thing is, when the old woman had said the words she was staring directly at Austin, as if it were meant just for him. Ashley had a feeling of unease building in the pit of her stomach. She had suddenly lost her appetite. It's just my imagination, she kept telling herself. It's just my imagination.

Ashley kept her mind from thinking about what she thought she had heard by rummaging through Susan's things. The closets were stocked full of fashionable clothes and shoes. Note pads and pens lined the drawers. In the bathroom, make up and perfumes, shampoos and fingernail clippers where all laid out, just as if Susan was still here, just as if she may return at any moment from a day of shopping or sight seeing. God, how Ashley wished that were true, that her friend would prance into the apartment right this very minute. Ashley sighed as she closed a drawer in the bathroom containing tampons and deodorant. No clues here though, among these cubbyholes and cupboards. No personal notes jotted down, nothing that would tell of Susan Bishop's whereabouts. What was strange, Ashley thought, was the fact that there were no pictures. No photo albums filled with their crazy high school and college antics. No yearbooks or diplomas. As a matter of fact there was nothing very personal in the apartment at all. Could someone have taken these things...the abductor or one of the residents of the brownstone? How silly Ashley felt now, of course the police had already searched for all those things. They would have surely taken photos of Susan to identify her with. And any personal items they would have taken too, to try and find family and friends. Of course, poor Susan had no family. But what about friends other than the people in the brownstone? Maybe the police could tell her something. With a heavy sigh she closed a small side table drawer full of paperclips and pens. Here she was, playing Nancy Drew with her friend's life. Still, there must be something. Ashley rubbed her eyes. They were heavy and gritty. Her search in vain, she gave up for the night, determined to make a game plan tomorrow.

That night the dreams returned. Nightmares she had not had in years were now back, and with a vengeance. They had stopped when she moved into the little house across from the Church, but now, the safety of St. Andrew's was far away, and the dreams seemed to know this. Ashley struggled in bed, twisted in the sheets. Sweat stained her nightgown and beaded her face. Images flashed in her mind. Quick, fleeting things that reeked of rot. A blurred face was close to hers. Horrible breath that smelled of dried blood assailed her nostrils. She was struggling to get free from someone's grasp and could not. She had the uneasy feeling, no, a terrifying knowledge that someone else, a third person, was there too, someone other than the faceless person on top of her, someone more evil. Then, along with the horrible breath came a whispered name, "AZREAL" then, "DAEMONICUS", the words dripped with evil. Ashley woke up screaming. The sheets twisted in knots around her body like bony white hands. She was heaving and the droplets of sweat that covered her body chilled her as the night air hit her moist skin.

At first she did not know where she was, then realization dawned upon her as a fearful chill wiggled down her back followed by a trickle of sweat. Of course, she was in Susan's home, sleeping in Susan's bed, and she wondered, was she dreaming Susan's dreams?

CHAPTER FOUR

For all the terrors that had threatened her in the night, the morning rose with sunshine peeking into the bedroom. One single shaft of golden, yellow ray sliced through an opening in the drapes and rested across Ashley's face. Her eyes fluttered open. She stretched, smiled. Last night's dreams seemed distant in the wake of a new day. Ashley felt vibrant. Yes, it's going to be a great day, the thought skipped through her mind. Then she began making mental notes about the day's activities. First and foremost she would have to go to the telephone company, oh no wait, it was Sunday, she would have to wait until tomorrow, her mother would be worried sick.

Ashley sat up, swung her legs over the edge of the bed and ran her hands through her hair, yawning. The hardwood floors beneath her feet were cool as she stood, slipping into her robe. Her stomach growled angrily and she wished that she had remembered to get something to make breakfast with. Oh well, she and Austin could go out for food. They needed to explore the city anyway.

The steamy hot water of the shower beat away at Ashley's skin, washing away the last of the stress and tension of the previous night. Really, had she actually believed that after nine years Austin was just chatting away with old Harriet Winthrop? What had she been thinking, and rushing into the room like that? She could just imagine what the landlady must have thought of her. And the horrible dreams, they were worse now. But it was just this new environment, she reassured herself. This was a big move, culture shock. All she needed was time to adjust, relax, and accomplish what she had come here to do…find Susan. Ashley lathered up her hair with an herbal shampoo (Susan's) as she laughed at her own foolery. The shampoo smelled earthy and moist, not like most. She rinsed and watched the water and suds drain in a swirl, going round and round in a tiny whirlpool down the drain, and that's when she noticed something shiny. Ashley bent down and dug her finger into the drainage hole. She felt the object, pulled it up and out. It was a small gold cross on a thin gold chain. It swung back and forth as the shower's water hit it sending it into a spin. On the back, a name was engraved, Abigail.

Ashley stepped out of the claw foot tub, laying the necklace carefully on the edge of the sink and dried herself. Wiping the steam from the mirror, she held the gold cross up to her neck. It dangled there beside her own antique rosary. Ashley smiled and wondered who Abigail was, a tenant before Susan? Or maybe she'd been a friend of Susan's. Who could say really how old the necklace was. It could have been stuck in the drain for years, although it didn't look very old. She carried the piece of jewelry into the bedroom and dropped it into her small jewelry box that she had laid out on the dresser. The necklace was forgotten for the moment.

Austin was dressed in an orange T-shirt and jeans. His mother wore jeans too, old, comfortable broken in Levi's, a small hole was beginning to form at the knee.

Vacant Spaces

She wore a light cotton shirt, pale yellow, the color made her look dead and the shirt was a little wrinkled but she didn't care, it was a lazy, first-day-in-the-city-Sunday and she was comfortable. As they descended the landing onto the first floor, Mrs. Winthrop's door opened.

"Good morning lovelies," the old woman greeted them. She held a spatula in one hand and wore an apron that said 'kiss the cook and you might get burned.' "Where do you two think you're off too this morning?"

Ashley smiled, part out of kindness but mostly because of the apron. "We thought we'd go exploring," she nudged Austin, "Right kiddo?" Austin stared at her. "The strong silent type, gotta love them," Ashley said, still smiling at Mrs. Winthrop.

The old woman began pointing her spatula at them. "Well your not going anywhere until you've had a good breakfast, now come on in." She waved the spatula in a—come on hurry up—kind of wave.

"No we really couldn't impose, we can pick up something while we're out."

"Rubbish. You won't be imposing. I've cooked plenty. Besides," the old woman continued, "Mr. Robinson will be joining us, it will give you a chance to meet a neighbor."

Ashley looked at Austin who looked up at her. She could tell that Mrs. Winthrop wasn't going to take 'no' for an answer and her stomach's loud groan was the tiebreaker. They entered apartment A1. The door closed silently behind them.

They were gone, all of them. The books that had filled the room the previous day were now nowhere in sight.

"Is something wrong?" Mrs. Winthrop asked, looking around as Ashley was doing.

"Your books, they're all gone," she said.

"Oh that," the old woman replied with a smile, "Just thought I would tidy up a bit. The books were beginning to have the run of the place."

'Tidy up' Ashley thought, was an understatement. Even the books off the bookcase were gone.

"Now, let's get the table set before Mr. Robinson gets here, shall we?" Mrs. Winthrop said, offering no further explanation for the books.

When the old woman said she had plenty, she wasn't just being polite. She had cooked enough for an army. There were eggs, enough for ten people, waffles with pecans, bacon, sausage, biscuits and toast, an assortment of jellies and jams. Juice and milk and coffee sat about in carafes. Ashley began to wonder if Thomas Robinson might be extremely obese. Surely Mrs. Winthrop didn't cook like this everyday.

"I trust your bags got up to you all right last night?" Mrs. Winthrop asked, laying out silverware. "Topples didn't give you any nonsense, that sort of thing."

"No, actually I never even saw him. He just left the bags at the door."

Mrs. Winthrop looked at her, said, "Probably just as well you didn't meet him, he was drunk as a skunk last I saw him, not worthy of proper company till he sobers up."

Vacant Spaces

"Does he live in the building?" Ashley asked, "I mean I don't remember you mentioning his apartment."

The old woman shook her head, "He lives in the basement, like the rat he is," then she looked at Ashley and smiled. "Oh pay no attention to me dear, I just don't get along with the man. Why once, years ago, he nearly burned the place down, passed out drunk. He was in apartment 3C then, that's when his brother moved him into the basement. Fireproof, you know, what with the cement walls and all. Had it been left up to me I would have booted him out into the street."

"Did he and Susie get along?" Ashley asked, trying to sound casual as she set down plates onto flowered print place mats. Mrs. Winthrop was too quick for that.

"Well he didn't cause her disappearance, I can tell you that. No he was passed out dead drunk that night. Had to help him down to the basement myself. Besides, you know poor Susan, got along with everybody."

Ashley nodded, watched as Austin sat juice glasses out on the table. "Her apartment doesn't look as though it was broken into."

"Strange isn't it? We fixed the door, it was kicked in you know, but everything seemed to be in order. I left everything just exactly as it was too. So the way you saw it is the way it's been since her disappearance." Mrs. Winthrop said, looking at her watch. "Mr. Robinson is always running late."

Ashley continued, "Did Susie ever have any friends over?"

The woman shook her head, "Not that I can remember. No wait. There was this one young gentleman, very nice fellow. I thought they might be an item but then he just quit coming around. Anyway," she added, "that was a long time ago." She looked at her watch again, seemed agitated, Ashley thought. Maybe all the questions were making her sad, thinking of Susan. They must have been very close. Ashley was just about to ask her if she knew anyone named Abigail when there was a knock at the door.

"That must be Mr. Robinson now," Mrs. Winthrop said, taking off the apron and rushing for the door.

Thomas Robinson was an extremely attractive, older gentleman. About Fifty years old, Ashley thought, although he wore his age well. His hair was salt and pepper and he had a full head of it. A well tanned face, natural complexion, and strong sharp features. He wore a light blue button down and trousers and Ashley couldn't help but noticed his well-formed chest and arms barely contained within the clothing.

After the introductions were made they all sat down to eat. Austin ate as though he was famished and Ashley was just a little embarrassed at the noises he made as he slurped down his food.

"So, Miss Malone, what do you think of our little brownstone so far?" Thomas Robinson asked, blue eyes piercing hers.

"Please, call me Ashley," she replied, saw Mrs. Winthrop smile and had the strange feeling the old lady was trying to play matchmaker. "The building's beautiful, so—majestic, I guess is the word I'm looking for."

He chuckled, looked at Mrs. Winthrop then back at her. "Yes it is rather overdone, but a simply wonderful place to live. Have you been to New York before?"

She shook her head no. The question had caught her with a mouthful of food and she wiped her lips with her napkin. "My father use to come here on business a lot before he died. But this is my first time."

"Then maybe Mr. Robinson could show you around sometime. A single man like himself needs to get out occasionally."

Now Ashley knew the old woman was trying to play cupid. She smiled.

The man's blue eyes stared through her again. "Sounds like a splendid idea to me. Anytime your ready."

"Thank you Mr. Robinson, I may take you up on that."

"I can baby-sit Austin," Mrs. Winthrop piped in.

"There is one condition, though," he added.

"What's that?" Ashley asked, not sure if he was flirting or if she just wanted him to be.

"You must call me Thomas. Mr. Robinson makes me think of my father."

The three laughed as Austin noisily sucked up his eggs.

After Thomas Robinson had left, Ashley stayed and helped with the dishes. Austin sat at the kitchen table, assorting a large jar of jellybeans by color.

"You and Thomas seemed to hit it off very well," Mrs. Winthrop said, handing Ashley a saucer to dry.

Ashley took the small plate. It was so thin and frail; she thought it might be expensive china. "Why do I have the feeling I've been set up?"

The older woman looked at her for a moment, "Why, whatever do you mean dear?"

"I mean I think you were playing cupid this morning," she said smiling, set the saucer in the drainer as she was handed another.

"Rubbish. Thomas Robinson comes over for breakfast every Sunday like clockwork. The two of you were bound to meet sometime, with or without my help."

Ashley noticed a slight smirk on the woman's face as she was passed another paper thin plate.

They took in some sights near their neighborhood that day. Antique shops, gift stores. Ashley bought her mother a tiny pewter Statue of Liberty then stopped at a payphone and called her collect. Yes, they had made it okay. No, the apartment wasn't a dump. Yes, she was keeping an eye out for muggers. For goodness sake, Ashley thought, next she'll be asking me if I'm prostituting.

They had lunch outside at a small cafe. Austin fed the birds and dozens and dozens of pigeons kept coming, demanding crumbs. They covered the gray sidewalk like a feathered skin, ravaging the meager handouts. Ashley watched as her son laughed. Strangers passed by and smiled at the mother and son duo. How normal the two of them must look from their eyes, Ashley thought. When the bread was all

Vacant Spaces

gone and the crumbs all gobbled up by the endless stream of hungry birds they left the park, hand in hand. It was beginning to look like rain. They made it back to the brownstone just at dusk. Ashley felt the first tiny pellets of rain begin to fall. In the distance thunder rolled. They rushed in to the safety of the old building. Windows lit up its stone cold face like eyes. Like a thing alive and Ashley noticed it looked kind of creepy at night. She felt as though she was entering the mouth of some great creature. But as intimidating as the outside of the brownstone seemed tonight, her apartment was warm and inviting. Rain had begun to fall heavily outside. The bay window was steamed over and streaked with water.

"Let's get your bath run," she said to Austin. He never turned down a bubble bath and Ashley made sure it always had extra suds. Sometimes they foamed up so high they covered Austin like a mountain made of soap. Bubbles popping. Him smiling. Tonight she added even more.

As her son bathed she fixed herself a cup of hot, herbal tea. The liquid soothed her, warming her throat as it went down. Ashley stood at the bay window, trying to see out. Lightening flashed off in the distance, electrifying the sky. A storm was approaching, heading right for them. She watched for the longest while as angry clouds gathered together like an army of smoke and rolled in, pushed by distant, groaning thunder. Ashley heard splashing in the bathroom and then the slurping sound of the water as it was being sucked down the drain. The small gold cross flashed in her mind, Abigail. She looked down the dim hallway and saw Austin in his pajama bottoms leaving the bath and heading for his room, his back glimmering with tiny droplets of water.

"Goodnight honey," she called to him. He paused, gave a slight nod of the head and disappeared into the dark room, closing the door behind him. He had never been afraid of the dark like Ashley was when she was his age; as a matter of fact he preferred it.

Rain began it's light beat at the window now, even more fog forming at the corners. The angry, dark clouds were right overhead, picking up speed as a north wind drove them. More were right behind these, stretching on as far as the eye could see. Yep, this one would be an all-nighter. Ashley wished she had telephone service. Then she could simply unpack her computer and plug into the Internet and work the night away. That was how she had learned to cope with so many things, pouring herself into her work. That way the silence wasn't so bad, the loneliness didn't stab at her like a knife, at least not until her work was over, and then it would sometimes come rushing over her, hitting her like a tidal wave. Just then a huge clap of thunder and at the same time a loud crashing noise above her snapped her out of her thoughts. Ashley jumped. Hot tea splashed over the edge of her cup, landing on bare feet. What was that? She thought, it sounded like something in the attic but she couldn't be sure, it could have been thunder. Walking to the middle of the room where she thought the noise had come from; she stood still and listened. Nothing. And then another rumbling of thunder made her jump again. Oh for goodness sake, get a grip on yourself. She was heading for the kitchen when she heard the noise again, the crashing sound up in the attic. Not as loud

Vacant Spaces

this time but not masked by thunder either. Ashley paused; she was trembling and had a chill despite the warmth of the room. All was quiet above her, then, over her head, a creaking floorboard. Footsteps. Slow and deliberate, as though they were trying to be silent, walked the space above her. Ashley watched as the chandelier swayed slightly, crystal clinking together like wind chimes. The footsteps stopped directly above where she was standing. Yes, someone was definitely up in the attic. She was aware of her own heavy breathing. She held her breath. Silence. She waited. Still nothing. That's when she noticed something at her front door. Shadows played along the bottom of it, interrupting the light from the hallway. Someone was outside her door. Had she turned the lock? She couldn't remember and she couldn't tell from where she was standing. Ashley waited for a knock. One never came. Inching toward the doorway, she held her breath. Her heart was beating fast and she could feel the blood pumping to her head.

"Who's there?" she called out. Suddenly a rush of footsteps in the hallway as the person fled. Ashley leapt for the door, tried to jerk it open, her fear replaced now with a burning curiosity. She tugged at the door but it refused to budge. It was indeed locked. She fumbled with the latch, slung the door open and stepped out. The hallway was empty but she had just enough time to catch a glimpse of apartment 3A's door closing.

The Briar sisters' apartment.

CHAPTER FIVE

Monday morning and the city awoke.

It was a mad place, and its effects were not unlike that of a drug. There was this certain kind of rush, a building excitement to a climax that never seemed to come. The streets were vast and Ashley explored them in great strides. People with faceless expressions carpeted the sidewalks and storefronts and despite the fact that no one smiled back, she gave a big, wide grin to everyone she passed. Harriet Winthrop was baby-sitting for her and for the first time in a long while she felt free. The city really did make you feel alive. This is how Susan must have felt.

How Ashley wished things had been different. How she wished she had not gotten ill in college and that Susan had not moved without her, she always dreamed of them living here together, Susan with her strength and Ashley with her...well, with her good taste in friends at least, her good judgment of people.

The telephone company was more difficult to find than she had expected. She went two blocks off and had to double back. When she finally entered the building, she found that it was packed like sardines. She stepped into her line, new accounts, which seemed to stretch on forever. She was standing behind a plump, gray haired woman in front of her who smelled of fried chicken and onions. Ashley noticed she was wearing a fast food restaurant uniform, God how that smell must stick to you. She stood and stood but the line never wavered, her feet ached and she wished she had worn more comfortable shoes. Up in the front of the line a man was arguing with the lady behind the window, eventually two uniformed guards came to see about the problem, they led the man away. Ashley let out a heavy sigh, which caused the chicken lady to turn and give her a snarl, the lady, turned back, rolling her eyes. Well, Ashley thought.

Forty five minutes later Ashley made it to the window, the lady behind it was about her age, hair pulled back tightly, glasses, no make up and a big gold name plate that read 'I love my customers' and under that 'Candice.'

"Hi," Ashley smiled stepping up to the glass. Candice did not smile back. "I need phone service at my new apartment," she went on.

It was Candice who let out a heavy sigh this time as she positioned her hands over the keypad of her computer. "Name, address and two forms of I.D., preferably drivers license and social security card."

"Oh," Ashley began to dig around in her purse. "They do it different in Atlanta, that's where I'm from. Just moved here." She kept digging.

"Name?" Candice repeated.

"Ashley Malone, 311 Beech St. apartment 3B." She found her drivers license and pushed them through the tiny slot. "I'm sorry, but this is the only thing I brought with me."

Candice typed her information with incredible speed and picked up the I.D. "I'm sorry, but we must have two forms of identification. Also, if you plan on being a permanent resident you'll need to have a New

York City drivers license." Candice pushed the little laminated card back through the slot.

Ashley could feel her face getting hot, customers behind her were grumbling angrily, "But—" she began to protest but Candice seemed to expect it.

"Thank you for your patience and please return when you have the items we requested. Next."

Ashley shoved the license back in her purse, furious, then—" Miss, excuse me miss," Candice was calling her back. Ashley stepped up to the glass again.

"Yes?"

"Our files are showing an unpaid balance from the previous occupant of that apartment, do you by chance have a forwarding address."

"No." Ashley thought for a moment, and then said, "I will pay the bill, the person is a friend of mine."

Candice shook her head, said, "Okay we'll mail it out to you. You should receive the last bill in the mail within two to three business days."

"Thank you," Ashley said, leaving. The trip had not been a total waste then. She would receive Susan's phone bill. Had her friend made any long distance calls the last few days before her disappearance they would be listed and Ashley could follow up. She left the phone company in high spirits.

She had lunch at a quaint little coffee shop. Its walls were lined with books and paintings. Ashley had an egg salad sandwich on rye, chips and a latte. The atmosphere of the place was tranquil, dimly lit with soft music playing in the background. Ashley took a big bite of her sandwich and began to chew, when—" Well, hello there. Fancy meeting you here," It was

Vacant Spaces

Thomas Robinson standing above her, smiling his million-dollar smile.

Ashley, surprised to say the least, held a—wait-just-a-minute-finger up as she chewed and swallowed. This man seemed to always catch her with food in her mouth. "Thomas, hi how are you?" She asked wiping her mouth with her napkin and taking a sip of her latte. It scalded her tongue but she pretended not to notice. "Please sit with me," she motioned to the chair across from her.

"I don't want to intrude on your lunch," he began, but pulled out the chair anyway.

"You won't be I promise. I hate eating by myself. It's kind of degrading, you know what I mean?" she crinkled her forehead. "Like watching a movie at a theater by yourself, as if you didn't have any friends." Then Ashley thought to herself, wait, I don't have any friends.

"I know exactly how you feel," Thomas told her. "You are, after all, talking to a world renown bachelor."

"By choice?" she quizzed, wanting to know more about this man.

He laughed, which caused small wrinkles to form around his eyes, what a smile. "No, not by choice at all. I guess you could say it's because of my writing. I spend most of my time at home coming up with other peoples imaginary lives that I have no time for my own."

"I understand," she nodded. And she really did, she wasn't just saying that.

"I work from home too, medical billing. Not really the social butterfly my mother had hoped for."

"And your husband?"

Ashley blinked, "What?"

"Your husband, the boy's father. I'm sorry I just assumed someone as attractive as you would be married." He looked deeply at her, interested in what she had to say.

Ashley paused and said, "No. Austin's father and I were never married. A boy I dated in college. I thought it was serious, but then I had to leave college, I became ill you see. When I returned four months later and told him I was pregnant, well, he denied being the father and I never saw him again." As she was telling him this she stared ahead, at nothing really. Her mind reeled in the past, that foggy haze of a time she couldn't quiet piece together. All she had told Thomas was true. It was just a college fling really, just a one time thing with the boy. But a few days later the headaches began, and then…well, she didn't like to think about it, even if she could remember.

"I'm sorry, I hope I didn't bring up any bad memories," Thomas said, still staring at her with that amazing stare. She felt like a bug under a microscope.

"It was probably for the best any way," she replied.

A waiter came to see if they needed anything and Thomas ordered water with lemon. "You said you became ill," he continued with the conversation after the waiter had left the table. "Was it serious?"

That bug under a microscope feeling was beginning to intensify as she replied, "I really can't say, that is, I don't remember much about that time. I was in and out of a comatose state. Everything's a blur really. The doctors think it may be the cause of Austin's autism though. Nothing like it has ever

Vacant Spaces

happened to me since. As my mother says when I ask her about it, leave the past in the past."

"Sounds like a very wise woman, that mother of yours," Thomas said as the waiter returned with his water. He squeezed the lemon wedge, Ashley watched as the juice ran off his fingertip and dripped into his glass. "Here's to your new life with us at the brownstone," he said, raising his glass and sipping.

Ashley did the same, watched as the ice cold water touched his pink lips, his tongue snaked out and licked them quickly, light shining off the moisture of them. Ashley was feeling hot, wished she had something other than coffee to drink but the waiter was nowhere in sight now. She hesitated, trying to think of something to say, anything. She just didn't want him to leave.

"So three books published, huh?" She tried.

"I see Harriet has been singing my praises again," he chuckled. "Do you read a lot?"

She nodded. "Yes, often," she lied. God! What was wrong with her? She felt like a schoolgirl. She smiled, and said, "No, not really, never enough time for it."

This time he laughed wholeheartedly. "An honest person, I can't believe it. Listen would you like to come over to my place for dinner tonight. Just you and I?" he added.

She thought for a moment, said, "I would love too, only I've been away from Austin all day, I really must spend some time with him tonight. Could I get a rain check?" She tried, and hoped desperately that she could.

"Friday then," Thomas smiled.

Thank God, she thought, tried not to answer too quickly and said, "Friday will be great."

He stood up and her heart sank. "What do you have planned for the rest of your day out?" he asked her.

"Well, my next stop is the police station. I want to talk to the detective in charge of Susan's case. See if anything has turned up."

He shook his head, "Great minds think alike."

"What do you mean?"

"That's where I was before I came here. I wanted to make sure they were doing their job."

"And? Anything?" she asked rising a little out of her seat.

He shook his head, "No, I'm afraid not."

She sat back down. Oh well, she still had the phone bill to go on.

"Listen," he began. "Since that part of your plan has already been accomplished, why don't you come see a movie with me?" He smiled a half smile and added, "I hate watching a movie by myself, so—degrading."

She laughed then, left some money on the table with her uneaten sandwich and she and Thomas Robinson walked away together.

As the afternoon dwindled away, they walked back to the brownstone. Ashley had really wanted to go talk to the newspaper reporter who had written the article that was mysteriously sent to her. But after the movie Thomas had insisted on showing her the city, and she was all too willing to accept.

Vacant Spaces

Now they stood out in front of the building, smiling.

"Looks like this is where we get off," Thomas said.

"I almost dread going up to my apartment." A breeze whipped a strand of hair into her face. She brushed it away.

"Why do you say that, do you not like it here?"

She shook her head, told him it wasn't that at all and told him also about the person or persons outside her door, and how she suspected it was the Briar sisters.

He laughed, and seeing that she was offended, he held up a hand and apologized, "I don't mean to laugh really, I know you must be scared out of your wits after what happened to Susan. You're probably right though. It was more than likely the Briar sisters. They're very-let's say curious, and your a new tenant. I'm actually rather surprised they haven't made themselves known yet."

The wind was blowing more fiercely now and Ashley wondered if it would storm again tonight, she hoped not. "I wish they would," she replied. "It would be a lot better than creeping outside of people's doors."

He placed a hand on her shoulder, said, "They really are harmless, I assure you. Older than Harriet herself and probably a bit senile as well, if it will make you feel any better I'll have Harriet have a talk with them," he added.

She shook her head no, better to not rock the boat when you're the newest passenger on board, she told him. She was about to tell him about the noises she had heard up in the attic when he came closer toward her. He was gazing at her so intently that she was sure he was going to kiss her. She wasn't sure how to respond. Was it prudent to kiss on the first sort of date these days? What would her mother say?

At the last minute he pulled back though, smiled at her, "Friday night then, say around eight?"

She nodded and he went in first. Staying outside awhile longer, looking up at the sky, she wondered how many nights Susan had stood in this very spot. Large puffs of night blue clouds were blowing by, fast. They reminded her of Austin's bubble bath. The wind still whipped at her, as if trying to move her. It seemed something was constantly trying to move her lately.

Mrs. Winthrop delighted in hearing about her day with Thomas Robinson. Ashley felt that the old woman was living vicariously through her, that she might even have a slight crush on the author herself. Of course Ashley knew she would never admit it if she did.

Austin looked happy. He was smiling and making noises that could be mistaken for humming. Apparently the old woman had had him in her garden out back all day. She told Ashley that he loved helping her with the flowers, marveling at all the colors, and that she would love to have him over every day through the week, if that was okay with Ashley. That would be wonderful, she told Mrs. Winthrop and asked her if she could keep him Friday night.

"Even better," the woman replied. "Since it will be near his bedtime, how about I come up to your place?"

"Perfect," Ashley said. She took Austin's hand and was about to leave when she turned, and as she opened the door, said, "I heard noises in the attic last night."

The old woman looked at her, seemed speechless for a moment then asked, "Noises?"

Ashley nodded. She thought that the old woman had suddenly gone pale, but maybe it was just the light pouring in from the foyer chandelier.

"That's impossible dear," Mrs. Winthrop smiled now. "There's nothing up there, and besides, I told you, it's locked up tight."

"It sounded like a crash," Ashley continued. "Two of them, and then footsteps."

"Well, I can assure you that no one was up there." She led Ashley and Austin out the door. "Ah, yes, wasn't it raining last night? Remember I told you the roof has began to leak a bit in some places. These old rafters can make some horrid noises when they get wet and sag. Why, oh dear, one could have fallen, even. That would explain the crashing noise, wouldn't it? I better tell the landlord, thank you so much for bringing this to my attention dear. Goodnight."

And with that she closed the door, leaving Ashley with her mouth open in reply.

Rafters?

Austin took his bath and went to bed. Ashley found the remote to the television in the living room and turned the set on. At least the cable was still on, or maybe it came with the apartment, she wasn't sure. She should really meet the landlord sometime. Maybe Mrs. Winthrop could arrange it. Ashley was just about to flop down onto the luscious sofa when there was a light knock at the door. It was so soft as a matter of fact that Ashley wasn't really sure if someone had knocked or if it was just the television. Thumbing the off button on the remote, she listened, then rose.

"Who is it?" she asked as she walked over to the door, pressing her face close to it, smelling varnish and polish. She was getting use to that smell.

"It's your next door neighbor," a young woman's voice said, muffled by the heavy, thick door. One of the Briar sisters, Ashley thought?

Then the voice said, "Cross."

"Oh," Ashley said out loud and unlocked the door, opening it.

A young girl stood in the hallway. Ashley remembered Mrs. Winthrop telling her that Cross was only nineteen, but Ashley could almost swear she wasn't a day over sixteen. Her hair was indeed colored jet black, but Ashley could see brown coming in at the roots. Thick, overdrawn mascara lined her eyes. It was smudged in places and gave the girl a raccoon look about her. The clothes she wore were thrift-storish and Ashley thought, wouldn't it be odd if something she had donated way back in Atlanta wound up on this girl here in New York? But then, she thought again, she didn't own that many black tee shirts with rock bands names across the front.

"Sorry to bother you," Cross said. "I'm Cross, I live next door," she repeated. "I know this is going to sound all Mayberry and all, but can I borrow a cup of sugar?" She held up a white ceramic mug with a small crack forming on it's outside. It looked homemade.

"Mayberry?" Ashley asked, a little unsure.

"Yea, you know, Andy Griffith, neighborly. I mean, this isn't a cry for help or anything I just really need a cup of sugar."

Ashley opened the door wider, "Sure come on in."

Stepping across the threshold, Cross looked around. "Nice," she said. "Makes mine look like the size of a bread crumb."

Ashley went toward the kitchen, "I think I saw some sugar in one of the cabinets," she said. Cross heard her opening and closing doors and followed her into the kitchen.

"Here we go," Ashley said, lifting down a large bag from a top shelf. She took the mug from the girl. "So this is the first time you've been in this apartment?"

She questioned.

"Yea, it is. I only lived here a few days before the lady disappeared, man what a real bitch she was."

Ashley stopped pouring. "She was my best friend," she said, looking hard at the girl.

"Oops," Cross said out loud, looking away from the harsh glare. "Look, "I'm sorry. I can't believe you two were friends though. I mean you seem so nice and your friend—well, she just wasn't."

Ashley shook her head and started pouring the sugar again. It ran over and spilled onto the counter. Damn it. She was getting more and more like her mother everyday.

Cross saw Ashley's hands shaking as she cleaned up the mess. Said, "Hey look, I'm sorry for what I said about your friend. That was wrong of me, I only met her a couple of times."

Ashley smiled at the girl, handed her back the mug. "It's okay, it's just I never knew her to be mean to anyone a day in her life. Maybe people change, though. It's been awhile since I've seen her."

"More like this place is what makes people change," the young girl looked around as she said this. Looked up actually. "What with all the creepy noises and all, it's enough to make anyone snap." She looked at Ashley suspiciously now, as if she were testing her. Baiting her for something. Seeing if Ashley was trustworthy.

Ashley bit. "Noises? Like in the attic?"

The girl nodded. So Ashley wasn't the only one who heard it. She began to feel a little less crazy.

Without warning the girl turned and began walking out of the kitchen. "Gotta go," she said. "I've got coffee brewing. Thanks for the sugar."

"Wait," Ashley said, following her to the front door. She wanted to talk more about the noises. "Maybe you can come over sometime, we could talk."

The girl eyed her wearily. "Maybe rent a movie or something?" Ashley tried again.

"Friday?" Cross asked.

Ashley bit her lip, "Ooh, no good. How about Thursday? We'll call out for pizza."

"Double cheese?" Cross asked. "I don't eat meat."

"Double cheese it is then." Ashley replied, and then, "Oh wait, I don't have a phone yet to order it with."

Cross dug into the pocket of her loose jeans with her free hand, pulled out a tiny cell phone. When had they started making them so small, Ashley wondered?

Vacant Spaces

"Problem solved," the girl said. "Never leave home without it."

Ashley smiled, "Great see you about seven?"

The girl nodded and left. Ashley closed the door and locked it. She rested her back against its cool surface, still thinking about the noises in the attic.

She dreamed of Thomas that night. He was leaning in to kiss her and this time he did. It was soft and warm, she felt the brush of his small, pink tongue and smelled the smell of...dried blood on his breath. No, the dream had changed suddenly. She was in the nightmare again. The person was on top of her, hot breath on her face, assaulting her nostrils. The other voice in the room was laughing. Where was that other voice coming from? Who was in the room while this stranger held her down? Then something new in the dream, a floorboard creaking. That was when Ashley realized she was awake now. The creaking floorboard wasn't part of the dream at all. She opened her eyes, heard the noise again. There were footsteps in the attic. She turned her head, looking out the window. It wasn't raining tonight. Mrs. Winthrop wouldn't be able to use that as an excuse this time. Again a floorboard groaned. Not a rat, either, Ashley thought, unless it's Mickey Mouse that would be a helluva large rat.

She slowly rose in bed, looked at the clock. Four A.M. Silently, she crawled out of bed. With a shuffle she slid into her slippers and robe. She knew what she was thinking. Susan. Maybe she was locked in the attic somehow. But she would have starved to death by now, even if she was hurt and couldn't call out for help. Not if she's being held captive up there by someone in the brownstone. But who? She asked herself as she fumbled in her suitcase for a flash light, found one, tested it. The Briar sisters? Thomas said they were too old. The beam of the flashlight came on sharp then dimmed, faltered, and then came back on bright again. A rustling sound came from the room above her. Now was the time to act, she told herself. Do it for Susan.

Ashley left her apartment silently. The hallway was dimly lit with the four wall lamps. All was quiet. Ashley pulled her door closed. It did so with a click. Reaching into her robe pocket, She brought out her keys, locking the door behind her. There, Austin would be safe. As she skulked slowly down the corridor she stayed close to the wall, stepping carefully so as not to hit any noisy floorboards. Passing Cross' door, she wondered if the girl had been waken by the noises too. The dark attic stairway lay just across the hall. Ashley crossed over to it; hit a floorboard that creaked, she paused, the sound echoed in the stillness. It seemed amplified a thousand times. When nothing happened she moved into the stairwell. The hallway's insignificant light didn't reach into this narrow space and Ashley could only see darkness ahead. She switched the flashlight on. Nothing happened this time. Damn. She smacked the plastic lamp lightly a couple of times. The beam tried to come on and failed. She was trembling and this part of the brownstone seemed cold and uninviting. You know how something seemed like a good idea at one time and later you're like, what was I thinking? This was one of those times. Oh well, she had come this far. Starting up the first step, Ashley felt it bow a little under her weight. She felt for a banister, there wasn't one. If the door lay open at the top of the stairwell she could not tell, for the darkness here was thick, increased somehow and Ashley felt that it could suffocate her had she breathed in heavily. Slowly, what seemed like a snail's pace she took the stairs, carefully, one at a painstakingly slow time until she reached the top. She held her hand outward in the darkness, felt for the door. It was closer than she thought. Her hand glided down, fumbling, finding the cold metal knob, she prayed it was locked like Mrs. Winthrop had said, and then she could turn back without being a coward. It wasn't locked though. The knob turned with ease and the door opened.

A rush of cold, stale air smacked Ashley in the face. Her heart pounded in her chest, threatening to burst. Go back, something told her. You won't like what you will find here. She stepped over the threshold; felt as if someone, something else was controlling her movements now as she entered the brains of the brownstone.

The darkness did not give way, save for the three large porthole windows that lay in the far eve. She moved in that direction, careful of the low ceiling. She felt spider webs catch in her hair, tried to brush them away but they only clung to her hands and spread. Smacking the flashlight again she prayed it would come on. Suddenly, it flashed, put out a bright beam of yellow light and went black. But in that instant the light had come on she had seen something, no, someone in the far right hand corner of the room. She stood frozen in fear now, her eyes had begun to adjust and she could make out the silhouettes of boxes and old furnishings. They loomed before her like great and unknown creatures that fed off the shadows and cobwebs. She was about to ask who was there, opened her mouth to do so, when a rustling noise snapped it shut again, the intruder moved, swiftly. Outside the moon must have peeked out from behind the clouds because a shaft of pale blue light waded in through one of the portal windows, falling just across the face of the intruder in the attic. Ashley stifled a scream as a pale face came into view, staring at her and grinning. That face, my God, she knew that face. The voice in her head had been right, she didn't like what she had found here.

CHAPTER SIX

Ashley had grown suddenly cold, there, in the attic. Her eyes were wide and glassed over. She opened her mouth to speak, her lips trembled, the word came from a hoarse, dry throat. "Austin?" She said and the voice did not sound as if it even belonged to her. How could this be, her son in the shadows of this attic? The boy moved swiftly back into the confines of the darkness. Ashley took a step forward and tried to follow. Water splashed under her feet. So the roof did leak. Then another movement in the room, this time from behind her. Ashley turned. From the thin veil of light that framed the doorway she had entered through, a tall, dark figure loomed. He came toward her and in Ashley's mind flashed images of her dream. That distant missing time in her life that constantly tugged at her memory was surfacing. The person on top of her, the evil voice in the room laughing as she was bitten and licked and this time Ashley did scream, a bloodcurdling scream that echoed from the rafters of this damned attic she was trapped in. The tall figure moved quickly at her now, arms outstretched and Ashley thought, no, not like this, not here. She turned in the darkness to run, hit her head hard on a low hanging rafter and fell into a mound of heavy boxes. They came tumbling down around her as she was sent to the cold, dusty floor. Her head throbbed and something wet ran down it and into her left eye. A small scurrying sound to her right. Austin? My God was he still in the room? Hide, she thought. Hide. Then the dark figure was above her. Her head was spinning and the image of the person spun with it. She could tell the person looming over her was huge from his silhouette, probably about three hundred pounds, she guessed, as her vision started to blur and she realized that the wet stuff running from her head into her eyes was blood. And Ashley was unusually calm as the figure bent over her body and she felt his hands on her. She didn't even panic as the darkness began to envelope her and she slipped into a pain induced unconsciousness. She did, however, think, as wakefulness became a mere pinprick, is this what happened to poor Susan? The thought rang through her head another second…and then the lights went out.

CHAPTER SEVEN

In the darkness she felt hands on her, smoothing her hair back from her face, caressing her cheek. And she heard voices too, soft and low. "It's been so long since I've seen you," one voice said. And, "The seeds we have planted are finally bearing fruit," other voices said. "What shall we do next? Ah yes, your right, training, preparation." The voices drifted away then, back into the darkness where Ashley was now. It's warm here, she thought. Yes, I like it here. Maybe I'll stay. Then she thought of Austin and she woke up.

At first it took time for the events that had transpired in the attic to catch up with her mind, but when they did she shot up in the strange bed she was sleeping in and when the stabbing pain shot through her head, threatening to put her out again, she slowly laid back onto the deep pillows. They smelled of raspberry. A heavy quilt laid over her, made of small, multicolored squares that were intricately stitched together forming an overall spider web like design on the cover. The bed itself was big and high with four rolling oak post that didn't quiet reach the tall ceiling. A small tiffany lamp was on beside the bed, an empty and fragile looking teacup rested solemnly beside it. Heavy wood furnishings decorated the room, against the backdrop of a rose colored wallpaper with intertwining vines faded into its design. Was she at Mrs. Winthrop's apartment? Another sharp and sudden pain stabbed at her head, it really did hurt to think, she almost giggled. Putting a hand to her head she felt a bandage high upon her forehead and remembered the rafter, the looming figure and then…nothing.

Just then the door to the bedroom opened and an elderly lady, very thin and very gray, entered with a tray. A tea pot and another tea cup that matched the one beside the bed rested upon it, steam rising from the cup whisped up in front of the wrinkled, smiling face. Set in the ancient skin covered skull was two sparkling eyes.

"I thought you might be awake by now. I brought you some tea." The elderly lady sat the tray down by the bed. The dishes on it made clinking noises as she did so and Ashley noticed that the old woman's hands shook uncontrollably. The old woman then sat herself in a rocking chair nearby, her face half in shadows, but Ashley could still see her bright eyes, almost shimmering, and thought it must just be the reflection of the tiffany lamp.

Ashley opened her mouth to speak, tried, failed. Her throat was dry and it hurt as it rubbed, trying to form words.

The old woman leaned up in her chair and said softly, "Drink some tea first, it'll help."

Ashley reached over, unsteadily, and took the tiny, thin cup by the handle. She noticed her own hand shaking too. She brought it to her lips. Steam rose filling her nostrils with the smell of chamomile and honey. She blew the liquid and sipped. It was warm in her mouth and even warmer going down. She sipped again and again, coating her parched throat.

Vacant Spaces

The old woman just smiled patiently, rocking in her rocking chair.

Ashley tried again. "Where am I?" Her voice sounded light and frail like the teacup she held in her shaking hand, as if it might break at any minute.

"You are in mine and my sister's apartment," the old woman smiled, never stopped rocking. "My name is Elizabeth Briar. My sister Lillian, everyone calls her Lilly, is napping right now. We've been taking care of you while you've been out."

How long had she been out? "What time is it?" Ashley asked. Dark, heavy, maroon curtains were pulled tightly shut at the window so that she couldn't tell if it was morning yet. She couldn't imagine that she slept here all night.

Elizabeth Briar stopped rocking at the question, looked at Ashley and said, "It's Wednesday afternoon dear."

Ashley only stared at the old woman as her mind tried to retrace steps lost to it. "Wednesday?" she said. She was out for over a day.

"You took quiet a bump to the head up in the attic. What were you doing up there anyway?"

"Austin!" Ashley exclaimed, trying to sit up in the bed again and again the excruciating pain sent her falling backwards, exasperated.

"Your son is just fine, young lady. Harriet is in your apartment right now taking care of him. Has been since your little misadventure in the attic."

Ashley sipped more of the tea, drained the little cup as Elizabeth Briar rose and walked to the bedside, refilling it.

"Now, why don't you tell me why you were up in that old attic," she said again, repositioning herself in the rocker.

"Austin. I heard noises, went to see what it was and..." she tripped on her words. Her head was spinning out of control. The room kept going around in circles, as did the old lady.

"Yes, go on dear," the Briar sister said. She sounded distant, faraway.

Ashley tried to shake the dizziness but her eyelids were heavy, kept wanting to close. "It was Austin, in the attic. Then the man...came at me."

Then again the faraway voice of the Briar sister, "But that's impossible. Your son was asleep in bed when we found you."

Ashley knew it was no use trying to fight it, sleep was coming whether she wanted it or not. The tea left a funny taste in her mouth and she began to wonder, was it the hit on the head that was putting her out, or was the tea drugged?

"How are you feeling, dear?" Mrs. Winthrop smiled down at Ashley as the young woman woke. This time she was in her own bed, well, Susan's bed actually.

"Like a freight train hit me," Ashley replied. The bandage was still on her forehead and she felt light, almost giddy. "I feel so strange."

Mrs. Winthrop smiled, "Pain killers. The doctor gives them to me for my back. When you get my age you get all the good drugs. Codeine, even morphine, you know."

Vacant Spaces

"Oh," Ashley said. She didn't know. "Where's Austin?" she asked.

"Playing with a set of leggo's I gave him. The boy really is quiet amazing you know?"

This Ashley did know and nodded.

Mrs. Winthrop pulled the covers up to Ashley's chin, said, "Elizabeth told me what you said. About why you were up in the attic I mean."

Ashley realized she was still nodding. "Yes, Austin got up there somehow."

"But that's impossible, dear. Topples heard noises, went up to see what was going on. He must have frightened you. He is rather scary I must say. That's when you panicked, screamed and hit your head on a low rafter. Topples carried you down to the Briar sister's, Elizabeth use to be a nurse. But when they sent for me, I went straight in to check on Austin. He was fast asleep."

Ashley was feeling more like herself now. She hoped the medicine, whatever it was, was wearing off. "I'm telling you Mrs. Winthrop," she said, attempting to sit up and found she could do so with only a slight throbbing in her head. "I know my own son, and I know what I saw. Austin was up in that attic."

The kindly old woman came over to the bed now, sat on its edge, gently pushing Ashley back down into the pillows. She smiled at the young woman, smoothed a loose strand of dark hair from her face. The old woman's hands were cold and smelled of lotion. Her amazing green eyes bore down on Ashley and she said, "When I saw you after Topples brought you down from the attic you were covered from head to toe in dust and cobwebs. But when I saw Austin asleep in bed he was clean. Still smelled like soap. Now how do you explain that?"

Ashley shook her head. She couldn't explain it, but she knew she wasn't dreaming or whatever it was that Mrs. Winthrop thought. Crazy. That's probably what she thought. But she wasn't crazy. She wasn't.

"Listen dear, that attic is dark and this old building makes noises and throws out shadows. Why sometimes I think I see things. The imagination is a tricky thing. What with you living here in poor Susan's apartment and all, I'd be surprised if you didn't hear or see things. Anybody would. But we can't let our imagination get the better of us. Sometimes we have to step back and look at things in the light of a new day." She looked at the clock then and added, "Now it's getting late. I'll stay and put the boy to bed. Tomorrow you'll be as good as new." And with that she got up, turned off the dim lamp and opened the door to leave.

Ashley watched her from the shadowy confines of the bed. "If no one was up there then how do you explain the attic door being unlocked?" she asked, but if the old woman heard her she made no notice as the door closed behind her, shutting out the last of the light. Ashley lay there in total darkness for a while and thought about what was going on. She remembered unlocking the door when she left the apartment to go up to the attic. Austin didn't have a key, how could the door have been locked from within if he went out it? And why hadn't he been covered in dust? Mrs. Winthrop said he was spotless when she saw him. Unless she was lying? But why would she do that? She had been so kind to Ashley and her son.

Then maybe she's scared of something, Ashley thought. Scared of something up in the attic. She yawned, stretched and felt restless. She needed to go back up to that attic, in the daylight this time. She felt sure that the answers to her questions lay there. Maybe the answers to what happened to Susan too. Yes, that's just what she would do. But tonight she would sleep, and, she prayed, not dream.

Thursday morning Ashley still felt as though some of the drugs that were given to her were still in her system. She felt sluggish and couldn't shake the drowsiness. A hot shower only helped a little. Wiping the steam from the mirror with her hand, she examined the black and blue gash on her forehead. What a beautiful thing to have the day before her date with Thomas. She'd have to be sure to wear a dress that matched. Then she noticed it, or rather the lack of it. Her antique rosary she wore around her neck, it was gone. But she never took it off. It was the last gift her father had given her before he died a couple of years later. Going to the bedroom, she checked the bed, in the blankets, the floor but found nothing. Maybe the Briar sisters' then, or, she shuddered, the attic. Last night in the warmth and safety of her own bed she felt brave making plans to return to that room. Now, however, the thought made the hair on the back of her neck stand up. The horrible, foreboding feeling she had gotten there. And the man, Topples. He had lunged at her, she was sure of it. Or was she just frightened and thought he was coming for her. She pushed the memory from her mind. If her rosary wasn't at the Briar sister's apartment, then she would have to return to the attic, whether she wanted to or not. Until then, she thought to herself, walking over to her jewelry box, opening it and removing the small gold cross, she would wear Abigail's. She fixed the clasp on the thin chain and stared at her naked reflection in the full-length mirror. She looked pale and thin. The gash on her head didn't help any either, adding to her sickly demeanor. It's no wonder Mrs. Winthrop thought her a loon, she looked like one. The poor old woman was probably worried about what she had gotten herself into, inviting Ashley to move here. "Just keep reminding yourself," she said to her reflection, "you're not crazy." Then she remembered hearing somewhere that talking to ones self was the first sign of mental health problems. If that's true, she thought silently to herself this time, then I've been going crazy for years.

Mrs. Winthrop had left a note in the kitchen that said she had brought up a few groceries for Ashley and Austin. Opening the fridge, Ashley gawked in wonder. It was full of orange juice and sodas, cold cuts and fruits and vegetables. She went to the cupboards, opened them, one after the other, they were all full. Canned soups by the dozen, pasta, sauces in jars, boxed goods and bottles all lined the shelves. More food than the two of them could eat in a month. Then Ashley remembered her bony image in the mirror and thought, but we can try.

She cooked bacon and eggs with toast and jelly. Poured two large glasses of orange juice and went to wake Austin. Her heart skipped a beat. His bed was empty. "Austin!" she called out loud, knowing she wouldn't get a response. She checked all the rooms

Vacant Spaces

and her son was nowhere in sight. Oh no, she thought, the attic! She ran for the front door, the throbbing pain returning as the adrenaline-pumped blood rushed to her head. Turning the knob Ashley lurched the door open and ran right into a smiling Harriet Winthrop who was holding hands with Austin. When Ashley saw her son she gave him a big hug, he pulled back.

"I see you're up and at 'em." Mrs. Winthrop started but Ashley cut her off.

"What are you doing with my son?" She snapped and the old woman stepped back, visibly shocked. "Do you know how worried I was after the incident in the attic, to wake up and find my son missing?"

"I'm sorry dear, I let Austin spend the night with me," Mrs. Winthrop began again. "I wasn't sure when you would wake and I didn't want him to wander about. I'm so sorry."

Ashley closed her eyes, put a hand to her now throbbing head. Why had she been so harsh, of course Mrs. Winthrop was only trying to help.

Tears welled up in the old woman's eyes as she said, "I've overstepped my boundaries, I'm afraid. Please forgive me Ashley. An old woman can get lonely sometimes and think of others as family, it doesn't mean that others think the same way."

Oh for goodness sake! Look what she'd done. It wasn't even nine o'clock in the morning yet and all ready Ashley had succeeded in making an old woman cry. And for what really? Looking out for Ashley and Austin's own welfare, that's what. Giving them a place to live, baby-sitting, nursing Ashley after her ridiculous trip to the attic, stocking her kitchen with food, and now this is how she's repaid. Way to go Ashley, what a champ.

"Well, I should go now," Mrs. Winthrop said, pulling a handkerchief from her sleeve and wiping a stray tear.

As the old woman turned to go, Ashley said, "Wait. Mrs. Winthrop I'm sorry. I shouldn't have snapped like that, of course you were only trying to help. Please don't go. I'm just a bundle of nerves after the attic and all." She looked at the old woman, "Forgive me?" She asked.

Mrs. Winthrop smiled and hugged Ashley. She actually hugged her. Ashley stepped back a little, caught off guard by the sudden gesture of affection.

"Thank you dear. That was just what this old battle-ax needed to hear."

"Friends?" Ashley put her hand out and the old woman took it.

"Friends," she replied, and, "Now let this old bat cook you two some breakfast." Ashley shook her head, "Nope."

Mrs. Winthrop looked confused, had she offended the girl again, already?

Ashley smiled and said, "Got that base covered, today you eat with us. And I'm not taking 'no' for an answer," she added, taking Austin's hand and going into the apartment.

"Okay," Mrs. Winthrop shrugged, following her in. "But I'm doing the dishes."

After the breakfast dishes were all cleaned and put away, and Austin was off looking at a cartoon on the television, Harriet Winthrop put a cup of coffee in

Vacant Spaces

front of Ashley. The girl sat at the small breakfast nook table, throbbing head in hand.

"Is the pain still there, dear?" Mrs. Winthrop asked, taking a seat across from her.

Ashley smiled lightly and nodded, taking the warm coffee mug with both hands and letting the aroma waver about and stimulate her senses before taking a cautious sip. It was good, and not too hot. She watched as Mrs. Winthrop dug around in her purse for a moment, and then produced a tiny brown bottle with no label.

"I thought it might be. Here, take these." She pushed the bottle in front of Ashley. "They'll help," she added.

Ashley shook her head, looking at the prescription medicine bottle. "Thanks anyway. I don't like pills."

Mrs. Winthrop shrugged, "Keep them anyway, just in case the pain gets to be unbearable at night and you can't sleep. They're not very strong, really."

"Thanks," Ashley said and then slid the pills into her own purse, safely away from Austin. "Mrs. Winthrop," she began, lost her words and had to start over. "Mrs. Winthrop, I just want to apologize."

"Why, whatever for, dear?" The old woman asked in surprise.

"For being so much trouble. It's only my first week here and already you've had to feed us and babysit, and now you've had to play doctor for me too."

Harriet Winthrop reached across the table and laid her hand on top of Ashley's, her eyes were glassing over and she said, "You and Austin could never be any trouble. I consider it a privilege to help." She looked far away now and the glassy look turned to tears that welled up, one escaped and streamed down the aged face, catching in a wrinkle and taking an alternate route. "When I was around your age I had a baby that died at birth, I was never able to bear children after that."

"Oh, Mrs. Winthrop, I'm so very sorry." Ashley said, placing her other hand over the old woman's. She felt like she was playing a game. Who's hand would wind up on top?

Mrs. Winthrop smiled a weak smile. "It was a long time ago. But I think that is why I'm so concerned for you and your son. You remind me of myself." At that she quickly wiped the tears from her eyes with the ever hidden hanky she kept up her sleeve. She could be a magician, Ashley thought. Magic tricks and all.

"I really must be going now dear. Thank you so very much for breakfast."

"Anytime, Mrs. Winthrop," Ashley said rising and walking the old lady to the front door.

At the door Harriet Winthrop turned and said, "And don't forget about your date with Mr. Robinson tomorrow. I'll be here at seven thirty sharp for baby-sitting duty."

Ashley smiled, "Thanks for the reminder." As if she could forget.

Ashley tried to catch up on some work. She knew better than to let personal matters interfere with her job, all ready she was behind on sending out notices to past due accounts. She worked vigilantly, completing what she could without phone or internet service, and as day turned to evening she remembered her plans with Cross was for tonight. A knock at the door told her she had remembered too late.

Cross stood in the hallway with tiny cell phone in hand as Ashley opened the door.
"Let's get the pizza rolling this way," the girl said, walking past Ashley and into the apartment. "I'm starved. You would think my boss at the bookstore would be a little more civilized, being literate and all. But do you think she gives breaks? No way. I have to pretend to be taking a piss just to be able to get a cigarette."
"Uh—hi," Ashley said.
Fifty-six minutes later they were sitting on the floor in front of the television set giggling at an episode of Gilligan's Island. Pizza crust lay discarded in the opened delivery boxes, whole slices of double cheese, now cold, looked less appetizing and was left to waste. Austin had finished two slices and fell asleep on the sofa. Cross looked at the sleeping boy and then back at Ashley, she whispered, "Looks like quite a spill you took up there in the attic."
"I see word spreads fast in the brownstone."
"Like wildfire on a farmer's ass," the young girl replied with a smile. "What were you doing up there anyway? I mean sure, I hear noises too, but do you think I'm going up in that spooky old attic? Not on your life." She took a sip of her diet cola as though she were washing down the words that she just spoke.
"It was Austin," Ashley whispered, looking at her son still sleeping on the sofa. "They all think I'm crazy but I saw my son in that attic. The apartment door was

locked from the inside, though," she added as an afterthought, as if she were arguing with herself.

"Well add me to the list of those who think you're crazy. If it was your son up in the attic then what about the noises I heard up there before you ever arrived here?"

Ashley looked hard at the girl. "So you have heard noises too, it's not just me?"

"It's not just you," Cross repeated, and then, "You think it has something to do with your friend missing, don't you?"

"I don't know what to think." Ashley replied.

Cross was looking far off now, seemed to be thinking hard about something. She spoke after a minute; the words came out slow and thick. "You're going to think I'm crazy but…" she paused, continued, "I think I was tricked into moving here. I think they want me here for a reason."

"They?" Ashley asked.

The girl nodded, "The mysterious landlord and Mrs. Winthrop."

Ashley almost laughed and saw that Cross looked offended, a conspiracy theory with Mrs. Winthrop as the conspirator? Ashley just couldn't see it. "Why would they want to trick you into living here?"

"Like I said, you're going to think I'm crazy."

"Good, then we can start a club," Ashley whispered back, trying to lighten the mood. She didn't like the solemn turn the conversation had suddenly taken. Something about the look in Cross' eyes was almost scary. "Everyone already thinks I'm crazy."

Cross drew in a deep breath and began her story. "Are you a religious person, Ashley?" she asked.

Ashley nodded, "Catholic," she added.

"Good, good. Then maybe you can believe what I'm going to tell you. I've never told a soul before." The girl in all black paused again. She seemed to be choosing her words carefully, or maybe she was afraid to say them at all because when she spoke, her voice was trembling. "Three years ago, when I was sixteen I became very ill. I would have blackouts and during these blackouts I would do and say horrible things that I couldn't remember later. The blackouts started to last longer and longer until finally I had lost over a month of my life."

A sudden dread was beginning to creep up on Ashley, washing over her. Her mouth went dry and she found her lips were severely chapped. She tried to draw some saliva to lick them but none would come.

Cross continued, "What I found out later was—was that I had been—" she waited a moment longer, trying to say the word aloud and when she did it rolled off her tongue and sounded dirty, "Possessed."

The feeling of dread now turned to icy cold fingers running up Ashley's back. Cross seemed far away and pain began to form at the base of Ashley's skull. What was this young girl telling her? Was she serious? Was this some horrible teenage joke?

"I told you you'd think I was crazy," Cross said. She heard heavy breathing, thought it was the sleeping boy then realized it was his mother. "Hey, you okay? You don't look so well."

Ashley Malone wasn't well. The pain now spread throughout her skull, a white-hot blinding pain that came in pulsating throbs of agony every time her heart pumped. Her stomach turned and became nauseated.

Before she knew it she was up off the floor and dashing for the bathroom, leaving Cross to wonder what the hell had just happened. Gagging and choking sounds echoed down the hallway and then, the unmistakable sound of vomit hitting water. Cross just sat there as gag after gag rang through the hall. Then she had a cold sensation. A feeling she was not alone. The girl looked at the sleeping boy from the corner of her eyes. Was he watching her? She turned her head swiftly and thought she saw his eyes snap shut but couldn't be sure. Water was running in the bathroom now, the toilet flushed and the water pressure she heard coming from the sink died down a little. The strange sensation was still with Cross. Something was here with her. She turned her head slowly this time to look at Austin. She gasped. His eyes were wide open and staring at her. This time he didn't even try to close them, and there was a crooked grin on his lips.

The bathroom door opened and Cross' head turned that way in sheer reflex and then snapped quickly back to the boy. His eyes were closed again. His breathing came in slow, steady rhythm. Peaceful sleep seemed to have hold of him.

"I'm sorry about that Cross," Ashley said, coming down the hallway. "It must have been the pizza mixed with some of the medication still in my system." She came into the living room and saw the teenage girl heading for the door. "Hey, you don't have to leave. I feel better now, we can talk some more."

Cross looked at her from the now open doorway. Ashley thought she saw a look of sheer terror in those eyes. "No, I really have to go. I shouldn't have told you that. I should never have even thought about that."

She bolted out the door and Ashley followed her into the hallway, leaving the apartment door ajar.

Cross fumbled for her key and, finding it, opened her own door and skulked inside.

Ashley reached it just as it was about to close and put her hand on it as a barrier. "Cross wait. You can't just tell me something like that and then leave. If you think there's something going on in this place then you have to tell me."

The pressure on the door eased and Ashley pushed it open and entered the girl's apartment.

It was indeed small. A futon still left out as a bed was in one corner, while a large stereo took up another wall. A small kitchen was separated from the living/bedroom space by only a small counter. Another door must be the bathroom, Ashley thought. Still, as 'cozy' as the space was, it still had that architectural flare that the rest of the brownstone shared, hardwood floors and high ceilings, intricate crown moldings and an arched doorway leading to the bathroom. Warm, rich paneled walls ran from the floor, halfway up to the middle of the wall, and above that, faded, but once bright and colorful wallpaper hung, draped to the ceiling.

Cross leaned against this wallpaper looking at Ashley. "Am I crazy? If I was I think I could deal with it. But to be sane and believe this, it's just too much."

Ashley knew what she meant. No she didn't believe this girl crazy, confused, maybe, but not any crazier than Ashley herself. Still, is possession possible? Even most Catholics knew that these were just misreported and misdiagnosed mental illness back in the dark ages of medicine and religion. Still this girl might know something that could help her find out what happened to Susan.

"Okay," Ashley began, "crazy or not, why do you think anyone would want to trick you into living here? What does your past have to do with that?"

Cross moved to a far wall where a little bookshelf, about knee high, stood. "Because of this," Cross said. Ashley watched as the girl moved the bookshelf and knelt down on the floor. The girls' hands glided over one of the square, oak wall panels, pressing gently at the corner. Ashley was beginning to think the girl was on some type of drugs when she heard a faint 'click.' She watched in amazement as the panel gently swung open, revealing a tiny closet, so tiny in fact a person would have to stoop down to go into it.

"I found this secret closet by accident a couple of weeks ago," Cross said, reaching inside. "This was the only thing in it." She produced a little leather-bound book with faded lettering that spelled 'journal.' "It dates back to nineteen fifty seven. It's a detailed journal a woman kept of her daughter being possessed by a demon. There's more, but you'll have to read it for yourself." She held the journal out for Ashley to take it. Ashley did so with trembling hands.

"Okay, I admit that is an unusual coincidence," Ashley said to the young girl. "But why do you think Mrs. Winthrop is involved?"

Cross sighed, as if explaining would be a difficult thing. "Just the way it all came about. She struck up a conversation with me in the bookstore I work at, then it was like she just happened to be everywhere I was. Movie theaters, coffee shops, you name it we'd be

Vacant Spaces

there at the same time. Then she offered me this apartment, dirt-cheap. I can't explain it; I just get a weird vibe, now. You know what I mean?"

Ashley nodded absently. Just like when Thomas happened to be at the coffee shop she was at, and just like he happened to have all ready visited the police station the same as Ashley was planning to do. She was looking at the book in her hands. "Do you know Thomas Robinson?"

"Sure," Cross replied. "The old dude in 2A."

Ashley almost laughed at the phrase 'old dude.' But she guessed he was. "Yea, but do you know any of his books from the bookstore you work in? He's had three published."

Cross shook her head, "No, but unless it's about the undead I don't read it."

Ashley nodded and remembered Austin asleep on the sofa and the door open. "I've got to get back to Austin, do you want to come back over, talk some more?"

Cross looked at the clock. "Thanks but it's getting late, read the journal, we'll talk tomorrow."

Ashley looked at the digital clock too and then at her own watch. They didn't match. "You know your clock is an hour slow," Ashley asked. "It's really almost ten thirty."

The girl rolled her eyes. "I know, daylight savings time a couple of months ago and I never bothered to 'spring forward'." She did quotation marks with her fingers as she said spring forward and then said, "I'm such a slacker."

Ashley smiled and said goodnight, Cross watched her as she entered her apartment then she shut and locked her own door.

Neither women had noticed the dark figure that watched them from the shadowy confines of the attic stairwell. Hidden in the recesses of the night, the dark, shadow of a person waited, then moved to the very edge of the opening, just at the threshold where the light ended and the darkness began. The figure stood there now, half in shadow and half in light, as if waiting for some silent epiphany. Cold eyes watched in unwavering vigilance, staring at the door of apartment 3B, at the space where Ashley Malone had stood only a minute ago. And if one could see the lips of the intruder, they would be able to make out a crooked, evil grin.

Ashley carried Austin to bed. He was getting heavier everyday. Soon he would be grown before she knew it, and when she died, what would happen to him then? It was a thought that came to her on a daily basis. A nagging, tugging worry she could do nothing about. She pushed the thought from her mind as she stared at her son sleeping. Ashley brushed the hair from his eyes and kissed his forehead. "Goodnight," she whispered leaving the room.

The pain had returned to her wound with a vengeance now. It had steadily worsened since Cross' story. The strange and sickening sensation was still at the pit of Ashley's stomach, like a burning ember building to a full blazed fire. She knew she wouldn't be able to get any sleep tonight unless it subsided soon. Then she remembered the pills Mrs. Winthrop had

Vacant Spaces

given her. Just one wouldn't hurt, and besides the pain was becoming unbearable. She fixed a cup of herbal tea and took the pill bottle out of her purse. It took her a moment to figure out how to open the white childproof cap on the little brown bottle. The pills were larger than she had expected. Ashley wondered if she could swallow a whole one without choking. She popped the pill in her mouth and took a swig of the tea. The pill went down but felt lodged in her esophagus. It left a bitter taste in her mouth. Funny how a lot of things were leaving a bitter taste in her mouth lately.

Once in bed Ashley lay snuggled under the blankets, the half empty cup of herbal tea at the bedside and the small leather journal resting on top of the covers. She picked the book up. A warm, fuzzy feeling was sneaking up on her. Ashley opened the cover and on the first yellowed and frayed page was a signature written in cursive with an exquisite penmanship. "Mrs. Laura Augustine Lyerly." Ashley turned the page. She felt as if everything was going in slow motion. It wasn't exactly an uncomfortable feeling, just different.

"November Eighth, Nineteen Fifty seven.

I can say with the utmost confidence that my seventeen-year-old daughter has been taken by the spirit. 'He' has her now, in control of both body and mind. He speaks in a language we cannot understand yet, we ask him to communicate with us in a way we can comprehend. We need to know what he wants."

Ashley's vision began to blur now as the drugs began to take full effect, her head kept dropping but she forced herself to continue.

"Lesions are beginning to form on my dear daughter. She looks sickly and I fear she may die. But she cannot, not yet. She is the chosen one. I pray to you my dark lord, do not take her yet."

Had Ashley read that right or was the drug messing with her. My dark lord?

"In the name of the evil one I plead, spare her soul for just a while longer, Azreal. So that she may be the chosen one, so that you may reign almighty. Praise all that is dark, damn all that is holy, in the name of the dark ones."

That was the point at which sleep overtook Ashley Malone. As hard as she fought it the battle was lost. But, she thought, in that foggy, drug-induced realm between wake and sleep, she had heard that name before. Azreal. She knew that name. But from where she could not remember. Ashley slept then, a heavy, undisturbed slumber, undisturbed by the footsteps that had started in the attic above her and undisturbed by the dark figure that now crept into her bedroom, looming over her sleeping figure. The same cold eyes that had stared from the attic stairwell now stared down at her seemingly lifeless body, and the same evil smile spread across the face of the intruder.

CHAPTER EIGHT

When Ashley woke the day was overcast. Even the wind seemed forbidding as it pressed against the old glass of the windows, making them rattle in their panes. She showered and made the bed, looking for the journal as she did so. Sure that it was tangled in the sheets somewhere, she smoothed the covers out one by one. It wasn't there. Nor was it under the bed or on the small nightstand with her cup of cold, unfinished herbal tea. This is impossible, she thought to herself. She vaguely remembered taking the book to bed with her, and she slightly recalled, without any real clarity, a couple of sentences and something about a familiar name, but she knew, without a doubt, that the book was in her hands as she drifted off. Frustrated she went to wake Austin. He woke sleepy eyed and with unruly hair; a cow lick causing it to stick up in the back. As the boy left his bedroom to go to the bathroom, Ashley began casually checking around his room. She felt as though she were snooping, betraying Austin somehow, but the book couldn't just get up and walk away on it's own. Still, though, the journal wasn't here either.

"Ashley?" a voice called from the living room, causing her to jump. It was Mrs. Winthrop.

Ashley rushed to the living room to find the old woman standing in the front doorway, hand still holding the knob of the door. She looked at the young girl wearily.

"Your door was ajar, dear. Has it been that way all night?"

Ashley shook her head, "I don't know. I mean, I don't think so." She thought back but the previous night was now just a hazy memory. But she always locked the door, and the journal was missing. My God! Had someone been in her apartment last night? She calmed herself, determined not to let Mrs. Winthrop see her freak out again.

"You really must be more careful dear, after what happened to poor Susan and all. I started locking the front entrance to the brownstone at night, but you can never be too safe. That reminds me." she said, digging into one of the oversized pocket of her gardening apron and removing a silver key. "Here's a key for the downstairs door. I lock them at nine sharp every night now. We don't want you to get locked out now do we?"

"Definitely not," Ashley said, taking the key from the woman, and then, "are you going to do some gardening?"

"Why, yes I am dear. That's why I'm here. I was hoping Austin could join me, if it's all right with you of course."

"You don't mind, even though you're baby-sitting tonight?" God, she hoped the woman had not forgotten about tonight, her date with Thomas. It was a date, wasn't it?

The old woman smiled a sly smile, "Don't worry dear, I haven't forgotten."

Vacant Spaces

That whole mind reading thing again, Ashley thought. "Okay, but he hasn't had breakfast yet."

"Then I'll fix him my special continental breakfast," Mrs. Winthrop replied, making a swirling, grand gesture with her hand.

Ashley smiled, "Please, don't go through a lot of trouble, really, he'll eat anything."

"Oh, no trouble at all dear. My special continental breakfast is also known as fruit loops." Both women laughed and Ashley thought, conspiracy theory, really.

"I'll just go get Austin ready." She headed for the hallway.

"Be sure to dress him in old clothes," Mrs. Winthrop called after her.

Some minutes later, mother and son emerged from the back regions of the apartment. Ashley was glad that Mrs. Winthrop was taking Austin for the day. That would give her a chance to visit the newspaper reporter who had written the article about Susan's disappearance.

"By the way, Mrs. Winthrop," Ashley began, as they left the apartment and she made sure to lock the door. "I noticed there's only one mailbox outside."

"Yes, that's right. All the mail goes there and I separate it and bring it up. Gives an old woman something to do. Are you expecting something dear?"

Ashley nodded, "Something from the phone company actually."

Mrs. Winthrop smiled, "Oh yes, you must have a phone. I'll be sure to bring it up to you right away when it comes. In the meantime, you're welcome to use mine anytime you like."

"Thanks," Ashley said, and meant it. As her son and Mrs. Winthrop went toward the stairs leading down, Ashley walked the opposite direction, to Cross' door.

The old woman turned and stared at her, "Not leaving yet?"

"I am, it's just that Cross left something at my apartment last night."

"Are you two becoming friends?"

Ashley smiled; felt interrogated, and said, "I hope so."

The old woman smiled back. "All right then, Austin and I are off. Ready young man?" She looked at the boy. Ashley watched as the two of them disappeared down the stairs. She felt a strange twinge of jealousy inside of her. It was good for Austin to associate with others though, she knew that. And Mrs. Winthrop was so good with him. No reason to be jealous, no reason at all. She knocked on Cross' door, waited. No answer. Oh well, she would have to tell her about the missing journal later. Ashley reached in her purse and unfolded the page of the New York Times. She looked at the heading of the article and then at the name below and to it's left. Dan Phillips. Well Dan, ready or not, here she came.

Ashley had no idea that the New York Times office would be so big, or so busy. No one seemed to know Dan Phillips until finally she found a mail boy. Third floor, down the hallway, take a left, then a right, you'll see a set of doors but don't go through them and bam, you're at Dan Phillips office. The directions were accurate and Ashley found herself entering a small,

Vacant Spaces

cramped office space, overflowing with papers. A male receptionist sat at the front desk. "Can I help you?" He asked as Ashley approached. He was young, about twenty-two probably, with freckles and reddish brown hair.

"I was hoping to see Dan Phillips," she said politely, smiling.

"Is it important?" The young man asked. He had coffee stains on the front of his baby blue button down.

"Well, yes it is, actually."

The boy shrugged, "Sorry, just missed him." He looked at his watch. "Ooh, by only a minute or two, too. What a bummer." The kid was being cynical on purpose.

Ashley felt infuriated. Why did everyone in this city have to be so rude? She kept her anger down, and then asked, "When do you expect him back?"

The boy smiled again, "Monday morning. He just went to the parking garage for the news van. Some big story breaking, probably take the rest of the day. Had you not been standing up here wasting my time you probably could have caught him."

"But I really must speak with him now, about an article he wrote." Ashley pleaded. This snot nose kid needed a good slap, she thought.

The boy smiled again, shrugged, "Oh well, sucks to be you."

She left the office red faced and saw an open elevator and made a dash for it. Catching the doors just as they were closing she stepped inside the compartment and fingered the button for the parking garage. The motion of the elevator made her stomach do flip flops. Hurry, she thought, tapping her foot.

Maybe she could still catch him. Finally the elevator door opened with a 'ding' and she found herself in a dimly lit garage with rows and rows of white news vans. At the far end of the garage she could see reverse lights and one of the vans pulled out and began coming toward her. Hoping that this was indeed Dan Phillips, she began waving at the van. It didn't slow down. I have to talk to this man, now, Ashley thought, and she stepped out blocking the exit. The van blared its horn at her as it continued its course. Ashley didn't move. At the last moment when she was almost sure the driver wasn't going to stop, the sound of screeching brakes on concrete echoed deafeningly throughout the garage. Ashley ran to the passenger side window, it rolled down with a push of a button.

"Are you fucking nuts lady?" The driver screamed at her. "I could have killed you!"

"Are you Dan Phillips?" she demanded.

"Not if this is about a paternity suit, otherwise yea, and I'm in a hurry."

"Your receptionist told me where you were, I have to talk to you."

The man looked confused, "My receptionist? Oh, you mean Greg." He chuckled and Ashley wondered what was so funny. "Look, there's a story going on I'm not about to miss, so you want to talk? Then you better get in."

She looked at him, was he serious? Looking around the garage she realized she really had no other choice, not if she wanted to talk to this man today. Oh well, what the hell, she thought. Ashley opened the van door and climbed in just as the elevator doors

Vacant Spaces

dinged open again. Greg, the receptionist boy ran toward the van yelling, "Dan, wait!"

"Oh for goodness' sake, It's just one of those days," Dan said, hitting the steering wheel.

"Why is your receptionist flagging you down?" Ashley asked.

Dan smiled, "He's not my receptionist, he's my cameraman. New cameraman I should say. My secretary called out today so I was making him man the phones. The kids a real ass."

Greg ran up to the passenger side window, saw Ashley inside and snarled. "Dan, your secretary showed up, I can go now."

Dan looked at Ashley and shrugged, "Sorry lady, too much equipment in the back to shove you back there, I guess this is were you get off."

"Mr. Phillips, You don't understand, I really need to talk to you." Her voice was raising angrily now.

"Screw you, lady, I'm his camera man," Greg yelled.

"Gotta have a camera man," Dan said to her apologetically.

Ashley looked at him, started to get out, and then said, "I'll take your pictures."

Dan Phillips laughed out loud this time, "You're serious? You'll be my cameraman?"

"Dead serious," she replied.

With the smile still on his face Dan looked at Greg, said, "Sorry kid, she's prettier than you. Go help Mary answer the phones."

The boy's face was flushed with anger now, "You can't do this, she doesn't even work here!"

Ashley looked at the young boy and smiled, "Oh well, sucks to be you," she said. With that, Dan punched the accelerator and the van sped out of the parking garage leaving a trail of fumes.

Ashley squeezed the door grip with white knuckled fingers as the van sped through heavily congested intersections, weaving in and out of traffic. Once, Dan Phillips even swerved into the on coming lanes to avoid a near miss with the rear end of a delivery truck.

Ashley shut her eyes tightly as he turned a corner, hitting the curb and causing cars with the right of way to come to a screeching halt, blasting their horns furiously at the news van. "Where are we going in such a hurry?" she asked, barely opening her eyes. She let out a small scream and snapped them shut again as the van cut across three lanes of traffic suddenly to make an illegal left turn.

Dan smiled a great big smile at the sound. Was he driving like this to purposely scare her?

"There's a shoot out at a Vietnamese grocery store. The police have the guy who's been abducting young women cornered in the place."

"Abducting women?" Ashley blinked, looking at him. A quick turn slung her into his shoulder. He smiled, there faces close. She quickly straightened herself back up in her seat.

"Yea, it's a story I've been following for about five months now. He abducts and then kills them, even raped one. You haven't heard this before? What, are you new in town or something?"

Ashley nodded, "Actually, yes I am. This may have some relevance on what I need to talk to you about."

Vacant Spaces

"It'll have to wait," he said, slamming the van to a stop. Ashley was jerked forward and was caught painfully across the breast by the seatbelt. "We're here. Grab the camera out of the back, I've got to get a statement from one of the police officers."

"Wait," Ashley said as he crawled out of the van, "What should I take pictures of?"

"Anything you'd want to see on the front page of the paper." And with that he slammed the door and was running toward the barricade of police cars with flashing lights.

Ashley got out and went around to the back of the van, opened the door and gawked, there were about six different cameras in back, along with various recording equipment and files in boxes. She grabbed the most expensive looking camera, turned it over. It had lots of gadgets and she wasn't exactly sure if she was holding it upside down or not.

"C'mon!" Dan yelled from somewhere in the crowd of police.

Ashley ran toward the mob just as gunshots rang out from the small grocery store fronting the scene.

She ducked and covered her head out of sheer reflex as the police returned fire. The big picture glass window that framed the stores front was shattered and went crumbling toward the pavement in a million, sparkling shards of light reflecting the sun.

Someone grabbed her arm, she looked up, saw that it was Dan Phillips.

"Start snapping," he demanded.

She looked at the camera and then at him and shouted over the police sirens, "I don't know how. It's not like my Polaroid."

He took the camera, turned it right side up. "Just look into this digital screen and hit this button. If you hold down on it, it will take pictures continuously." He handed the camera back to her just as more gunshots were fired from the store. This time the bullets hit one of the police cars that were acting as a barricade, spider webbing the windshield and shattering the blue bulb that was rotating atop the car, so only the red one was flashing.

Again the police returned a spray of bullets. Slanted tables that held an array of fruits and vegetables were hit, sending produce flying through the air and exploding into pulp as if they were target practice, their remains landing on top of broken glass and pavement below.

"We're going to gas him!" One police officer yelled out and a handful of others started dawning mask. They looked alien and just a little bit frightening. Ashley fumbled with the camera and hit the red button, snapping sounds came from it as balls of smoke were fired from a large tubular device. Loud pops caused her ears to ring as a total of three of the smoking balls were shot through the gaping hole that was once the store's window. Clouds of gas bellowed out of the building's orifices now and the police officers with the masks positioned themselves to go in, all the while Ashley held down on the little red button. She saw Dan Phillips near the front of the barricade talking with a man in a white button down, the sleeves of the shirt rolled up. Sweat stains spread from the man's armpit and he seemed to be yelling at Dan, or was he just yelling over the racket? Ashley couldn't be sure.

Vacant Spaces

Rapidly and without warning a figure emerged from the gray recesses of the pillows of smoke. Gun in both hands, waiving them like prizes, the man that was held up inside the store came barreling out, running straight toward the barricade. As though it were happening in slow motion, Ashley watched as fiery blasts came from the barrels of the man's guns. Something whizzed past her right ear and policemen began to fall. Glass shattered from windshields all around Ashley. Sounds of metal being punctured and flesh and bones hitting the ground with nauseating cracking sounds could be heard as the man kept pulling the triggers. The sounds mingled with the repetitive and deadly shots. She saw Dan looking at her from near the front, he looked angry. Did he think she wasn't taking pictures? Then she saw a stream of blood trickle down from his hairline just as his knees buckled and he fell out of her view. An explosion of gunshots from the stunned police now, and Ashley watched in horror as the man from the store was literally picked up off the ground by the army of bullets and thrown backwards, his body jerking in mid air as if he were having a seizure, as bullet after bullet was fired into him. Splatters of blood and skull flew and finally he hit the concrete with a sickening thud. Smoke and the smell of gunpowder hung heavily in the air. Suddenly the mob of cops and reporters became a stampede and Ashley found herself forced into it or be trampled. She tried to fight her way to where she saw Dan Phillips fall but police officers were holding the public back now. More sirens wailed in the distance as another herd of ambulances arrived. A short, wrinkled man was yelling at the police in Vietnamese and pointing at the damage to his store. Standing on tiptoes and holding the camera above her head, Ashley could see paramedics loading the newspaper reporter onto a stretcher. She broke through a yelling policeman's arm just as they were putting him into the back of the ambulance.

"I'm with him!" Ashley yelled as one of the young paramedics grabbed her hand and helped her into the back of the wailing vehicle. The doors slammed shut and Ashley found herself on yet another fast paced ride in a van.

It was almost four hours later when Ashley Malone and Dan Phillips left the emergency room. Dan wore a bright, white bandage on his head and joked that the two of them would have matching wounds. Thank God the bullet had only grazed him.

"Listen," he said, turning to her in the parking lot just as an ambulance sped by. "I have to drop this camera off to developing and print my story, do you want to meet in a couple of hours and talk about— well, whatever it was you wanted?" He smiled and so did she. Nodding, she told him that that would be fine. They made plans and he gave her directions to a little coffee shop nearby. Saying their good-byes, they both walked away in opposite directions.

What a city, Ashley thought as she walked. It was filled with murderers, rude people, teenage girls who thought they were once possessed, and eccentric old land ladies who lurked about, stocking your cabinets at night. She couldn't help but smiled to herself, despite the day she'd had. More had happened to her in the past week than had in her whole life. Then she thought about the dead man at the grocery store too. It was the first time she had ever watched someone die. Her own father passed away alone in the hospital from cancer, in a drug induced sleep. She still remembered the phone ringing that Sunday morning seven years ago. Her mother, calm and collected, told her that her father was dead. Ashley hadn't understood her mother's seemingly uncaring reaction. To her the calm and collective demeanor seemed more like cold and calculating. But she figured her mother had just gone numb on the inside. It wasn't easy waiting for the one you love to die, knowing there was no other route to be taken. Still, even though she knew the man that was shot down earlier was a killer and a rapist, she couldn't help but feel sad. She wondered if he was the one responsible for Susan's disappearance. Maybe Dan could clarify some things for her over coffee. Ashley found herself wishing she didn't look such a mess.

Dan was right on time at the Java Hut Gourmet Coffee Shop. Ashley had purposely gotten there early and made use of their facilities. She dug out the meager items of make up that were buried at the bottom of her purse, applied lipstick, powdered her face, and tried in vain to make her disarrayed hair look a little less like a bird's nest. Sitting in front of Dan Phillips now, though, she felt a little less self-conscious. He was unshaven with an early five o'clock shadow. Ashley giggled to herself as she thought maybe he hadn't springed-forward either, like Cross. His blondish brown hair was a mess too, windblown and pushed up by that ridiculous looking bandage. His baby blues were red and bloodshot.

Still, in spite of the rough exterior, Dan Phillips was an extremely attractive man. Ashley ventured a guess that he was probably around thirty-two years old and he didn't wear a wedding band. Not that she cared, she thought quickly to herself; it was just something she'd noticed. She also noticed his lean, muscular arms that stretched the sleeves of his fresh white tee shirt, and his well-defined chest and hard nipples that out lined his torso. Not that she was at all interested, she reminded herself again.

"What exactly is a latte?" Dan asked her after they had ordered. He stuck with regular coffee.

"Well," Ashley started, cocked her head to one side and said, "It's kind of like a cappuccino."

Dan shook his head, "What's the difference between the two?"

"A cappuccino is espresso and steamed milk and a latte is—well espresso and steamed milk too, but it's—uh—is it to late to say I don't know?" she asked crinkling her nose.

Dan laughed and then produced a white envelope. "I thought you might like to see some copies of the pictures you took today," he said, reaching inside and pulling out a stack of large, glossy photos."

"Oh, I'd love too," and scooted her chair closer to his.

"Well then," he handed her the first one. "Here's a picture of your feet, and this one's the back of some cop's head, the sky, another one of your feet, nice shoes by the way." One after another he handed her the pictures. Trash all of them.

Vacant Spaces

"I'm so sorry Dan. I didn't mean to ruin your story." She put the pictures down on the table; she couldn't look at them anymore.

Dan smiled at her and said, "You didn't ruin my story," and then he produced one last picture. "Because among all the bad photos was this one jewel that will be gracing the special edition of this evening's paper."

Ashley stared at the shiny picture. It was the perfect shot of the man, bellowing out of the smoke, guns blasting, and his face a contorted mask of rage.

"That is by far one of the best pictures I've ever seen in my career. Not only that but probably the only picture of this guy alive." Dan added.

"And this is going to be on the cover of the New York Times?" Ashley asked, in amazement.

He laughed, "Not just the local paper, but it was sold to every news magazine and network news across the world."

Ashley's eyes were wide as she stared down at the picture.

"Of course," he added, "You'll get a percentage of the sale, and not to mention credit. I even made sure they spelled your name right. Your name was Dan Phillips, wasn't it?" he laughed and she said very funny. There was a moment of silence as they stared at each other. Finally, Ashley broke away and Dan cleared his throat.

"So," he began, back to business at hand. "What is so important that you would step in front of a moving van and risk your life to talk to me about?"

"If I knew how you drove then I wouldn't go within ten feet of that van, moving or not," Ashley kidded as she produced the folded newspaper page. Unfolding it in front of the man, she pointed to the article circled in magic marker. "This was sent to me anonymously when I was still living in Atlanta. Do you remember writing it?"

Dan read the article silently as Ashley continued to ramble on nervously.

"I didn't know about this guy abducting women until today. Do you think he's the one who abducted Susan, Dan?"

He looked up at her and said, "I wouldn't know. I'm not the one who wrote this article."

"What?" she asked confused, taking the paper from him. "Your name's right here, Dan Phillips." She pointed at his name, showing him. He nodded.

"I see my name," he said. "But I'm not the one who wrote this article, trust me I would remember."

"Then who did?"

Dan shook his head and stood now, "I don't know," he said laying money down on the table. "But we can find out. Come with me."

Ashley stood and followed the reporter to the door. "Where are we going?"

He replied, "The newspaper's archives. I want to check something out."

"Did you drive?" Ashley asked him.

"Yea, why?"

"I'll take a taxi and meet you there, give me ten minutes head start." She laughed and cut in front of him.

He watched her as she went out the door. Nice ass, he thought, not that he was interested.

Vacant Spaces

The New York Times archives office was just a long narrow room filled with floor to ceiling shelves. The shelves held metal canisters that had past issues of the paper on microfilm.

"They're trying to update it all to computer," Dan told her, as she stared in awe at the vast array of stored data. "You should see the archives office for anything before eighty four, all on hard copy."

Ashley whistled.

Dan located the date and took the microfilm to a slide viewer and began turning the knob, the blue electric light of the machine illuminating his face.

"Just like I thought," he said.

Ashley peered over his shoulder. "What is it, Dan?"

He looked up at her and nodded for her to look at the screen. She did so. It was the exact same page of the New York Times that was sent to her, except that where the article about Susan should've been was a story on the first woman abducted by the man that was shot and killed earlier today, and it wasn't Susan!

"That's the story I wrote," Dan told her. "Not what you showed me."

"What does it mean?" Ashley asked, more to herself than to him.

"It means someone played a rather elaborate hoax on you."

Ashley shook her head, "But it doesn't make any sense. Susan really is missing. I'm living in her apartment right now. Why would someone send me a fake newspaper article about a real event? It just doesn't add up."

"Unless someone wanted to get you here to New York," Dan put in.

"But Susan is the only person I know that lives here."

"Do you think she could be behind it?"

Ashley looked at him, confusion behind her eyes. "I don't know what to think anymore, Dan. I feel like I'm going crazy." She felt tears tugging at her eyes and desperately didn't want him to see her cry. He took her by the shoulders and lifted her chin with his finger so that she was staring right into those baby blue eyes.

"Hey, It'll be okay," he told her, and, "Let me do some checking before you commit yourself. There's got to be an explanation. You have a phone were I can reach you?"

She shook her head no.

"Okay, well I've got your address then," he said, holding up the article. "Give me a day or two, let me see what I can come up with."

She looked down and he tilted her head up again. "Okay?" he asked.

Ashley smiled and nodded.

CHAPTER NINE

Ashley felt like Cinderella rushing home from the ball as she ran down the massive concrete steps of the New York Times building. She lost a shoe and had to double back up two steps to retrieve it. After the shoot out and coffee with Dan, and now the discovery of the fake article, Ashley had all but forgotten about her date with Thomas. If it was a real honest-to-God bonified date. She wasn't exactly sure what Thomas considered it. Maybe she was reading too much into it. Perhaps he was just being nice to the new tenant. Regardless of his intentions, Ashley was running late. She glanced at her watch for the fifth time. Six forty five and she wasn't anywhere near ready. She watched as taxi cabs zipped by her one after the other despite her frantic waves. Finally one pulled up to the curb, "Hey, I know you," a voice said from the driver's seat. Ashley crouched down and peered into the open passenger side window. Inside was the cabby who had picked her and Austin up at the airport. "311 Beech street right? Get in."

Ashley rolled her eyes and climbed in the back seat of the urine-scented cab. She closed the yellow door and the cabby turned and smiled at her with that same rotted tooth smile.

"Nice to see you again," he wheezed as he punched the accelerator.

Ashley was never as glad to see the brownstone as when she stepped from the cab. She took in a lung full of fresh air, well, as fresh as the air gets in New York. It was seven fifteen. She had forty-five minutes to work a miracle on herself.

Once inside the foyer, she stopped to let Mrs. Winthrop know she was home and apologized for being so late. She did not explain why, she simply didn't have time for all of that.

"Stop worrying about me," Mrs. Winthrop insisted. "Just go upstairs and get ready, Austin and I will be up in a bit."

Ashley took the stairs two at a time, practically tip toeing past Thomas' apartment.

After a quick shower she realized she had nothing to wear. The only two 'going out' dresses she owned were too wrinkled from the move to wear and dry clean only. Susan, she thought, heading for the closet. Susan always had fabulous taste and was Ashley's size. At least she was almost ten years ago, the last Ashley had seen of her. The closet was lined with clothing. Blouses and skirts and slacks, aha! Here was what she was looking for, a beautiful blue satin dress with thin shoulder straps and floor length with a thigh high slit up one side. Ashley slipped it over her head; let it slide down her body, gliding over her hips. The material felt good. Like soft hands caressing her thighs. She glanced in the full length mirror. Perfect. The fit couldn't have been any better than if it was bought for Ashley herself. It hugged to her in all the right places, showing off her hourglass figure and just enough cleavage to make a man want to see more. The gold cross of Abigail's sparkled and Ashley thought again of her missing rosary. She would have to make time to stop by the Briar sisters apartment, she prayed her rosary would be there. Her eyes moved to the black and blue gash on her forehead. It was still noticeable, but with the right hairstyle she could cover most of it up. Just as she was about to turn away from the mirror, she noticed a tag hanging from the satin material of the dress. Ashley gave it a jerk and it gave way. She whistled when she saw the price. Brand-new and Susan had never even gotten to wear it. The name of the store was on the tag too. "Chantal Litharge fine apparel." Even the name of the place sounded expensive. Ashley knew Susan had good taste, but to spend such an outrageous price for a dress and then never wear it? Oh well, success must be nice, she thought.

Mrs. Winthrop and Austin arrived just as Ashley finished readying herself.

"Oh my!" the older woman exclaimed, putting a hand to her cheek. "You look absolutely stunning. A man would have to be blind, deaf and stupid not to snatch you up."

Ashley giggled and turned for the woman. She had to admit to herself, she did look exceptional tonight. She wished she had time to show Cross and tell her about the missing journal, but already it was five till eight. She noticed now that Mrs. Winthrop had a strange look on her face. She was staring at Ashley, actually she was staring at Ashley's neck.

'Mrs. Winthrop," Ashley walked over to the woman who's eyes never wavered from her neck. "Are you okay? You look like you've just seen a ghost"

At that the old lady snapped her head and smiled at Ashley. "Just fine dear, just remembering days gone by. You know, I was quite a looker in my day. A real heart breaker."

Ashley smiled, "I bet you were Mrs. Winthrop."

"That's a lovely cross you're wearing," Mrs. Winthrop said, again looking at Ashley's neck and the small piece of jewelry that hung there. "Is it an heirloom?"

Ashley touched the tiny gold cross and looked down, "I really don't know. I found it in the bathtub drain; it says Abigail on the back. Do you know her?"

"Abigail?" The old woman said the name as though she was tasting it, then, "No I can't say I do. A friend Of Susan's perhaps."

"Could be," Ashley said.

Mrs. Winthrop took a step forward. "You know dear, as lovely as that cross is, it really doesn't match your outfit at all. Something diamond maybe."

Ashley laughed, "Diamonds. Wouldn't that be nice? I'm afraid I don't own much jewelry though."

The old woman smiled and winked at Ashley, reached down her flower print blouse and removed a small, sparkling diamond on a silver chain. She began to unclasp it and said, "A gift from my last husband. Quiet valuable really." She handed the necklace to Ashley.

"Oh Mrs. Winthrop it's beautiful, really, but I can't. If anything were to happen to it I'd never be able to forgive myself."

"But I would. Besides nothing is going to happen to it." She stepped behind Ashley and fastened the chain around her neck at the same time unclasping the

Vacant Spaces

cross. "Wear it for luck," she added, and "I'll put this in your jewelry box." she held up the gold cross on it's thin chain.

Ashley thanked her and gave her a kiss on the cheek. She thought she actually saw the old woman blush. She gave Austin a peck on the forehead, "See you later, kiddo. Mommy loves you." He stared at her, bright eyed and Ashley could have sworn that she'd seen a ghost of a smile on his lips.

"Have a good time," Mrs. Winthrop said, walking her to the door.

"Thanks for everything," Ashley replied, stepping out into the hallway and almost running in to Cross.

"Ashley, thank God your here I've got to talk to you," the girl looked disarrayed.

"Oh Cross, hi," Ashley said, "I want to talk to you too but can it wait, I'm already late."

Cross started to say no, then saw Mrs. Winthrop standing in the doorway smiling.

"Yea," she replied instead. "It can wait no biggie." The girl never took her eyes off of Mrs. Winthrop.

Ashley placed her hand on Cross' shoulder, "I'll stop by later, okay? Promise."

"Yea, sure whatever," she tried to sound casual.

"Cross," Mrs. Winthrop looked at the girl and stepped from the doorway. "Austin and I were just about to have some hot chocolate, would you care to join us?"

Cross shook her head, didn't speak for a minute then, "N-no thanks. I got a lot to do." And with that she fumbled for her keys and went to her apartment door.

Mrs. Winthrop smiled and winked at Ashley as Ashley headed down the stairs.

The old woman sighed as she shut the door, leaned up against it and stared at the cross in her hand. She turned it over, looked at the engraved name upon it's back. "Abigail." She said with disgust. Mrs. Winthrop clutched the cross in her fist and walked down the hall into the bathroom. She raised the lid on the toilet and let the small cross dangle over it; it swung from the thin gold chain. Her eyes reflected the cross' swaying motion, she squinted, smiled, then opened her hand and let the piece of jewelry fall into the toilet. "Oops." she said, pressing the handle of the commode and flushing it. Mrs. Winthrop watched as the cross glittered and went round and round in the water until it went down and out of sight. As she turned Austin was standing in the doorway watching her. The old woman smiled.

CHAPTER TEN

"You look beautiful," Thomas smiled at her, beckoning her into his apartment. He didn't look so bad himself, Ashley noticed, his dark gray slacks and matching jacket with a white button down underneath. The collar of his shirt opened just enough to show a little toned and tan skin.

Ashley looked around the apartment as she entered; this unit was bigger than hers. The man had amazing taste; impeccable antique furnishings were spread about. What looked to be a hand carved redwood curio cabinet lounged in one corner, close to the dining room. It stood high on claw feet, deep cut grooves spread up and out in unusual designs. Ashley walked over to it and peered through the glass doors at what rested safely on the shelves within. Statues of all sorts, unlike anything Ashley had ever seen before. One large one that seemed to dominate the others, looked familiar though. It was a Pan like figure. His legs were like that of a goat, his feet hooves. A hairy torso led up to a twisted and contorted face, two long and spiraled horns sprang from the forehead of the creature. But the most noticeable things were the two large wings that twisted from the creatures back and spread out, as though it were ready to take flight. It was the most ugly thing Ashley had ever seen.

"Quiet beautiful, isn't it?" Thomas asked, so close behind her that she could smell the scent of his cologne, could feel his hot breath at her neck. She felt his hand touch her bare shoulder, rested it there, warm and firm. "I used to do a bit of traveling back in my younger days," he said softly, his head bent down beside hers now, his words putting hot breath in her ear. She tried not to breath heavy. "That particular piece is the prize of my collection. I located it in a remote region of India. There are only two more like it in the entire world."

"What is it?" Ashley asked, a break in her voice.

Thomas chuckled at that. "Superstitious nonsense, really. It's the image of the oldest and most powerful demon, Azreal, the first angel to rebel and follow Lucifer. The demon of rebirth, it is said that Azreal is neither male nor female and that Satan will one day birth the antichrist from this demon."

"How grotesque," Ashley stated. She was still looking at the statue. That name, Azreal. Wasn't that the same name from the journal? She couldn't be sure, but the fact that the journal had never turned up terrified her beyond words. If there was someone in her apartment they could have killed her and Austin.

"Is something wrong?" The man asked her, gently rubbing her shoulder now. Ashley shook her head and smiled at him. "How about a glass of wine then?" He smiled back and walked over to the small bar on wheels. Her shoulder was still warm were his hand had been. "What will it be, red or white?" Thomas held up two bottles.

"Red please," Ashley replied, walking away from the ugly statue. "India doesn't worship the Christian God though, right?" she asked as he poured, the bottle top clinking against the sparkling, crystal cut wine glasses.

He shook his head and handed her one of the glasses, she made sure his had the same amount in it, it did. Just in case he was trying to get her drunk.

"Not particularly, no, although Christianity is being taught widely around the world now. That's what makes the statue so valuable, though, you see. The fact that it was found in a non Christian country, and dated to be over two centuries old." He smiled now, held his glass up. "But enough of all this boring mythology, here's to us, and our first date together."

So it was a date. The clinking glasses rang in the air for another second as they sipped the wine. It was warm, with a sweet after taste as it slid down Ashley's throat. Her left dress strap slid off her shoulder. Thomas smiled lightly and with two fingers glided it gently back into place, caressing her arm and shoulder as he did so. Chills of pleasure ran down Ashley's back as she stared deep into the burning pools of his eyes. He took her hand and led her to the table.

"You sit, while I check on dinner. There's some bread and cheese here," he motioned to a basket on the table were bread still steamed and a dozen varieties of cheese lay cut in thick blocks. "I hope Cornish hen in a cranberry and honey glaze is all right," He said as he disappeared into the kitchen. Sweet smells of spices and sauce wafted in causing her stomach to growl.

"That sounds delicious," she called back. Cornish hen? Ashley wasn't even sure if she had ever had Cornish hen. She was more of a fried chicken kind of girl.

"Almost ready," Thomas said, coming back in through the door and carrying the aromas of the food into the room with him. "Here have some French bread and cheese." He began slicing.

At the same time that Ashley was breaking bread With Thomas Robinson, Cross was pacing back and forth nervously in her small apartment. She held a large black book in her hands. It's hard cover worn with age. She had to speak with Ashley. Damn, why had Mrs. Winthrop been standing there. And where was Ashley going all dolled up like a Barbie? Cross wondered. A date probably, dressed like that it pretty much had to be a date. She continued to pace. Every time she reached the middle of the room, a loose floorboard would creak painfully. The house's way of reminding the residents of it's age. After Ashley had told Cross that Thomas Robinson had had three books published, she checked at the bookstore were she worked, and this is what she had found. Oh just wait until Ashley got a load of this. Conspiracy theory wasn't the half of it. As she paced, Cross looked at the suitcases on her futon. She had packed what she could a little while ago. She was getting the hell out of here, a.s.a.p. The only thing she was waiting on was Ashley. As she paced one loose floorboard creaked each time she came to it. Her mind raced as she gripped the book tightly with both hands. As the creaking rang through her head, interrupting her thoughts, she realized it was coming too soon. She wasn't at the creaking floorboard yet. She halted. Listened. CREAK. It was coming from above her, in the attic. Light footsteps ran across the ceiling. Someone was walking up there.

Vacant Spaces

Her heart began to race. She backed up to the large bay window that looked down into the front yard of the brownstone. Her back against its glass, she listened. Silence. Leave now, something told her. Don't wait. But if she left by the hallway Mrs. Winthrop may see her. She looked out the window. She was three stories up with no fire escape. She would have to take the chance of being caught with suitcase in hand. There was no other way out. Just then, she saw shadows dance across the crack at the bottom of her front door. Someone was in the hallway. There was a scuffling sound. Cross was afraid to move. She could see the doorknob's lock from where she was. Thank God it was turned. She was locked safely inside. The chain was undone but Cross never thought they were really any help anyway. Anyone could bust through a door with only a chain lock holding it.

In the hallway the shadows still played at the bottom of her door. Go away, go away. Cross said silently. Her heart was pounding and her mouth went suddenly dry as she watched the doorknob being slowly turned from the outside. My God, she thought. The lock wouldn't let the knob budge but the person still twisted it back and forth slowly, as if trying to be quiet. Cross brought the book up to her chest and hugged it for safety.

Then with sheer terror penetrating her mind she heard the jingling of keys. Blackness began washing in around the edges of her vision and the girl was sure she was going to faint from sheer fright. Cross shook her head and with that shook off the surrounding darkness. Quickly she ran to the small bookshelf that hid the secret closet, pushed it away and let her hand glide over the wall panel. Come on! Come on! She said quietly, and the door of the little hidden closet swung open. She placed the book inside, closed the wall panel and pushed the bookshelf back into place. Another noise now, metal sliding into metal and she looked at the doorknob, watched in horror as the lock turned. Her phone! She had to call for help! The door opened slowly, silently.

The red stain spread quickly across the throw rug, absorbing into the fabric. Ashley was on her hands and knees, dabbing at it with a cloth napkin. Her wine glass lay next to her on its side. "Thomas, I'm so sorry," she apologized as she dabbed, doing little good except ruining the cloth napkin too. "I guess I should have warned you what a klutz I am."

"Nonsense," Thomas said, kneeling down next to her and stopping her nervous dabbing. He took the napkin from her hand. "No stain is permanent." He said smiling, setting the fallen wine glass on the table and helping her up from the floor.

"Dinner was wonderful," Ashley wasn't sure what to do now, Thomas was still holding her hand. He stared intently at her. His other hand went up to her cheek and he rubbed it with the back of his fingers. Their heads leaned in close to one another, both were breathing unsteadily. Ashley closed her eyes in anticipation of a kiss when the shuffling of feet caused her to open them again. Thomas pulled back. Someone was in the hallway.

"Must be Father Jerod coming home," Thomas stated dropping her hand. "Have you met him yet?"

Ashley shook her head, "No, I haven't."

Vacant Spaces

"Splendid fellow, really. Always out at one charity convention or another. I swear, he's here so rarely, you wonder why he has an apartment at all." The man chuckled and walked to the bar, he poured another glass of wine and handed it to her.

"Are you sure you trust me with this?" she smiled, taking the glass.

Somewhere from the back regions of the apartment a telephone rang. Ashley looked around.

"The phone's in my office were I write," he explained, "That's were I spend most of my time. Excuse me for a moment"

She watched as he strolled down the dark hallway toward the muffled shrill of the phone. His tall, lean figure moved with preciseness. This man was very sure of himself. Confident. Everything Ashley was not. So how did it come about that she was standing here in his apartment, on a date with this man? She heard his voice speak, couldn't make out the words. The wine had made her feel light, almost giddy. She was more relaxed now. Ashley walked about the room, wine glass dangling at her side, free hand gliding over furnishings. The hallway loomed before her and at the end was a tiny shaft of light penetrating the darkness where the office door had been left partially open. She would love to see were he wrote, what he wrote. She waded lightly down the hallway, following the sounds of his voice. His words were becoming clearer now.

"How could you have been so foolish!" His tone, though hushed, sounded angry. "Yes, I understand perfectly and if this ruins things you will be the one to pay the price."

Ashley stopped at the door, was about to push it open, when it swung inward suddenly, Thomas loomed before her, red-faced and glaring at her.

"I - I thought I would like to see your office," she stammered.

The man smiled, softening the anger in his amazing eyes. "It's a mess, really," he said pulling the door shut behind him and guiding her back into the living room. "I'll give you the tour next time, I promise."

Next time. He definitely said next time. That was a good sign, Ashley told herself then tried to stifle a yawn.

"Tired?" he asked.

"I think it's the wine." She looked at her watch. "It's getting late and Mrs. Winthrop has had Austin all day with out a break, I really should go."

"Must you?" he asked and she nodded, setting her wine glass down and walking to the door.

"I had a great time," she said turning, longing for a kiss from this man.

He walked toward her. "Maybe we could go see a show next week? Broadway, or anything you like."

She smiled up at him, her own eyes bright tonight too. "I'd like that"

Thomas touched her cheek again, "I really am fond of you, Ashley." And this time there was no hesitation; he leaned in and kissed her, deep and warm. She had to stand on her tiptoes just for her lips to be able to reach his. It lasted only for a moment when they both pulled back slightly and looked into each other's eyes. He leaned in again. His lips were soft and new, she tasted the wine on them and then there tongues were probing. Ashley felt a hot stirring inside

Vacant Spaces

of her that she hadn't felt in years. His hand was placed firm against the side of her neck, the other flowed down her bare shoulder, moving in between her shoulder blades and down to the small of her back were it rested and he pressed her against him.

Then the sounds of sirens coming closer, getting louder, interrupted the two. They paused looking at each other, neither moved, waiting for the wails to pass, sure that the noise would go on by the brownstone so that they could continue their embrace. The sirens did not pass, though. They stopped in front of the building. Red and blue lights strobed through the window, penetrating the sheer fabric of the drapes.

"What in the world?" Thomas exclaimed and walked to the window. Suddenly there was a stampede of footsteps coming up the first flight of stairs. They rambled by Thomas' door causing Ashley to jump. The herd of footsteps continued their course up to the third floor. Ashley was struck with a quick and terrible fear. "Austin!" she said aloud and lurched for the door, jerking it open. She was heading for the stairs with Thomas at her heels.

As the two of them reached the third floor landing, Ashley saw Mrs. Winthrop standing in the hallway. The girl ran to the older woman. "Where's Austin?" she demanded as Mrs. Winthrop took her by the shoulders.

"He's fine, Ashley. He's in his room," she said. "The noise scared him.

"What's happening, Harriet?" Thomas asked, coming up behind the two women.

Ashley noticed that Cross' door was open, busted open actually, voices coming from within. The crackling static of police radios filled the air.

Mrs. Winthrop looked at Thomas then at Ashley as a policeman came out of Cross' apartment and approached the three of them. He looked at Mrs. Winthrop.

"We'll need to ask you some questions, mam," he said to her.

"What's going on?" Ashley demanded, tried to move to Cross' apartment and found that Thomas was holding her back.

Mrs. Winthrop looked at Ashley now, tears forming in the old woman's eyes. "It's Cross dear," she said, finally. "I'm afraid she's dead."

Ashley felt as if she'd just been slapped. The words rang in her ears. It couldn't be true, it couldn't. But she knew better, reality set in bitterly, Cross was gone.

Death had come to the brownstone.

PART TWO

REMEMBRANCE

Mark Andrew Ware

CHAPTER ELEVEN

Ashley sat in her darkened living room, a glass of sherry in her hand that Thomas had brought up for her. He had wanted to stay but Ashley had sent the man away, she needed to be alone, well alone other than Mrs. Winthrop, that is. The only light came from the hallway behind her, casting the front of her silhouette in shadows. Mrs. Winthrop had insisted she take another one of the pills she had given her, no, don't worry, the alcohol wont affect them, she had said. They're not very strong, really.

The police left an hour ago, spoke with Harriet Winthrop briefly because she was the one who had heard the horrible crashing sound. Ashley wanted to talk to them and find out exactly what had happened, to find out about Susan too, but when she had entered her apartment and looked out the window at the commotion below—well, then she went numb, talk wasn't important. She had seen it, three stories below on the dew wet grass, Cross' crumpled body, hands curled, fetal position. One might have thought her asleep except for the impossible way her neck was twisted. Ashley almost became hysterical then. Thomas and Mrs. Winthrop tried to calm her. Ashley was jabbering, getting louder. Her hands were moving in uncontrolled motions, flying up from her sides. She kept talking about the man she saw shot down today and now Cross and how someone had tricked her into coming here. The police said it was a suicide, that the girl had flung herself out the apartment window, there was a page ripped from a poetry book that was pinned to her shirt, it read: I am a lonely soul, alone I wonder, to and fro, filling vacant spaces, with times strong hold, waiting for death to bring me home.

Mrs. Winthrop came rambling down the hallway now, causing noise in an otherwise perfectly silent apartment. She sat down beside Ashley on the sofa, placed a hand on the girls arm. Ashley didn't move, didn't even blink. Instead she kept her stare, straight-ahead, eyes glassed over with future tears. The half drank glass of sherry held precariously in her hand, resting in her lap.

"Are you okay dear?" The old woman asked softly, and when Ashley did not answer looked about nervously. "Can I get you anything......Ashley?"

With only the slightest of movement, Ashley shook her head.

"Austin is in bed, sound asleep. I didn't tell him what happened."

Silence still, and then—" Do you think she did it?" The words came from the girls' mouth as a hoarse whisper, spilling into the silence.

Mrs. Winthrop didn't understand at first, then she realized what Ashley had meant and said, "The police say it's definitely suicide dear. There was no foul play. What with that horrible poem and all, she had a history of mental illness too, did you know that?"

Ashley's head turned to look at the old woman now, at what she had just said.

Mrs. Winthrop nodded and continued, "Seems her parents had institutionalized her two years ago. When she turned legal age she just checked herself out. That's what the police told me anyway. Her parents have her listed as a missing person, that wasn't her real name, just as I suspected."

Ashley turned her stare straight ahead again. "Do you know what she told me? She told me she had been possessed once, that a demon had taken over her body. I just laughed at her. It was probably a cry for help, and I just laughed."

Harriet Winthrop looked intently at this person in front of her now; she stood slowly and walked to the bay window. Her back was to Ashley so that her auburn dyed hair caught highlights from the hallway. "Just because she had a mental problem doesn't mean that that wasn't true." The old woman said, face toward glass, moonlight shining in a blue night hue. Her voice sounded suddenly different and Ashley felt a chill.

"W-what did you say?" She whispered at the old woman who did not turn to look at her.

"I fully believe that a person can become possessed by a demon." she turned now and looked at Ashley. Her green eyes almost glowed, they were glassy and seemed to look not at Ashley but stare at what she spoke of, some distant knowledge of the past and she was there now, as she spoke. She began to walk about the room, letting her fingers glide over the stone of the fireplace, the panels in the wall. "Did you know this old brownstone used to be one dwelling? Oh yes, quiet majestic in it's time. The family who owned it was wealthy and threw huge parties. The largest parties you've ever seen. The father had dealings all around the world, so people from far away lands would show up, with strange tales and stories hidden from us here. There are places in the world were dark things are still practiced, for wealth, fame, eternal life. They had three children, the youngest a daughter. The bedroom where you sleep now, that was hers." The old woman continued to walk as she talked, lost in the story. Ashley watched her nervously. She wasn't feeling well, she wasn't felling well at all.

"There came a time, after one of these parties, after a friend of her father's had told them, taught them incredible things, dark and evil things that filled them with a knowledge of greed and power that the youngest daughter began to act strange, vile. Spitting out curse words and clawing at people's eyes, but after a while she would be back to her old self again, with no recollection of these things. Eventually her condition worsened though, she began speaking in a language foreign to her, she prophecised and the prophecies came to be. Her entire appearance began to change until it became that of something unearthly." The old woman looked at Ashley now, eyes boring into her. "She was possessed!" She spat the words at Ashley like venom and they struck. Ashley could not move, maybe it was the drugs and the alcohol causing the room to spin. A chill had wrapped itself around the young woman and was now squeezing. Her teeth chattered and she shivered visibly.

If the old woman saw this though, she paid no attention as she babbled on. "The mother and father had been practicing the black arts, devil worship you see, and there daughter's body to Satan was there greatest sacrifice. He would have her birth his image through a child, the daughter had no say so in the matter but soon came to crave the blood sweet taste of evil herself. She became pregnant during her possession, and the baby was to be the son of demon and man, the spawn of the devil bred into this realm for one purpose and one purpose only, to bring darkness and evil into the world, to damn all of that which was good and holy." She walked closer to Ashley now, Ashley backed away a bit, trying to bury herself in the sofa, a fear and dizziness had a hold on her, sweat poured from her brow, plastering her hair to her forehead. "Stop, please," she said to the old woman, but her voice broke and it came out only as a hoarse whisper.

The look in Mrs. Winthrop's eyes spoke of murder now, she blinked rapidly as she continued with the bedtime story from hell. "The baby died in it's mother's womb though, a horrible stench stayed in this brownstone for days afterwards, the parents thought the girl tainted and not worthy of being part of the devil's coven after that, only she had different plans. The family noticed that the milk started tasting funny," a sly grin crooked the corners of the woman's lips now as she said this. "It should have," she went on. "The daughter had poisoned it. She had offered them as her sacrifice to Satan. If she could not be the one to bear the antichrist, she would have eternal life by finding someone who could." With that she stopped and it was a good thing she did. Ashley had a hand held to her mouth, her own eyes glassed over now and her skin had become white as a sheet.

"Are you okay dear?" Mrs. Winthrop asked and came closer. The tone in her voice sounded sarcastic to Ashley. This old woman didn't care if she was okay or not.

"Get out." Ashley said softly, almost inaudibly.

"Excuse me dear?" The old woman looked shocked now.

Ashley snapped out of her trance, stood up and began to usher the old woman towards the door. "You have to leave. Now." She opened the door and practically pushed Mrs. Winthrop through it. The old woman opened her mouth to say something but Ashley closed the door in her face, locking the lock. She stood there with her hand still on the knob for another moment, felt a stirring in her stomach that turned to a wrenching and then, without warning, she vomited up Cornish hen in a raspberry and honey glaze.

CHAPTER TWELVE

The weekend passed. Ashley worked and took Austin on tours of the city. The two of them ate all three meals, breakfast, lunch and dinner, out. She shopped, visited museums, antique shops and thrift stores, anything to stay away from the brownstone and away from Cross' apartment and away from Mrs. Winthrop. In a drug induced hazed memory she recalled the story that Mrs. Winthrop had told her, in sickening defiance it kept springing up in her mind.

Cross' parents had sent movers for her meager belongings. They were having the body sent back to Cleveland so there would be no funeral to attend. That was what Cross had been reduced to now; Ashley thought sadly, a body to be shipped. All hope she had of finding Susan was vanishing quickly. If the police couldn't find anything how could she? Then she remembered the phone bill. It should have been in the mail by now, but that would mean asking Mrs. Winthrop for it. She couldn't avoid the woman forever though, and what was she avoiding her for really? For believing in something Ashley didn't, for being a tad bit eccentric? She had been a good friend to Ashley, and to Susan too. Ashley owed her an apology. She thought about this as she and Austin returned to the brownstone Sunday evening. Looking at the woman's door however she decided that now was not a good time.

Quietly, mother and son climbed the landing to the second floor. As they were about to pass apartment 2A muffled voices drifted out. Ashley stopped and Austin did the same. The voices sounded odd. Ashley couldn't make out any words, just the fact that the voices sounded monotone. She could make out three, and they seemed to be all talking at once. An argument, perhaps? But the voices didn't sound angry, more like chanting. Chanting? She'd thought. Austin pulled on her hand now, demanding to go. Ashley couldn't believe herself. One date with the man and now she was snooping outside his door. What was she now, a stalker? Did she think Thomas had a young woman in there, tied up or something? Really Ashley. Get a grip.

The young woman looked at Thomas Robinson, she was laying on her back, naked, spread across the black satin sheets of his king size bed. Thomas opened a drawer on the nightstand and pulled out leather ropes and a ball gag.

"Oh you are kinky," the blonde girl said, rubbing her breast, pinching her nipple until it became hard and rigid.

"Shhh." Thomas raised a finger to his lips. "Don't speak, just lay there." He could tell she was a whore from the moment he saw her, drinking a Tom Collins at the bar, barely able to stay on her stool. Still though, she was quiet beautiful, and her body, perfect. His mind couldn't help but drift to Ashley. How he wished it were she lying in his bed right now. He began tying the girls' wrist to the post of the bed. She smiled up at him, stupidly, making sounds of pleasure, her eyes closed. Whore, he thought silently as he made the ropes tighter.

In the living room the sounds of chants set to music played on the stereo, covering the noise of the front doorknob turning, the door creaking open slowly. Feet shuffled into the living room, cautious of loose boards in the hardwood floors. Cold eyes look at the statue of Azreal as they passed the curio cabinet and continued down the hallway toward Thomas Robinson's bedroom door.

CHAPTER THIRTEEN

Ashley woke early Monday morning. She was determined to find her rosary. Hoping that the Briar sisters would discover it and return it to her, she had waited. Now, however she would have to go to them. Ashley hoped and prayed that the two women had it, otherwise the only place it could be was the attic.

She walked over to her jewelry box. Also, she really must return Mrs. Winthrop's diamond necklace. It would be her excuse to see the old woman, to apologize and ask about the phone bill. Ashley opened the small metal box, took out the sparkling diamond necklace and noticed, that among the few priceless trinkets she kept there, Abigail's gold cross was nowhere to be seen. Maybe Mrs. Winthrop placed it somewhere else, she would have to remember to ask her later. She slid the diamond necklace safely in the pocket of her pants, and while Austin still slept, she left the apartment and crossed down the hall to the door with the big brass 3A on it. Ashley rapped her knuckles across the door. After a moment she heard shuffling on the other side and then, "Who is it?" a frail voice called out.

"Your neighbor, Ashley Malone. From apartment 3B?"

The door crept open, only an inch, and an old wrinkled eye peered out at her from waist level. Apparently this was the sister, Lillian, Ashley thought.

Vacant Spaces

Was she a midget? "What do you want?" The eye asked.

"I was here—with your sister Elizabeth? Well, I was wondering if I lost something here?"

"Lost 'something?'" The eye asked. "You don't know what?"

Ashley laughed nervously, looking down at the eye and answered. "A rosary. I think I may have lost an antique rosary, in your guest bed maybe?"

A familiar voice from behind the door said "Lilly! Open the door and let the poor girl in." The voice snapped. The eye disappeared just as the door was slammed shut. Ashley waited for a long uncomfortable minute and when the door was reopened Elizabeth stood smiling at her. "Hello again young lady, you look like you're feeling better."

Ashley nodded, "I am, Thanks." She raised a hand to her now fading bruise.

"Do come in, you'll have to forgive my sister." Elizabeth turned her head and spoke loudly toward the hallway, "She always has been antisocial." Then back at Ashley, smiling. "She hates it when I say that."

Ashley laughed as she entered the living room. "Wow, this place could make a fortune if the residents ever had a yard sale." The room was stocked full of antiques. So many in fact, that a small walkway trailed between them to let you out of the room. It was cluttered and claustrophobic. The smell of age dominated the room.

"Sister and I are avid collectors. Some of these things date back to the sixteenth century." The old ladies eyes gleamed with pride.

"They must be worth a fortune?" Ashley said looking around, wondering how Lilly had left the room so quickly with all the antiques blocking the way. "They probably should be under lock and key somewhere."

Elizabeth chuckled at the girl. "Oh no, they're quiet safe here, in our little brownstone."

Safe? Ashley wondered. After what happened to Susan how could she possibly think that these priceless relics were safe, unprotected save for two little old women?

"I heard you say something about losing a rosary?" Elizabeth asked, breaking the girl's thoughts.

"Yes, I was hoping it was here."

"I'm afraid not dear. I don't remember you having one on at all."

Ashley nodded her head. That's what she was afraid of. The attic then, was the only place it could be.

"I'm sorry you lost it, was it valuable?" Elizabeth asked.

"Only sentimental value. It was a gift from my father," Ashley replied, "I'm sure I'll find it though, sorry to have bothered you and your sister."

Elizabeth opened the door for her and with the ever-constant smile said, "No bother at all young lady. Come by anytime." And with that she closed the door. She was about to walk away when she heard: "How could you let that girl back into our home?"

"Oh Lilly, really, she's such a lovely thing." She heard Elizabeth reply.

How had the sister returned to the room so quickly, a person of her age and with the mounds of

Vacant Spaces

furnishings? Had she been hiding in the room all along, listening, watching? Hidden behind one of the large antique armoires or the china cabinet? Ashley shook her head, more and more curious, she thought.

There was no answer at Mrs. Winthrop's door. Ashley looked at Austin and said, "Maybe she's in the garden you love so much."

At that her son took her by the hand and led her out of the brownstone, down the steps and around a small stone pathway that led to a little white picket fence. Ashley found a gate, unlatched it and walked into a bright and sunny backyard, blooming with flowers of all colors. Austin smiled up at her with pride. Was it just her, or was he acting more normal today? Then she thought, what is normal lately anyway? The two of them walked through pathways between rows and rows of sweet smelling roses and petunias. Son led mother to a small vegetable garden then, in the back of the yard. Cabbage grew in purple heads. Red tomatoes plumped so largely on the vines that they looked as if they may pick themselves at any moment. And, dominating it all was Mrs. Winthrop's rear end poking out of a small bushel of corn.

"Hello down there." Ashley smiled as the old woman crawled out backwards on all fours.

"Ashley! Hello darling," she said, standing. One gloved hand held a small digging tool while the other brushed dark, rich soil from the knees of her purple slacks. "I see you spotted my rather large derriere poking out of the corn. Probably frightened you." She giggled. "I was hoping to see you today. After what happened to poor Cross and not seeing you all week end I was beginning to worry."

First poor Susan and now Cross had been given the prefix to her name too.

"I just needed to get out a bit, you know?" Ashley asked her and the old woman nodded. "I wanted to apologize too, for the way I acted the other night."

"Oh, forget it," she waved a dismissing gloved hand at Ashley, then spotted a weed and crouched down to pull it up. "You could make it up to me however," she added with her head down, "By letting Austin help me in the garden today. That is," she looked up at Austin now, "If he wanted to."

Ashley smiled and looked at her son, who in turn beamed up at her. Ashley clicked her tongue, "I think that's a yes." She said, and then added, "I may go out in a bit, and I'll pick him up say around five?"

"Whenever your ready, dear. I love having him around."

Ashley kissed her son on the forehead and turned to leave when she stopped. "Mrs. Winthrop, I almost forgot, did the phone company ever send me anything?"

"Oh yes, dear they did. It came Saturday, actually. I didn't see you to give it to you though. Would you like me to get it for you now?"

Ashley looked at the woman's dirty hands and at Austin all ready digging away. "No, that's all right. I'll get it when I pick up Austin this evening."

"Okay dear, have a good day." The old woman went back to picking weeds as Ashley returned to the front of the brownstone. She looked up at the portal windows of the attic, squinting in the sun and raising a

Vacant Spaces

hand to shade her eyes. The windows were dark and she half expected a face to appear in one only to vanish suddenly, like you see in the movies. There was no face though, and her eyes wondered down to Cross' window. That's when Ashley realized she was standing in the very spot were Cross' body had landed, neck twisted and contorted. She stepped away quickly. Poor Cross, she thought as her eyes squinted back to the cold, faceless glass of the attic windows. Oh well, no time like the present, and Ashley Malone entered the brownstone, destined for the top floor of the house.

On her way to the attic Ashley passed Thomas' door. All was quiet. No more mysterious chanting. Walking past apartment 2B she listened and Ashley wondered about the priest that lived there. She would very much like to meet him, but his apartment was quiet also, as was the Briar sister's and her own, and of course, Cross'.

As she climbed the stairs to the attic, she tried to think of other things, of the flowers in the garden, of Thomas of anything really, other than the cold recesses of the room that lay at the top of the stairs. The room were all of her troubles had began, were she was sure she had seen her son, even though that was impossible.

Be brave, Ashley told herself as she reached the top and put her hand out for the knob. With the bright sunlight pouring in from the hall window below, she could see in the dim stairwell this time, and what she saw was a new pad lock securing the attic's door. She laughed, relieved and sorry at the same time. Relieved that she didn't have to go into the room again and that now Austin couldn't get back in. Sorry that she wouldn't be able to get her rosary. Wait, she thought. Topples, the handy man. He would have a key. He was probably the one that installed the lock in the first place. She would simply get him to look in the attic for her. She bolted down the stairs and at the last step, let out a small scream as she crashed into someone, sending both, herself, and the other person flailing to the hallway floor.

The person stood quickly, dusted himself off and held out his hand for Ashley who regained her senses and looked up at the smiling face of Dan Phillips.

"You walk like I drive," he said, as she put her hand in his and was pulled up close to him. Too close, and she backed away, straightening her clothes.

"What are you doing here?" she asked, his blue eyes glowing from the stream of sunrays that broke the dimness of the hall's insufficient light.

"Nice to see you too. I told you I'd come by after I did some digging."

"And?" Ashley asked with new hope, stepping closer to the man. He smelled good. "You found something?"

Dan nodded, and then said, "Yes and no. Not exactly what you're looking for. But—look, I don't want to discuss it here. How about dinner tonight? About seven?"

Was he asking her out on a date? "I don't know," Ashley replied, "I'll have to see if I can find a baby-sitter." There she thought, that'll take care of it, the whole' you have baby?' thing.

Dan looked at her, "You have a baby?"

Right on cue. "A son, nine years old, hardly a baby."

Vacant Spaces

"Oh, well then if you can find a baby-sitter, tonight at seven okay?" He asked looking at her.

What's this? He's still pursuing. Ashley didn't speak.

"That is," he added, "Unless you have a husband stashed away too. But I'm betting since you have to get a baby-sitter, you don't."

"You would win that bet," she replied.

Dan dug around in his pocket and handed her a card. "If you can't make it call me. If you can then I'll see you at sevenish at the Java Hut, kay?"

She nodded and before she realized it he was gone. Ashley stood in the hallway holding his card, she still wasn't sure, was this a date? So many things were happening at once that Ashley just needed to take a breather. Still, if Dan Phillips had information on Susan, then Ashley would sure as hell go out with him. Not that she was the least bit interested in this man, she kept telling herself. But first things first, she needed to see Topples, and that meant leaving the top floor of the brownstone and going down to it's bottom floor. Ashley hoped it was more inviting.

Dan Phillips left the brownstone whistling. He liked Ashley that he couldn't deny. But the girl had problems, problems he wasn't even sure she was aware of, and the last thing he needed in his life was more problems. As he left the yard of the majestic building he had a strange sensation of being watched. Dan turned, looked up at the brownstone just in time to see the drapes swing close in an apartment on the second floor, apartment 2A to be precise. He shrugged his shoulders, nosy neighbors, there's one everywhere you go, he thought as he walked on, his whistle fading in the distance.

Ashley wasn't sure if she should knock on the basement door or not. She decided not and tried the knob. It turned. Opening the door only an inch she could see a narrow stairway, illuminated by a dim bulb hanging from a wire. The damp smell of mildew filled her nostrils.

"Hello," she called down the stairs, "Mr. Topples?" Mr. Topples, she thought? C'mon Ashley, get it together. "Topples, are you down there?" She called out again. There was no answer but Ashley couldn't be sure how deep or big the basement was, maybe he couldn't hear her. She placed a weary foot on the first step. It gave a groaning creak under her weight and she could feel the wood bow. Cautiously, one foot after another, one groaning step at a time she descended into the bowels of the house. Ashley was surprised to find a narrow hallway at the bottom of the stairs, lit by yet another bulb on a wire, this one swinging, yet there was no draft. Had someone been here? Now you're being paranoid, she told herself and waited a moment longer as her eyes adjusted to the shifting light. Shadows swaying to and fro, and Ashley's mind went to the poem that was with Cross' body. I am a lonely soul, I wonder to and fro. She shook the poem from her head, not wanting to remember the rest. There were two doors, one just a few feet away and to her left, the other at the end of the hallway. Ashley walked to the closest. Cold concrete floors echoed the clicking of her shoes as she walked. Ashley stopped at the door, raised her closed hand to

Vacant Spaces

knock, hesitated and then rapped on the door. The sound seemed incredibly loud in the confined space and she was sure the door would be swung open at any moment by an angry and red-faced Topples. Ashley tapped her foot nervously and hugged herself, rubbing her arms. The warmth was lost down here in the dampness. Behind the clicking sound of her tapping feet she could hear water dripping somewhere, maybe behind the door at the end of the hall. She stopped her tapping, listened. Drip......Drip......Drip. It echoed, wafting down the thin hallway, muffled only by the other door, blocking the source of the leak. Tired of waiting and just a little scared, Ashley checked the knob and it wasn't locked. The door opened with ease and Ashley was led into a room about the size of her living room. An unmade bed with disgustingly filthy sheets rested along one wall, a small reading lamp glowed, casting it in a spotlight like circle. A Formica table with one upholstered vinyl chair (badly torn) stood in front of a tiled counter top, a hot plate and dirty dishes resting upon it. Ashley moved closer toward the makeshift kitchen, saw a roach scurry away under a half eaten sandwich, the bread covered with mold. Dirty clothes were strewn about the floor and another door, this one opened, revealed a small bathroom. Ashley didn't even want to think of what the toilet may look like. Having her fill of the disgusting quarters, knowing that Topples wasn't here, she wanted desperately to leave the basement. How could a person live down here, she wondered, like an animal? She hurried out of the room, softly closing the door behind her. Drip......Drip......Drip. Damn that dripping. What was behind that other door anyway?

Water pipes probably, or maybe a laundry room. Mrs. Winthrop certainly didn't mention a laundry room. Ashley looked up the hallway, at the stairs, then back to the door at the end of the hall. Oh what the hell, she thought. If she could help it she would never come back down to this basement again, might as well snoop around now. She clicked down the hall, the sounds of her shoes mingling with the monotonous sounds of the leak. Drip…Click…Drip…Click. Ashley stopped just in front of the door, thought she smelled something, something with an almost sickly sweet odor blending in with the smell of mildew. The dripping noise was definitely coming from here, it's source just beyond this door. Ashley put her hand on the knob, started to turn it when suddenly the hallway went dark. She spun on her heels, looked to the stairs. They too were shrouded in blackness. Had the bulbs blown? The darkness was thick and complete. Her breath came in heaves with that damned dripping noise mocking its rhythm. She tried to move back up the hallway, her hand touching the damp wall for guidance. Ashley heard movement then and froze. Heavy footsteps clambered down the basement steps, they groaned even louder in agony. The noise sounded eerie here in the pitch black. My God had someone turned off the lights on purpose? Did they even know she was down here?

The footsteps stopped now at the bottom of the stairs. Ashley couldn't move, frozen with fear she felt like a deer caught in the headlights of an on coming vehicle. She would just stand there and wait for her slaughter. Snap out of it, she told herself. She called out in the darkness. "W-w-who's there?" She heard breathing that was not her own.

"Who's there?" she repeated, this time her voice was more bold.

Laughter and then, "Here piggy, piggy, piggy." The voice was deep and wet with cruel intentions.

My God, Ashley thought, this wasn't really happening. The footsteps picked up again, steady and coming right for her. In a blind rush she felt along the wall, found the doorknob to Topples' room and rushed in. She slammed the door closed behind her. Even the dimness of the small lamp was blinding after being in the black hole of the hallway. She fumbled with the knob, locked it and backed away, bumping into the table, upsetting a stack of dishes that fell over. Ashley screamed at the sound and screamed again as the doorknob was rattled back and forth and again the voice. "Little pig, little pig, let me in."

"Go away!" Ashley yelled and stumbled her way around the table to the counter. She found a drawer and pulled it open. It came out too far and went crashing to the ground, silverware spilling out and sliding across the floor. Ashley quickly dropped to her knees, hands feeling through the mess of metal. She found a small slicing knife and stood, facing the door. She waited, aware of her own heavy breathing. Her heart beat rapidly in her chest, pumping blood to her head causing it to throb. She held her breath, heard nothing. She waited. A phone? Her eyes searched the room but did not see one. She couldn't just stay here. Maybe they left. Slowly she moved toward the door, careful not to let her pumps click on the floor. Her breathing started again, as she got closer, closer, all the while keeping her eyes on the doorknob. Standing now in front of the door she cautiously placed her ear against its cold wood. She could hear her own heart beating but nothing else. Ashley stepped back, reached for the knob, and just as she lay her hand on the cold brass metal it was twisted furiously from out in the hallway. Heavy blows now shook the door on it's hinges.

"Little pig, little pig, let me in," the voice bellowed as fist pounded.

Ashley screamed at the top of her lungs, backing away. She screamed again and again until the pounding stopped. There was silence for what seemed like an eternity. Ashley waited; shaking, and then she saw the doorknob, watched in horror as the lock began to turn. Tears streamed down her eyes now and she shook her head, "No, no, no," she cried softly, raising the knife, her only meager means of protection. The door opened slowly and...

"Who's in here?" It was Mrs. Winthrop's voice, and then the old woman was squinting into the room. Her gaze fell wide eyed on Ashley, mascara streaked face, knife held up, gleaming in the lamps dim light. "Ashley? My God what's wrong?"

Ashley dropped the knife and ran to the woman, throwing her arms around her neck.

"Oh Mrs. Winthrop, it was awful! Someone turned out the lights and chased me in here. They were pounding on the door and—" she couldn't finish, only shook her head as the tears streaked down her face and clung to her chin. She buried her face in the old woman's shoulder.

"Oh you poor dear! Is that what all the screaming was about? Thank God I heard you."

Vacant Spaces

Ashley looked at her. "Did you see who it was?"

Mrs. Winthrop shook her head, "No, but I have a pretty good idea. Topples." she said, then added, "And I can guarantee he won't be back in this building. I'll contact his brother...and the police."

Ashley clung to the woman, sobbing into her blouse. The sweet smell of earth and flowers clung to her.

The old woman led her out into the hallway the lights were back. "Lets get you to my apartment and get a hot toddy in you, you poor thing."

Oh, don't call me poor, Ashley thought to herself. It makes me sound like poor Susan and poor Cross.

Mrs. Winthrop led her to the stairs, her aged and liver spotted arm around the girl's shoulders. Ashley glanced back at the doorway at the end of the hall. "Mrs. Winthrop," she asked, "What's behind that door?"

"Oh nothing but a storage room and leaky pipes, dear." The old lady replied.

"Oh," Ashley said, climbing the stairs, "That's what I thought."

Down the basement's hallway, behind the door at its end, a dark figure listens as the two women leave the bowels of the house. A grin spreads across the face and behind the dark figure the body of the blonde girl that was in Thomas Robinson's bed the night before, hangs upside down from the low ceiling. Her feet bound together. Blonde hair and arms dangling down, the body swaying as her long nails scrape along the concrete floor. The girl's throat is sliced, gaping open as though her head were hinged, and blood not yet clogged runs from the wound, down to the dead girls tilted chin. The ruby red droplet clings there for a second before dripping into a silver metal saucer below. Drip…Drip…Drip.

CHAPTER FOURTEEN

"Is that better?" Mrs. Winthrop asks, looming above Ashley as she lay on the woman's sofa, sipping the hot drink.

Ashley nodded, a mouthful of the liquid inhibiting her speech. She swallowed it and to her surprise it was incredibly smooth. She had never been one for alcohol, but in the past week alone she had gotten tipsy on wine, been soothed by sherry and now calmed by a hot toddy.

The old woman seated herself on the arm of the sofa now, sounds of Austin in the kitchen licking the bowl after a chocolate cake batter was prepared carried into the room. "What were you doing down there in that basement anyway, Ashley? More noises dear?"

Was the old woman mocking her? "No, I was looking for Topples. I wanted him to search the attic for me. I think I lost my antique rosary up there. Now I wish I hadn't found him."

Mrs. Winthrop patted her hand. "A horrible thing for that man to do, scaring you like that. Drunk as usual, I'm sure. I have to say though, as cruel as it was, Topples would never hurt a fly, I truly believe that."

Ashley shook her head. "I wish I could say I felt the same, but that voice, it was just—evil."

The old woman chuckled at that. "Drunk perhaps, but I wouldn't say evil. Don't worry about him any longer though. As I told you in the basement, he won't be coming back into the brownstone. Now why don't you take a nap here on the couch, while Austin and I bake that cake I've been working on?" She rose then, was about to walk away, when, "Mrs. Winthrop?" Ashley said, and the old woman turned, looking down at her.

"Yes, dear?"

"Thank you." And Ashley closed her eyes.

She awoke to the smell of warm chocolate drifting in from the kitchen. Ashley smiled, felt better now, and rose from the sofa and walked to the kitchen. Mrs. Winthrop was at the sink wiping her hands on a towel, while Austin sat at the table, behind the largest cake Ashley had ever seen.

"What do you think?" The old woman asked, still drying her hands. "Double chocolate fudge cake."

"It's huge," Ashley said, wide-eyed. Then added, "and it looks delicious." Her stomach growled lowly as she looked at the cake.

Mrs. Winthrop laughed and walked over to the girl, squeezing her shoulders. "Then after dinner, we'll have a huge slice. You will stay for dinner won't you?" She asked, looking at Ashley with pleading eyes. Austin's eyes beamed, still watching the cake. Dinner! Ashley thought and looked at her watch. My God, it was a quarter till eight, she was supposed to meet Dan at seven or call first. How could she have slept that long? Oh well too late now.

"Of course we'll stay," she smiled at the old lady. "I just need to use your phone first, is that okay?"

Vacant Spaces

"Of course, it's in the living room, right beside the sofa. And that letter you were expecting from the phone company is there too, dear."

"Thanks," she said, and left the old woman and young boy alone with the giant cake.

Ashley dug the card out of her back pocket, punched in Dan Phillips' cell phone number and waited. The phone rang six times before she gave up and placed the receiver back in its cradle. She picked up a stack of mail then. The phone bill addressed to her was on top. Finally, she thought, maybe I will have something to go on. She folded the mail and shoved it into her back pocket with Dan's card. Was he angry with her, she wondered? Thinking that she stood him up on purpose. She would have to go to his office tomorrow, apologize, tell him what happened. And of course it would sound like an excuse. Sorry I couldn't make it, I was attacked in my basement. He wouldn't buy that for a minute. Smells of the cake still carried into the room, her stomach demanded some and the cake made her think of birthdays. That's when she realized that Austin's tenth birthday was next week. My God she had almost forgotten. What a horrible mother she was, not to remember her own son's birthday. Still with everything that was going on, she couldn't blame herself. She would have to get Mrs. Winthrop to bake one of those huge cakes. And they could have a party. Yes, that would be fun, just Austin and her and Mrs. Winthrop. And she thought with a smile…she could invite Thomas.

As she returned to the kitchen the old woman smiled at her, Austin's mouth was ringed in chocolate batter. "Everything a-okay?" Mrs. Winthrop asked.

Ashley nodded, then suddenly began to dig around in her pocket, "Before I forget," she says, pulling out the diamond necklace, its many facets shimmering in the kitchen's light. "I need to return this."

"Oh thank you dear. I had forgotten all about it," she took it and slipped it into the large pocket of her apron. "Of course I'd forget my head if it wasn't screwed on. And it's not on too tightly anyway," she chuckled.

"I was looking for the cross," Ashley said then, as the old lady returned to her cooking.

"Cross dear?"

"Yes, the one that said Abigail on the back of it, I didn't see it in my jewelry box."

She was still talking to the old woman's back and at first she wasn't sure if Mrs. Winthrop had heard her at all. There was a long moment of silence and then, "Oh yes, I probably just laid it down somewhere," She turned now and smiled at Ashley, raising a finger. "I can guarantee you it's somewhere in your apartment. Like I said my head isn't screwed on all that tight."

Ashley smiled then too. Good old Mrs. Winthrop, she thought.

As Ashley tucked her son snugly into his own bed she smiled down on him. His eyes closed almost immediately, his breathing slowed and became rhythmic. She wondered what he dreamed about, what he thought. Almost ten years old and really Ashley didn't know her son at all. Autism was a horrible thing, to be able to steal someone's reality, someone's personality. Mother leaned over and kissed her son on the forehead. The boy stirred slightly but did not open his eyes. "I love you, Austin." She whispered, turning out the light and casting the world into darkness. She left him there, in the shadows.

The ordeal in the basement had taken a lot out of Ashley. Heavy circles framed her eyes and they were heavy, still though she didn't feel like sleep. The nap earlier at Mrs. Winthrop's had lasted too long, she doubted she would have much rest all night. Maybe some tea, she thought and tried to push the thought of taking one of the pills Mrs. Winthrop gave to her out of her head. She sat on the sofa, flicked on the television set and thought about Thomas. Was he still up, she wondered? Typing away on a new novel perhaps? She was tempted to sneak down to his apartment, but she didn't want to seem presumptuous. Besides, she wanted him to come to her.

And then there was Dan Phillips. Ashley dreaded facing the man tomorrow. Mrs. Winthrop would have Austin so Ashley would have the entire day free. She hoped he wasn't too angry with her. She stared at the television screen, not really seeing it, not really hearing it. It cast an electric blue hue across her face as her mind reeled with the events of the past week; the attic incident, the missing journal, Cross' suicide and now with what happened in the basement. She realized then that tears were forming in her eyes and she wiped one away as it tried to escape. Ashley was suddenly overwhelmed with a sense of melancholy. She missed her mother and Atlanta. She missed the comfort of the little house across from the church and she missed her friend Susan. Where are you, she thought? I need you to be all right. I need you to be alive. Then she remembered the telephone bill. Taking the folded envelope out of her back pocket and looking at her own name printed above Susan's address she thought about how their lives were mingled, intertwined by the cruel hand of fate. Ashley began to rip the envelope open and then paused. She had heard something. She waited, began to open the mail and paused yet again. There it was again, like a muffled telephone ring. She grabbed at the TV remote and thumbed the mute button just as the ringing returned. Ashley laid the envelope on the sofa and rose. Walking the room she would pause every time the ring would come. She followed it down the hallway and then to Austin's door. Outside of it, she pressed her ear against its wood. The ring came again and Ashley quickly opened the door. Austin still slept soundly, the phantom phone not disturbing his slumber a bit. There was no phone service in this apartment; Ashley had checked the line herself. Maybe it was coming from the Briar sister's place. But would the noise carry across the hallway? Or the priest's apartment, perhaps? It was right below hers, it wasn't unlikely in an old house such as this that the acoustics made his phone sound as though it were ringing in Ashley's apartment, in Austin's room. She shrugged. Wherever it was coming from it had stopped now. Ashley was sure it was from the apartment below, though. She turned and was about to leave the room when the ringing started again. She froze, startled, heart beating fast. It had definitely come from this room. She stood now, waiting for the next ring and when it came her eyes followed sound to the bed…under the bed, to be exact. Ashley walked closer and stopped when it rang

Vacant Spaces

yet again and this time she began to realize why the ring sounded so strange, it was the electronic ring of a cell phone. My god, she thought, mind racing, was there someone under the bed? She fumbled in the darkness for the light switch and flicked it up, bathing the room in light. Austin stirred in bed as another ring came and Ashley dropped to her knees peering under the bed, certain she would see an evil figure waiting to grab her. Instead what she saw was a thousand times more horrific.

CHAPTER FIFTEEN

Ashley stared wide-eyed at the tiny cell phone, Cross' cell phone, as it's persistent ring filled the still air, demanding her to pick it up, to answer it. Ashley reached under the bed and grabbed the phone, looked at it's face trying to locate the answer button, found it and slowly raised the phone to her ear.

"Hello," her voice shook out the greeting.

"Hello, this is operator two-eleven calling you with a one time only offer. To whom am I speaking with, please?"

Her mind didn't comprehend what was happening as, in a hoarse voice that was barely above a whisper, she said, "Ashley."

"Hi Ashley, are you ready to save up to twenty percent off of a yearly subscription to Better Budgeting Magazine?"

Ashley let her hand drop to her lap, the tiny cell phone still in it. She stared at her son who was now wide awake and staring at her too, half his face buried in the pillow. What was Cross' cell phone doing here, in Austin's room? My God, the implications that were running through her mind were just too incredible, to ridiculous even, for Ashley to comprehend.

Austin smiled at her now, then closed his eyes. Ashley stood, her legs shaking, operator two-eleven's voice buzzed from the phone, "Hello, ma'am, are you still there?" Ashley pressed the 'clear' button and the operator vanished. She turned and looked at her son one last time before turning out the light and leaving the bedroom.

Ashley took one of Mrs. Winthrop's pills after all. Her nerves were wrecked. She lay in bed holding the cell phone up in front of her, studying it. Figuring out how to work the redial button she pressed it and groaned out loud at what she saw. The last number Cross had dialed on her phone was 911. Conspiracy theory, she thought, as her mind drifted into unconsciousness and her hand clung tightly to the dead girl's tiny cell phone.

CHAPTER SIXTEEN

Morning came with a wind that rattled the glass in the windows, waking Ashley Malone with a start. Outside, she could see bellows of gray clouds rolling swiftly over the treetops, their thickness snuffing out the sun like a puff of smoke. A storm was coming, rolling in fast and it suited the mood that hung in the brownstone today. In the distance thunder rolled in over the ocean and streaks of lightning set the ash colored clouds afire with electricity. Ashley picked up the cell phone that lay beside her, dropped from her hand in the middle of the night during a vague and fitful dream. Cross' cell phone. My god what did this mean, really? Was Cross right all along? Was there some reason Mrs. Winthrop wanted the young girl here, and if so, for what? Did Cross commit suicide like the police had said, or was she pushed from the third floor window, to the concrete walkway below, and if so by who? Mrs. Winthrop…or…no the thought was too much, too utterly ridiculous, but still, the cell phone was under his bed, and she had seen him in the attic. But Austin was just a boy, none of these things started happening until they moved here, into Susie's apartment, into this brownstone. And Austin wasn't capable of such things, he wasn't. She knew her son and knew that a little boy with problems like his couldn't be cold, caculating, not Austin. She desperately needed to talk to someone, someone she

Vacant Spaces

trusted. God how she wished Father Malley were here. Or even her mother, although her mother would only say 'I told you so.' Outside the clouds thickened, the distant sound of thunder crackled with a ferocity that seemed to be more of a warning. The storm was coming in quickly. Ashley felt that it was going to be a bad one.

Forty-five minutes later Ashley found herself in front of Thomas Robinson's door. Austin's hand was gripped tightly in hers, her palms sweating. The door opened just as the first drops of rain began to batter at the slate roof of the old building.

"Ashley," Thomas smiled, and then looked down at Austin and his smile widened even more. "What a pleasant surprise, come in, please." He stepped aside and Ashley needed no second invitation as she hurried past him into the safety of his apartment. "Can I get you some coffee, maybe some juice for the boy."

Ashley shook her head, looked around nervously, "No thank you, we're fine." Austin went to the fogged over window and pressed his finger to it, began to draw shapes in the mist.

"Is something wrong, Ashley?" Thomas asked in a lower voice now. He saw that she was near tears and went to her, put big, strong hands on either of her shoulders and squeezed. "Talk to me, please. Tell me what's bothering you."

She tried to speak, didn't know where to start. From the curio cabinet she saw that damned ugly demon statue staring at her, eyes mocking. Azreal, that's what Thomas had called it, the demon of rebirth.

He put a finger under her chin, lifted her head so that she was staring into the pools of his blue eyes, drowning in them. "Talk to me," he demanded, voice stern yet caring. And that's when it all spilled out. She told him everything. The incident in the basement, Cross' conspiracy theory, finding the cell phone under Austin's bed, and now, how she thought that Mrs. Winthrop may somehow be involved in the girl's death.

Thomas led her to the couch when she had finished, sat her down and then seated himself close to her. "You say the girl was at your apartment the night before?" Ashley nodded. "Then isn't it possible," he continued, "That she left her phone behind, you said yourself she left in a hurry."

Ashley nodded, stared off at nothing as she thought about this possibility, then said, "But how did it wind up under Austin's bed, and the last number that was dialed was 911, it should have been the number to the pizza delivery place."

"Austin." He said matter-of-factly. "He could have found the cell phone, he couldn't tell you if he did. And have you ever taught him how to call for help during an emergency?"

"Yes, 911. As a matter of fact it's the only number he knows how to dial. Ohhh," she groaned, slapping her hand over her eyes and falling back into the sofa. "I feel like such a moron. Of course that's how it happened. How could I suspect poor old Harriet Winthrop of murder?" She laughed at her own silliness and Thomas chuckled with her.

Vacant Spaces

"I can vouch for Harriet," he said, still smiling. "The only crime she's guilty of is that hair color. Auburn. At her age."

Ashley stood, feeling better now. "I've got to go out, I promised Mrs. Winthrop she could baby-sit. To think I was scared to let her less than half an hour ago."

"Everything will be fine, Ashley. You're safe here."

"Please don't tell Mrs. Winthrop about this," she asked him, her eyes pleading. "I've been so much trouble already."

"Don't worry, my lips are sealed. Now you two go on down to Harriet's. You're going out you say?" Ashley nodded.

"I'll call you a cab, it's pouring out." At that, Thomas Robinson walked to the telephone and picked it up as the woman and boy left, the door closing quietly behind them. Thomas dialed a number quickly and waited impatiently as it rang, someone answered on the third ring. "Hello," He smiled as he spoke into the receiver, "You won't believe the conversation I just had with young Miss Malone." He chuckled as wind blew sheets of rain at the window behind him, Austin's drawing decorating the fogged glass. The boy had drawn the demon from the curio cabinet, Azreal. Already the drawing had began to fog over, droplets of condensation running from it as though it were crying, slowly melting away.

Ashley leapt out of the cab and made a mad dash up the steps of the New York Times building. By the time she entered the glass doors of the lobby she was drenched. Her dark hair clung to her face and dripped onto her blouse. Did she always have to look like such a mess every time Dan Phillips saw her? She made her way to the elevators, her pumps making wet squeaking noises on the marble floors. A secretary looked up from her desk, irritated at the disturbance. "Sorry," Ashley mouthed silently to her as the woman rolled her eyes and looked back down at the mound of paper work atop her desk.

"Oh, it's you," Greg the cameraman snarled at her as she entered the tiny and cluttered office. Apparently he was acting as receptionist again today. Ashley wondered if her day would ever get any better. If Greg had disliked her before, she was sure the young man hated her now, after her picture made the front page, in all fairness it should have been his shot.

"Is Dan here," she asked, walking right up to the counter and tried to put on her best 'don't mess with me attitude.'

Greg snarled at her, "Hold on." He pushed a button and Dan's voice came over a small speaker, full of static.

"Yea Greg, what is it now?"

'That woman is here again," He replied, still giving Ashley a go to hell look.

"What woman?"

"The one who thinks she's a photographer." Greg said with disgust.

Almost immediately the door to Dan's office opened up and the man loomed in the doorway. He was unshaven and his clothes were badly wrinkled. He

Vacant Spaces

stood, buttoning the top buttons of his shirt, leaving Ashley to wonder if he had slept here all night.

"Ashley, come on back," He motioned her into the office. It was stuffy and only had one small window. Filing cabinets lined one wall, while the desk spilled over with papers and electronics. A computer, printer, fax, they all buzzed with a life of their own. On the walls were various awards and certificates for the school of journalism. There was a picture of a much younger Dan, shaking hands with the president.

"I missed you last night," he said, clearing off files from a chair so that she could sit.

"I'm sorry about that, it was a horrible night. I tried to call but I didn't get an answer."

Dan seated himself behind the desk, turned off the computer. "Yea, it was a bad night all around I guess."

"What do you mean?" She asked.

He handed her a folded newspaper and she opened it. "Oh no," she said, reading the main story.

Dan nodded. "Seems the guy that was shot and killed the other day wasn't the one doing the rapes and murders after all."

Ashley read in horror. Another woman's body had been found, there was a picture of her, young, blonde, very pretty. Her body had been found just after midnight, her throat was sliced.

"Forensics shows that her feet had been bound after death and the body hung upside down, to drain blood apparently. Just the same as the other victims that were found. That information was never made public, that's how the cops know it's the same psycho."

Ashley read on. "The midnight stalker?" she quizzed.

Dan smiled. "That's the name I dubbed him with when I first started following the story. It just kind of caught on."

"And you're sure a woman named Susan Bishop wasn't one of his victims?" Ashley asked, putting the paper back on his desk.

"I'm positive. Trust me Ashley, I've been over this story with a fine-toothed comb, over and over again. I know every victim by name, the scene of the abductions and the dumpsite of the bodies. Your friend isn't one of them…unless—" He paused.

"Unless what?" Ashley rose and leaned up in her seat.

Dan looked at her, "Unless they just haven't found her body yet."

Ashley sank back into the chair. Not exactly what she had hoped to hear, but still, she had to be prepared for the worse. "You said yesterday you had some information."

Dan nodded and then said, "Hey have you had lunch yet?"

The two stood on the curb trying to hail a cab, close under Dan's umbrella as the rain whipped around them splattering their ankles as it landed in puddles at their feet. They stood close together, trying not to get wet and Ashley could make out the scent of that woodsy cologne that he wore. His body radiated warmness as her own trembled and when a car flew by splashing water at them she leaned in close to his shoulder. Dan smiled down at her and she felt a

Vacant Spaces

strange stirring inside, something that burned even though she didn't want it to. Finally a taxi pulled up to the curb and their closeness was replaced with the cramped backseat of the car, Dan's woodsy cologne replaced with the odor of beer and cigarettes. The taxi sped off with the two sitting in silence in the back seat. What did Dan want to tell her? Before they left his office he had grabbed a yellow folder. He seemed to be avoiding what ever news he had to share, putting it off for as long as possible. Ashley stared out the rain streaked window of the taxi and in the sky lightning flashed, followed by claps of thunder, rain came down harder, making it nearly impossible to see the streets. The cab slowed as brake lights appeared out of nowhere in front of it. It came to a halt as sheets of water pounded at its roof and hood.

The cabby turned and looked at the two of them, spoke loudly above the noise of the storm. "Looks like a traffic jam. Happens every time it storms. Better get comfortable, we could be here awhile." He turned back to stare out the windshield, hands gripping the steering wheel as the wiper blades swished back and forth furiously, trying in vain to clear the water from the glass.

Dan smiled at Ashley. She stared down at the yellow envelope lying in his lap.

"What news do you have for me Dan?" She asked and waited for his reply.

He stared at her, saying nothing, then turned his head to look out the window.

Ashley's eyes went back to the envelope. What was he avoiding? What was so horrible that he couldn't find the words to tell her?

"Is it about Susan?"

"No," he said, refusing to look at her.

"Dan, look at me!" She snapped and he turned to stare at her. His eyes looked troubled and there was an atmosphere that suddenly filled the small compartment of the cab, Ashley was feeling claustrophobic, as if the walls were closing in. In a voice that trembled, from the cold of the rain or from something else she couldn't be sure, she asked, "Dan, what's in that envelope?"

He sighed, picked up the yellow package, turned it over and then said, "When you were eighteen you became ill, didn't you?"

Ashley looked confused for a moment. "How did you know that?"

"You slipped into a coma and lost nearly three months of your life," Dan continued. "Only you didn't remember anything afterwards, am I right?"

She was shaking visibly now. That damned yellow envelope mocking her. "How do you know all of this?" She demanded, her voice slow and calm.

Dan opened the envelope then, pulled out copies of newspaper articles. "When I was trying to find out information about Susan Bishop and came up empty handed I put your name in my search engine instead. You don't remember anything from that time in your life do you? You don't even know what happened to you."

Her eyes were beginning to blur now, "What happened to me?" she repeated. She could see one of the newspaper articles, it was a grocery store tabloid. Her yearbook picture was printed beside the article. A tear streamed down her cheek.

Vacant Spaces

"A rumor got started when your parents hired a priest to come to your house," Dan began. He was speaking to her but he was looking out the window. "He was there to exorcise a demon out of you. Your parents believed you were possessed." He said softly, casually as though it were a normal thing to say. In the front seat, the cab driver looked nervously in the rearview, then quickly back out the rain splattered windshield. He adjusted the defroster, trying in vain to keep the windows from fogging over.

Ashley just sat there, shaking her head. It wasn't true. This was crazy. Then she realized she was bawling, crying uncontrollably. The wiper blades gushed back and forth swiftly, cutting into her thoughts.

"Your parents didn't know what to do, the doctors didn't know what to do and the church wouldn't help. That's when a priest appeared out of nowhere, showed up on your doorstep, offering to help." Dan said all of this coldly, as though he were numb, all along looking out the window, avoiding her eyes, while those damned wiper blades made their God awful racket. He turned to her then, looked her right in the eyes and she could see his own eyes were filled with tears. "Only he didn't try to help you Ashley, he—he raped you."

"NO!" Ashley screamed, over and over again. "NO! NO! NO! It's not true!" then she was lashing out at him, slapping and clawing at him. She scraped her nails down his cheek and drew blood. "You bastard!" she screamed, "You lying bastard!"

Dan tried to subdue her, grabbed her hands as she fell into him sobbing in great heaves, hyperventilating.

"The only reason it was in the papers at all is because your Mother reported the rape," he said softly into her ear, smelled the sweet smell of raspberry shampoo in her rain dampened hair. "They never found the priest who attacked you."

She seemed calm now, and he was about to put his arm around her when suddenly Ashley was clawing for the door handle, found it and slung the cab door open. Sheets of rain blew in at them, battering them, the cabby yelled something from the front seat but Ashley didn't hear what as she bolted out of the automobile and out into the weather. Rain pounded at her as the wind whipped her skirt up.

"Ashley!" Dan called from the cab, rain beat at his face from the open cab door. He was about to follow her but lost sight of her.

Ashley weaved her way through the stalled traffic. Making her way to the sidewalk, she ran as fast as her shaking legs would carry her, bumping into strangers with umbrellas as they cursed her. She kept running, her feet splashing puddles. The rain mingled with her tears and ran into her mouth tasting salty. It wasn't true, it wasn't. She would remember something like that. He was lying to her for some reason. This was all some sick game. Damn him. Damn this city. Damn Susan for disappearing, damn her mother for lying to her. Damn them all, she screamed out loud, not caring about the people staring at her like she was a stark raving lunatic, not caring they all thought her mad. "Damn them all to hell!" Ashley screamed as she ran off into the raging storm.

Vacant Spaces

Dan sat in the cab, cold and shivering. He felt like shit. He felt like shit because that was not the way to deal with repressed memories, and that was not the way to deal with someone so fragile. He felt like shit because this woman's parents never pressed charges, but tried to cover it all up and hide a dirty little secret. He felt like shit because he had to be the one to tell this beautiful woman that her whole life was a lie. That she was all messed up on the inside. And, most of all, he felt like shit because he knew now that he would have to be the one to fix it.

Ashley found a catholic church, St. Francis, on the corner of 43rd and 12th. She stood in the shelter of its archway for a while, her hair plastered to her forehead. Her clothes were drenched right through and her small pink nipples, rigid from the cold, showed through her thin blouse. She wasn't worthy to enter this place, she told herself, not if what Dan had told her was true, she was unclean, evil. Still God could forgive her. He could forgive all sins. She stepped to the big doors and pulled one open. Inside was warm and the air was soft and calm, not like the storm that raged outside, not like the storm that raged inside of her.

Ashley walked the length of the aisle, passing pew after empty pew. There was no one in the confessionals and so she went to the altar, picked up a match with a trembling hand and lit a candle. She knelt before the statue of Mary who peered down from the altar. Above the entire scene, hanging from the wall high up near the tall ceiling of the church was the image of Christ, crucified, head tilted and eyes partially open and looking down on Ashley.

Ashley prayed then, prayed and cried and asked for forgiveness, asked for cleansing and salvation for her endangered soul.

"Would you like to confess?" a deep voice asked from above and at first Ashley actually thought that it was the voice of God. She opened her eyes, turned sheepishly and saw an old priest standing behind her, hands clasped in front of him.

Ashley wiped the tears from her eyes and nodded. He motioned her to the confessionals and she got up, her knees ached from being in the kneeling position so long, her right foot was asleep and she almost stumbled as she tried to walk. The priest caught her, held her lightly by the elbow and led her to the small, curtained booths.

Ashley sat, heard rustling through the small grate opening as the priest took a seat and shifted his weight to get comfortable. The confessional was stuffy and smelled like pine cleaner. An image flashed in Ashley's mind but it came and went so quickly that she couldn't make it out.

"Forgive me Father for I have sinned," she began and her voice was weak and hoarse and it sounded like someone else who said, "It has been two years since my last confession and—" Again the image flashed in her mind and this time Ashley saw her own reflection in a mirror, except her face was different. She shook her head, tried to get the fleeting memory out of her mind.

"Yes, go on child," the priest spoke soft and slow, with a caring in his voice, deep and genuine.

Vacant Spaces

Ashley stuttered, tried to find the words to begin. "It's just that I...I was told that I was..." she couldn't say it.

A flash of light and the past was playing like a movie reel in her head. Ashley was tied to the bed post and looking at her own reflection in a floor length mirror, only her face was contorted into an evil and horrific grin, and her forehead, my God her forehead! Out of her skull, just above the temples, protruded what looked to be two tiny, bony nubs of horns.

"You were what, my child?" The priest urged her to continue.

The sound of the man's voice on the other side of the small cube box snapped Ashley back to the present. She found she was sweating despite the fact she was freezing from her wet clothes. She trembled and her heartbeat sounded like the flapping of mighty wings in her chest as she said the words. "Possessed! I was possessed!" Ashley spat the words out like something vile in her mouth and they held in the air, hung there heavily in the cramped, little booth as she muffled her sobs with her hands. "I was possessed by a demon and now I'm afraid my soul may be damned for all eternity. Please forgive me father, please cleanse me of these sins." Her words came between sobs of tears that flowed freely down her face, dripping off her chin. She wiped her running nose with the back of her hand, waiting for a reply. The other side of the confessional was quiet.

"Father?" Ashley leaned in closer to the decorative grate opening, she could see the silhouette of the priest and she pressed her hand against the cold metal of the grate. "Father?" She repeated.

Suddenly the man jerked and moved, his face pressed up so hard against the metal that the fatty flesh of his face protruded through the small holes of the meshed grating that separated the two. Ashley jumped back with a small scream escaping from her throat. The priest was smiling at her, his face twisted by the metal, he had an unearthly gleam in his eyes, his lips snarled showing yellowed teeth and blood red gums. When he spoke his voice was no longer soothing and gentle, it was deep and demonic.

"There is no forgiveness for you, you'll burn in eternal flames with me, bitch." The priest laughed and his breath smelled of dried blood and sulfur. Ashley screamed as the laughing got louder. She tore at the curtain, stumbling out of the confessional and running up the aisle, toward the entryway of the church. She was almost to the doors when a loud scraping sound made her stop and turn, at first she thought it was thunder from outside, but then she saw it. High amidst the Church's cathedral ceiling the huge image of Christ's' crucifixion had come loose from the top brackets holding it, the bottom bracket the only one intact, it fell, scraping down the plastered walls of the church, sideways, then swung back and forth upside down. Ashley gaped in horror and crossed herself as she watched the inverted cross sway left, then right, swinging like the pendulum of some satanic clock before finally slowing down until it stopped in a mockery of all that was holy. Ashley could see the eyes of the virgin mother that adorned the altar, they were crying and then the laughter began from the confessional booth again. "Praise Daemonicus!" A voice straight from the depths of hell called from inside the box of horror. Ashley hit the doors of the church running and never looked back. It was true, she cried as pellets of rain stabbed her face and the wind tore at her clothes. God help her, it was all true.

Ashley made it back to the brownstone. But now the building held no safety for her. It did not fill her with the sense of security she desperately yearned for. It no longer looked like the dream home she had such high hopes for when she first arrived in the city. Instead it loomed before her like a tumor rising from the earth's wet face. As she entered the front doors, Ashley even felt as though she were entering the mouth of some cancerous entity. A breathing, living monstrosity of brick and mortar, of wood and glass, the place where all of her problems had started, and all of Susan's problems too. Ashley didn't stop at Mrs. Winthrop's apartment, or Thomas'. She clambered up the stairs noisily, clumsily unlocked her door. Ashley walked through the darkened living room, down the hallway. Entering her bedroom she didn't bother to turn on the light. She was running mechanically now. Not really knowing what was happening, or what she was doing, her mind was on autopilot. She lay down on the bed. She wasn't crying anymore, her breathing was a little heavy, she realized that, and she was feeling a little light headed. Other than that she was fine, just fine. She closed her eyes. Had she closed the front door? She let out a giggle. Did it really matter? Darkness began to envelope her mind and Ashley didn't try to fight it, she didn't care to. The darkness came in swirls behind her eyelids and then the whirlpools of black changed to waves of color and the waves of color changed to images of long ago—and then the memories came flooding back…

It was the scratching sounds that the two girls first noticed. Ashley and Susan stood still in the little college dorm room, like cats stalking prey, and they waited, listening.

"There it is again," Susan whispered, so close to Ashley's ear that Ashley could feel the girl's hot breath on her.

The scratching sound had started just two days ago, right after a surprise visit from Ashley's father. At first it came from underneath Ashley's bed and the girls were sure it was a mouse, but now, now they had determined it had moved, upward, and was coming from Ashley's mattress, from inside Ashley's mattress.

Ashley turned to her friend now, fearful. "Oh Susan, I can't sleep in that bed, not if there's a rat inside."

Susan just smiled at her, rolled her eyes and shook her head. She walked without pause over to the bed and began stripping it of its sheets and covers. She was fearless and Ashley admired her for that. She admired her friend for many things, but above all, that. Now, from a safe distance, she watched as Susan inspected the mattress all over, first the top and sides and then even lifting it up and inspecting the bottom. She let go of the bedding; it flopped on the box springs with a dull thud. "No holes," she said, a puzzled look coming over her face. "How would a mouse get—" the words dangled at her lips as the scratching sound started again, louder this time. Susan's face may have went a little pale, Ashley couldn't be sure.

"What are you doing?" Ashley asked in astonishment as she watched the other girl lightly lay her hand on the top of the mattress.

A smile spread across her face and she looked at Ashley. "It tingles," she said in a goofy kind of voice. "Kind of like an electrical shock, but it tickles instead of hurts." She just stood there, her hand resting on the spot of the mattress were the scratching sound was becoming ever louder. "Come here, you gotta feel this."

Ashley shook her head and took a step back. She had a strange feeling, had it for a couple of days now. Had someone asked her she would not be able to describe or explain it, just a sense of forbidding, of fear, a sense that something was about to reveal itself.

"C'mon," Susan pestered. "Don't be a wuss, feel it."

Yea come on Ashley, don't be a wuss, it's just a rat or something. Get a grip, she told herself, if Susan could do it then she could right?

Susan was still giggling at the funny feeling as Ashley approached the bed. She wasn't sure if it was just her but the scratching sound seemed to be getting louder the closer she got to the bed, as if something were about to claw it's way through the bedding. With her right hand Ashley was absently clutching the antique rosary that her father had given her two days ago.

"Feel it," Susan smiled up at her, removing her own hand.

Ashley leaned in towards the noise, held her hand out reaching down as if in some sick embrace. Her hand faltered and wavered an inch above the surface of the mattress for a second. She could feel an incredible heat radiating, a welcoming warmth. Just as Ashley rested her palm on the surface of the bed the scratching sound stopped.

Susan looked at her. "What happened?"

"I don't know," she replied hand still on the mattress. "It just stopped."

Suddenly the mattress began to move, as if vibrating from a force within. Ashley quickly snatched her hand back and stumbled into her friend. The mattress seem to take on a life of it's own as it began to bounce up and down on the box springs.

The two girls both let out small screams and clung to one another, backing away and climbing onto Susan's bed.

The mattress seemed to be doing some macabre dance as it continued it's flopping before finally projecting itself off the bed completely and, in an upright position, smacking into the wall next to the bed.

The two girls still clung to one another, staring wild-eyed at the now lifeless piece of fabric and foam lying motionless on the floor. Susan slowly turned her head to look at Ashley and said, "You can sleep in my bed tonight."

"Ashley, wake up."

Ashley's eyelids fluttered open heavy with sleep; they felt gritty as though they were full of sand. "What's the matter?" She asked pushing hair from her face. Her head felt funny, like it was on crooked or something everything was fuzzy.

Vacant Spaces

Susan looked at her for a long minute, just staring at her with her mouth open.

"What's the matter with you?" Ashley repeated.

"You were talking funny," her friend said, still with that strange look on her face. "In your sleep."

Ashley giggled and closed her eyes. "Funny how?"

When her friend did not answer her she opened her eyes, leaned up and switched on the bedside lamp. Across the room the mattress still lay tossed on the floor.

"Susan, funny how?'

"This is going to sound strange, and I only recognized it cause we're studying it in Professor Walsh's class but—" she paused for only a second then said in a hushed whisper as though she was afraid someone would hear, "Ashley, you were speaking Greek."

Ashley laughed aloud. "That's ridiculous, I don't know any Greek." She looked at her friend and saw that she wasn't joking. "Okay, if I was speaking Greek what was I saying?"

Susan shook her head. "Well as best as I could figure you were cursing……God."

Ashley and Susan lay there for the rest of the night with the light on. Neither slept, neither spoke. Ashley lay staring up at the ceiling, her mind racing with thoughts. What was going on? What was happening to her?

Ashley was on a plane trying hard not to look out the window because the airline had only one seat available and it was a window seat. She tried not to

185

look out because the thick and heavy clumps of vapor that flew by only made the headaches worse, as a matter of fact any motion whatsoever made the headaches worse. They had started about two weeks ago, shortly after the mattress incident. She wore her antique rosary still, clutching it, clinging to the little figure of Jesus crucified and prayed, begged that these headaches would go away. Ashley had fled to the doctor once they had worsened to the point where she couldn't even get out of bed, only lay there in the dark, in the quiet. She was sure it would be a tumor or some other life threatening condition but the doctor had said migraines. She wished she could get her hands on that doctor right now, she would make him think migraines. Ashley felt a warm hand on hers, opened her eyes a little and saw Susan smiling at her. "You sure you don't want to switch seats?" her friend whispered. Ashley smiled back, a weak smile and just nodded her head. She shut her eyes again; her rosary still squeezed in her fist and she thanked God for giving her a friend like Susan Bishop. It was Susan who had insisted that she take time off from her failing studies and return home to Atlanta and rest. Susan had even offered to stay with her a couple of nights, before flying back to Boston just in time for finals.

In the back of the plane Ashley could hear the clinking sound of dishes as the flight attendant began rolling the food cart down the narrow aisle. The smell of Salisbury steak wafted around Ashley's nostrils and her stomach turned. Her eyes snapped open as though she had been physically assaulted and before she knew it she was stumbling over peoples feet and down the aisle, trying desperately to get to the bathroom. Her mouth began salivating heavily, she bumped into the food cart and heard the attendant yell something at her as she made it to the bathroom's door but not inside as the contents of her stomach surged up and out, stinging as it shot out her nose and throat, leaving the sticky taste of bile in her mouth. Susan was beside her now, pushing her hair back from her face. Ashley looked up at her friend, stared deep into Susan's eyes searchingly, wanting her friend to give her some kind of answer as to what was wrong with her, instead a strange look crossed Susan's face. A look as though her friend had just seen a ghost.

"Susan what is it?" Ashley asked, wiping her mouth with her sleeve.

Susan stared back at her and opened her mouth, and when the words came out they came slowly, carefully. "Ashley," she began not taking her stare away from Ashley's. "What color are your eyes?"

Ashley couldn't help but smile. "Brown, you know that." she replied. Was Susan loosing it?

Her friend was shaking her head now, "No, they're not, not now anyway. Ashley they're green."

The smile left Ashley's lips as she realized Susan wasn't joking. Slowly she rose from the floor and stood before the tiny mirror above the sink. Behind her, Susan was as pale as a ghost. Ashley leaned in close to her reflection, her breath fogging the mirror as the green eyes of a stranger stared back at her. "My God Susan, what's happening to me?" Her voice trembled with fear; she was locked in place, unable to move, unable to tear herself away from her own glare.

Susan stood close behind her, whispering to her that it would be okay, that everything would be okay.

And the funny thing was, when Susan said it, you believed her.

The headaches had only worsened at her parents' and Ashley's dreams were tormented by horrible images that would flee her memory upon awakening. Her mother had taken her to a specialist who had x-rayed every part of her body and taken more blood than Ashley knew she'd had and then told her to come back in three days for the results. In the meantime he had sent her home with painkillers, which still sat unopened in their little orange prescription bottle. Ashley hated taking pills, but the pain was so bad that maybe…then her thoughts paused. What was that? There was a noise. She had heard something, something familiar, but it was gone now. No, wait…there it was again! It was coming from beneath her, coming from inside her childhood mattress, that scratching noise. Ashley almost laughed out loud, probably would have had she not been so terrified as she thought, it's followed me home. I wonder if mother will let me keep it? The thought struck her as hilarious and she was sure she was going mad as the scratching became louder and louder and then she sensed a warming sensation flowing over her skin, as though invisible hands were caressing her lightly. She closed her eyes gripped in between a state of fear and incredible pleasure as the warmth slid across her breast, down her stomach and brushed the inside of her thighs, leaving goose bumps in it's wake. This wasn't right, Ashley told herself, this was no hallucination this was really happening. She should get up and run or lay there and scream or something, do something. And then a voice, old and shuffling like the pages of a tattered and dog-eared book said, "GO WITH IT."

Fear immobilized her now as she realized the voice was not an outside source, it was coming from within her, from her own mouth.

Ashley's eyes fluttered open to a terrific pain between her legs. A burning pain that sent sharp stabs throughout her abdomen. Hot breath at her neck and ears, wet with the sounds of pleasure. That was when she first realized that there was someone on top of her, pressing down on her. She tried to move and could not. Her fingers wiggled but her hands were held above her head. Rope cut into her wrists as she struggled. A voice inside her head laughed, "Don't fight it," it said. It sounded old and familiar and tainted with evil. Now heavy grunts and the pain worsened. She wanted to scream but could not. Her head shook violently. Her eyes adjusted to the darkness and she realized then that she was in her own bedroom, in her own home. Somewhere in the house she heard the faint voices of her mother and father. My God, did they not know what was going on! Could they not hear their own daughter being brutally raped right under their noses? This must be a dream she kept repeating in her head. It must be a terrible nightmare. But the sharp pangs that now seized her body assured her that this was indeed real. The voice inside her laughed in unison with the moans of the intruder and as she tried to scream one last time she made the most horrifying discovery yet. She was smiling herself! Her own lips twisted in an evil grin of pleasure. There was darkness then as her eyes closed, the smile still on her lips as the intruder crawled off of her.

"Praise Daemonicus and all that is dark, damn those who evoke goodness. Glory to everlasting hellfire, to power and eternal suffering." The intruder's voice was low and heavy.

Ashley felt her own mouth move, words came from a dry and bloody throat, a voice that was not her own, deep and evil said, "Go now my faithful servant. You shall be rewarded greatly, all the powers of hell shall be yours and you shall reign at my side." She saw images flash in her head then, bloody corpses and rotting flesh. She smelled sulfur and decay. She heard herself screaming, heard herself cussing, speaking in tongues and damning the cross. She spat blood and revoked Jesus and damned all that was holy and she couldn't stop herself, couldn't gain control. Something had entered her body, her mind. Something had possessed her, body and soul, something evil and dirty and it had made her dirty too, and Ashley Malone knew she would never feel clean again. Her head twisted from side to side of it's own accord. She couldn't stop it; she no longer was in control of this vessel. That same evil grin was still plastered across her face as she caught the reflection of the intruder in the full-length mirror. He was whistling a tune, and she watched as he dressed in priest's clothing. A wolf in priest's clothing, she thought and she laughed more, the thing inside her laughed, and in the mirror, behind the mockery of the priest she could see herself, or at least what use to be her, what was left of her. Her face was contorted, lined and wrinkled and leathery. Her eyes were cat-like and just upon her forehead, two tiny little horns protruded. There was the voice inside her head whispering low and soft, as if whispering sweet nothings in her ear, "I AM AZREAL. PRAISE DAEMONICUS."

There was darkness more often than not, and the smell of sulfur assailed her nostrils. She heard voices screaming, cursing God, begging God for mercy, begging Satan for mercy and then her eyes were open and Susan was standing in front of her, tears streaming down her eyes. "What's wrong with you, Ashley, why are you saying all these horrible things?" And the demon that was inside Ashley smiled and made Ashley's lips move and say, "When I see your parent's again, I'll be sure their suffering is seven fold what it is now, they'll burn in the hottest flames of hell." And the demon laughed as Susan began lashing out at it, at Ashley, slapping her. Savagely attacking her, wanting to hurt Ashley, hurt the demon. Dear, sweet Susan who would never hurt anyone.

As Ashley slept, exhausted and flooded with memories of the past, her body twitched and jumped in bed, almost in seizures. In the living room a dark figure enters through the opened doorway, closing the door quietly, shutting out the light from the hallway. The intruder moves swiftly through the apartment, knowing every corner, every piece of furniture and creaking floorboard. Moving to the bedroom, the dark figure pauses and watches as Ashley's body shakes violently. The eyes move to the woman's purse lying on the floor beside her bed, the contents spilling out. Among the make up and address book, ink pens and fingernail clippers and Cross' cell phone, lay the bottle of pills Mrs. Winthrop had given to Ashley. The intruder smiles, yellow teeth showing through the evil grin. A hand reaches down and picks up the little brown pill bottle. It was time for Ashley Malone to die.

Ashley didn't wake as the handful of pills were shoved into her mouth, or as the glass was pressed to her lips and the wine forced down her throat. She did begin to regain consciousness however as the medication became lodged in her wind pipe and she began to choke. More wine was forced into her mouth, she had to swallow to breathe and still she didn't know what was happening to her. Were these more memories, more of her hidden awful past? She coughed, wine burned as it came out her nose. Suddenly a hand was clamped over her mouth and nose and she couldn't breathe. She tried to struggle but her arms were held under someone's weight. Her head throbbed and ached with pumping blood and lack of air and she felt as though her lungs would explode. Darkness and blue spots began to wash over her vision like a shade had been pulled down, she was sinking fast and just before she went under she heard Dan Phillips voice calling from far away, "Ashley?" She couldn't answer, she had already drowned in the darkness.

CHAPTER SEVENTEEN

Ashley woke to the smiling, unshaved face of Dan Phillips. She blinked, her eyes burned and felt crusty. She was in unfamiliar surroundings. "Where am I?" She asked from a dry, parched throat.

Dan brushed a loose strand of hair from her eyes. "You're at the hospital," he said, still smiling an 'it's okay, I understand' smile.

Ashley scooted herself up to a sitting position in the bed, white sheets were crisp and stiff, irritating her skin. "What am I doing here? Where's Austin?"

"Calm down, Ashley. Austin is with your landlady." He sensed that she might become hysterical at any moment and tried to persuade her to lie back. She did so, resting her hands on her stomach.

"Do you remember what I told you in the cab?" He asked. She nodded, looked at him and then saw the long, scabbed scratch marks running down his cheeks.

"Oh Dan, I'm so sorry," she reached out a hand to touch his cheek as he pulled back and smiled.

"Still kinda hurts," he laughed. Then his expression turned serious. "Do you remember what happened at the brownstone? Why you are here?"

Ashley thought for a second, everything was a blur, she looked at Dan and he saw the confusion in her eyes.

He rested his hand on hers, "Ashley, you tried to commit suicide. Tried to overdose on morphine."

Ashley shook her head, stared at this man in front of her who seemed to keep telling her lies. "No, Dan I didn't. I would never." She tried to sit up then and he put his hand on her white-gowned shoulder.

"It's okay. I came to your apartment, found the door open and you lying on the floor. There was a pill bottle and some wine...you don't remember?"

She brushed his hand away and sat up. "Don't tell me it's okay, and don't tell me that I don't remember. I didn't try to kill myself."

Dan sighed, put his head in his hands. God this was all his fault, for telling her about her past, for not going after her right away. He looked up, stared into her eyes then and said, "Then how do you explain the stomach full of wine and pills they pumped out of you, Ashley? How do you explain that?"

She looked as though she had just been slapped. His words struck her hard and she had an image of Cross' body laying crumpled three stories below, like a dead bird, neck twisted. And then with a strange calmness she said, "My God, they're trying to kill me."

Dan looked at her, "What?"

"Dan someone's trying to kill me, they want me dead!" She was up and out of the bed now, her fingers buried in her hair.

"Who are you talking about Ashley?" He demanded, going toward her.

She turned to stare at him, looked him in the eyes. "I don't know exactly, the same person that abducted Susan. They tricked me into coming here don't you see? They want to kill me, just like they killed Cross." She grabbed onto his shoulder, she had to hold on to something, she had to make this man believe her

Vacant Spaces

because she was all alone and needed help. "Dan, you have to believe me. Another girl died at the brownstone last week, another girl that had been...possessed." Ashley stopped then and became numb. It was true. She recalled in vague flashes images and evil laughter and...the rape. She watched Dan move away from her, realized then that he was calling for the nurse and snapped out of her memory induced trance.

"I've got to get out of here," she said, going to the closet and taking her clothes out. "I've got to get my son away from those people."

"Ashley, please, just take a moment and think about what your doing," Dan pleaded. A nurse and doctor came in then, both thin and pale, both wearing glasses. Dan whispered something in the doctor's ear. Ashley shook her head.

Traitor! She tried to pull her blouse over her head without taking the hospital gown off. She felt the nurses' hands on her then.

"Come along Miss Malone lets get back into bed. You're in no condition to go anywhere just yet."

Ashley jerked away, "Get your hands off me!" She glared at the nurse who backed off. There was a look in Ashley's eyes that frightened the woman, a wild, crazed look. The doctor then stepped forward.

"Miss Malone, I'm afraid if you don't get back into bed and calm down, we'll have to sedate you."

Ashley scoffed at the man, looked from him to Dan then at the nurse who quickly looked away. "You can't keep me here."

"I'm afraid we can," the thin doctor replied, light reflecting off his glasses so that she could not see his eyes. "Any attempted suicide patient can be kept for forty eight hours if we feel they are a harm to themselves or others."

Forty-eight hours. Two days! She couldn't leave Austin for that long. But he was with Mrs. Winthrop though, that was good. Or was it? Cross suspected that the old woman had lured her to the brownstone. But lured her there to kill her? That didn't make any sense. Ashley needed to clear her mind, she couldn't think straight.

The doctor came to her, took the blouse she was still holding out of her hands, he smiled. "It's late. Why don't you get a goodnight's rest and tomorrow a doctor from our psyche ward will speak with you. After a few simple questions, if he feels you are all right you can go home."

Ashley felt a pinprick, stared down at her arm. The nurse had stuck her with a needle. She began shaking her head no. She had to get back to the brownstone. She had to get to Austin. The room was now spinning. She felt hands on her and then felt the mattress under her. Stiff sheets were brought up to her chin and voices trailed away as her mind drifted into darkness once again.

The office had no windows. That was the first thing Ashley noticed as she sat in the small wooden chair across from the doctor's desk. A small desk lamp with an ivory green shade was the only illumination in the room. It cast a dim veil of shadows over the thin balding man with glasses that sat on the other side of the desk, reading over her chart. So this is what a psychiatrist looks like nowadays, Ashley

Vacant Spaces

thought, only the slightest trace of a smirk forming at the corners of her lips. Above her a central heating and air vent was blasting warm air directly into her face, smothering her. Surely the heat wasn't on, not in this weather? She felt closed in, trapped with no windows and this man that wanted to pick her brains. He couldn't help her. He didn't even know her. The smirk on her lips broadened as the thin man looked at her now, the lenses of his glasses reflecting the lamp's glare, hiding his eyes. Time to start, Ashley thought. She knew all the tricks of the trade. Psychology had been her major in college, and she was so close to graduating too, before the headaches, before the……

Anyway, she knew all the tricks. Like the dim lighting was probably suppose to give her a sense of comfort, so she would open up, the good ole' doc had probably been using this trick for years and the only real thing it did was ruin his eye sight. The man cleared his throat…time to start, Ashley grinned as the heated air stole her breath. She shifted to the left in the wooden chair.

"Uncomfortable?" The man asked, taking off his glasses revealing his eyes. They were dark and beady.

"No," she lied.

"Ashley, may I call you Ashley," he didn't wait for a response as he shifted through her file, "My name is Dr. Stanley Ross, I am a psychiatrist as you know. I've been reviewing your files and I must say you seem pretty normal to me," Dr. Ross chuckled and Ashley chuckled back, mocking him. God how textbook could you get, next he'd be telling her he wanted her out of this place more than she wanted to be out herself, and that he wanted to help her, to be her friend.

"Look," he scooted up closer to his desk staring intently at her now. "I want to help you, I know you want to go home, I probably want you out of here more than you want to get out," again the chuckle.

What a loser Ashley thought, her stomach was growling and her head was still fuzzy from the pills and shots and...memories. She wasn't feeling like herself at all.

"There are just a few things I need to clear up first. A few things that you told the doctor's and nurses when you arrived here." He put his thick glasses back on and picked up her file again.

What a jerk, Ashley thought and noticed that the smirk on her lips had widened into a smile, into an impish grin. She was feeling so strange. Not like her self at all. It was like the memories had awakened something, some trace of the evil that had possessed her body and soul, like some long dormant part of that demon had lingered here with her, trapped in her mind and they had awakened it. They should have left the past alone, left the memories buried because Ashley wasn't feeling like Ashley at all. She was so hungry, and this thin little man sitting at the desk across from her looked good enough to eat...

Dr. Ross was staring at her now. He didn't like that look in her eyes or that smile, why was she smiling like that anyway, he wondered, like the cat that just ate the canary. "It says here that you told the nurses that your attempted suicide was staged by the people in your apartment building, that they were trying to kill you and had all ready killed another girl who lived there." He looked at her now, waiting for an

Vacant Spaces

answer that would be satisfactory enough to let her out of this dark inferno of an office.

Ashley shifted a little, let the smile fall from her lips and looked up at him with wide eyes that were glassed over and on the verge of spilling tears down her cheeks. And when she spoke her voice sounded innocent, almost virginal. "I know what I said doctor, but of course none of it was true. You see I had just learned the truth about memories I had repressed when I was a teenager."

His interest peaked and his eyebrows raised now, "Really?"

'Uhuh," Ashley nodded and licked her lips quickly. "You see I had just learned that I had been raped by a priest that was hired by my parents who thought I was possessed by the devil." She let the words ramble out quickly, watching in great enjoyment as they hit their target.

"Uh-oh-I-I—see," Dr. Ross stuttered and started flipping through the papers on his desk. "None of that was in your file, no one told me." This woman was making him nervous; he had to regain his composure. He leaned back in his chair and took in a deep breath.

Ashley was watching him out of the corner of her eye but she was staring at the lamp on the desktop. Next, she thought to herself, he will say what happened to you was horrible.

"Miss Malone, what happened to you was horrible,"

Oh now it was Miss Malone, she saw how it was, he didn't want to be her friend anymore. No first name basis for the girl who had sex with a priest.

"Rape is an awful and personal thing and people deal with it their own ways, but it's something that I highly suggest you seek counseling for in the future. You were the victim of your parent's radical religious beliefs and for what happened to you I am truly sorry—" He paused for a moment, why was she staring so intently at that lamp, he wondered? "But even so I think you and I both know there is no such thing as demonic possession..." he waited for an answer. "Right, Miss Malone?"

Ashley took her eyes off the lamp for only a second to look at him, were her eyes a different color now? "Right," she smiled and then looked quickly back at the lamp.

Suddenly the bulb's dim glow began to waver and buzz. The lamp took on an eerie strobe effect before getting amazingly bright, too bright, then the bulb shattered and the tiny windowless office was cast into darkness.

Dr. Ross sat deathly still, the only sound he could hear was his own breathing, and then...growling?

He asked, "What was that noise?" in a shaky voice that sounded almost feminine.

"Oh, that was just my tummy growling, doc. I'm awfully hungry."

Then there was giggling, followed by a sudden movement from across the desk.

Half an hour later Ashley Malone was released from the hospital.

Two hours after that Dr. Stanley Ross turned in his resignation to a stunned and surprised chief of staff who was curious as to why there was a large, blood soaked bandage on the psychiatrist's neck.

Vacant Spaces

It was Wednesday afternoon when Ashley stood outside the brownstone again. Its majestic and comforting solidarity that had once seemed so safe and inviting now felt cold and dark. Its walls and doors that Ashley thought would keep danger out seemed to now harbor an evil within, giving it sanctuary and protection. This place was calling for her. She felt as though the house its self had tricked her here, to fulfill some dark and evil destiny. They let her out of the hospital. She had answered all of their questions right. Was she hearing things? Yes, but they could be her imagination. Did someone try to kill her and make it look like suicide? Ashley told them no, that it was all her. But she had to be honest with herself too, she couldn't be sure she didn't try to kill herself. The strange sensation she had in the hospital, the feeling of not being herself had went away now. Everything up until this moment seemed to blur together. She couldn't remember any of the conversation she had with the psychiatrist, she wasn't even sure why they had released her. She was in a bad way and the repressed memories of the rape and the…other thing. God she couldn't even say it. It was reeking havoc on her mind and body. It was impossible, wasn't it? Cross didn't think so. Even Mrs. Winthrop believed in…demonic possession. Still the fact remained, someone had sent her a fake newspaper article about a real incident. Yes, Susan was missing, Mrs. Winthrop and all the residents here confirm that, but someone wanted Ashley to know about it, wanted her here in New York; but why?

A light breeze began to blow, rustling the leaves on their limbs. Ashley felt a chill and hugged herself, despite the warmth of the day. She had to go into the brownstone, had to get Austin…and then what? Leave? She had nowhere to go really. And would she just give up on Susan so easily? Life seemed hopeless as Ashley walked the cobblestone-paved walkway, took the steps that led to the porch and through the lion faced doors into the brownstone at 311 Beech Street.

There was no answer at Mrs. Winthrop's door. Ashley wondered if the woman had taken Austin out into the city, or maybe they were in the garden. Either way Ashley wanted to go upstairs and change clothes first. She was still wearing the same blouse she was brought to the hospital in, and she wanted to shower again. The shower at the hospital felt cold and impersonal. She needed the warmth of Susan's shower, her shower. As Ashley climbed to the second story she passed Thomas' door. God what would he think of her now…a suicidal maniac with paranoid delusions. Everyone in this building seemed a bit eccentric and strange in his or her own little way and she topped them all. She was Ashley Malone, queen freak.

Then she paused, stood in front of apartment 2B, Father Jerod's apartment. She wondered if he was inside. She needed to talk to a priest right now, she needed guidance and understanding and above all, forgiveness, forgiveness from God for harboring that terrible secret ten years ago. She felt as though she must be evil herself to be the recipient of such evil. She wanted to repent. Ashley raised her hand to knock, let it waver there for a moment unsure and then lightly tapped on the door. She waited, leaned in closer and thought she heard movement inside, but no one answered the door. She started to knock again and thought better of it. Even if the priest had been home, she didn't know the man. How could she possibly tell him these things? No, what she needed to do was to go to church for confession. Confess her sins and beg the church and God and Jesus and the Holy Mother Mary for forgiveness. And pray that forgiveness would come.

The brownstone seemed unusually quiet today as Ashley dug in the pocket of her jeans for her keys. She slid the key into the shiny brass knob's keyhole but the knob turned easily without it and the door swung open. Had the paramedics left the door unlocked, or Dan? Surely Mrs. Winthrop would have locked it for her. She entered cautiously. Maybe Mrs. Winthrop was here, with Austin. Ashley moved quickly now, as if someone might try to grab her at any moment, down the hallway and to Austin's room. She pushed the door opened and looked...then smiled. Austin was asleep in his bed. Turned on his stomach, covers kicked to the floor. His breathing was deep and restful. How Ashley wished she could sleep in such comfort and bliss, without the threats of nightmares and intruders. She closed the door. So Mrs. Winthrop was here. But where? She heard sounds then coming from the bathroom. The door was only open an inch and the sound of water gushing, not running but gushing, echoed eerily down the hallway. What was that noise? Ashley approached the door, placed her hand on its face, pushing and at the same time said, "Mrs. Winthrop?"

Loretta Malone let out a little scream as she stood and turned from the toilet bowl where she was stooped over. She had on large yellow rubber gloves up to her elbows and a plunger in one hand. "Ashley you scared me to death," she said, dropping the plunger in the toilet and taking off the ridiculous gloves.

"Mother?" Ashley just stood there with a dumbfounded expression on her face. Oh please God tell her this was another one of those paranoid delusions she seemed to keep having. She really didn't need this right now.

"Oh how are you dear?" Loretta came to her, gave her a light hug that Ashley did not return. "That reporter man called me, told me what happened and I flew right out. That landlady woman, oh what's her name…Mrs. Whitwell—"

"Winthrop," Ashley corrected.

"Yes, well, whatever, she let me in. Honestly Ashley a perfect stranger watching Austin? That isn't safe."

Ashley rolled her eyes, turned to leave the cramped, little room. She really could not deal with her mother right now.

"Ashley wait," Loretta called after her.

Ashley turned; saw a look in her mother's eyes that wasn't there very often, a look of genuine care and concern.

"Dan told me about the pills, and—and he told me why you took them." Suddenly tears were springing from the woman's eyes and she tried to hide her face in her hands. "I'm so sorry Ashley, it's all my fault.

Vacant Spaces

Your father and I, we should have told you, we should never have tried to—to hide it from you." Her words were coming in sobs now and Ashley felt hot tears streak down her own cheeks. She had never seen her mother cry before. Not even at her father's funeral. And she had never, ever heard her mother admit guilt.

Loretta looked up at her daughter, mascara streaked down her face and she looked silly, "Can you ever find it in your heart to forgive me?" She pleaded, "I didn't understand what was happening, I didn't know what to do."

Ashley went to her then, put her arms around the woman and showed her the love and compassion that her mother never showed her. The woman who had always seemed cold and calculating was breaking down now, crumbling at Ashley's feet and revealing a mother that Ashley had always wanted.

"Of course I forgive you mom." She said as Loretta clung to her, bunching the girls blouse up in her fist as the sobs came louder, stronger.

"What happened to you, Ashley, it's not your fault, it's nobody's fault."

They stood like that for a while, neither woman wanting to let go. Finally Ashley pulled back, wiped tears away with the back of her hand and looked at the plunger still sitting in the toilet. She smiled a half smile. "What are you doing in here anyway?"

Loretta looked at the toilet then back at her daughter. "The damn toilet is stopped up, I was trying to plunge it."

For no reason at all, the entire situation struck Ashley as funny and she began to laugh, this caused her mother to look at her in earnest and say, "I don't see what's so funny about a stopped up toilet." And then, "Maybe Mrs. Butterworth can fix it."

Ashley lost it then and the laughter came nonstop until she doubled over in pain. Maybe she was crazy, she thought, as she continued laughing her way down the hall, but right now it felt pretty good.

Her mother cooked dinner for the three of them that night. She pestered Ashley constantly. You look thin. You look sick. You look tired. And of course it was all true, Ashley knew this, but she didn't need to be reminded of it.

As Loretta began setting the food out on the table, the smells of meatloaf and mashed potatoes filling the air, there was a knock at the door.

"I've got it, mom," Ashley said, looking over her shoulder at her dismayed mother who she knew was thinking, 'knocking on the door at dinnertime, really, how rude.' Ashley smiled to herself; opening the door her smile widened even more. The largest bouquet of flowers Ashley had ever seen hid whoever was at the door, she raised a hand to her chest, the smile still plastered across her face. She saw masculine hands gripping the bundle of sweet smelling floral.

"Thomas," she said, "they're beautiful."

The bouquet dropped then, revealing a grinning Dan Phillips, the grin disappearing quickly. "Who's Thomas?" He asked, a look of irritation, or perhaps jealousy spread across his face.

Ashley snarled. "Oh it's you. What do you want?" She was tempted to slam the door in his face. Why must this man keep pestering her? He had been no help to her at all, only trouble.

Vacant Spaces

"Look, I came to apologize, and to see how you're doing," he replied, holding the bouquet out to her, she refused it.

"Ashley, who is it?" Her mother called. Ashley rolled her eyes.

"No one mom," she yelled over her shoulder but it was too late, Loretta was already at the door.

"Well whoever you are your interrupting dinner so either leave or join us," Loretta demanded, waiting for a response. Good old mom, Ashley thought, always did have a way with words.

Dan's free hand shot out like a bullet. "Hi, Dan Phillips, we spoke on the phone."

"Oh my yes!" Loretta's face lit up like a Christmas tree. "You're the man who saved my daughter's life. You must definitely stay for dinner."

"Mother," Ashley started to protest but it was too late.

Loretta grabbed the man's arm and pulled him inside the apartment. "And look Ashley, he brought you flowers." Her mother took the flowers and headed off to the kitchen. "I'll just put these in some water and you two get comfortable with Austin at the table." She disappeared out of sight, then called out, "Dan, I hope you like meatloaf."

Dan smiled and called back, "My favorite." Then looked at Ashley.

"Dinner and then you leave," she said sternly, softly. "And eat quick," she added as she was walking away. Dan's impish grin returned as he looked at her rear end. He liked a woman that played hard to get.

Dinner was sickening. Oh the meatloaf was fine, the mash potatoes were a little lumpy but still good. No, the food wasn't it at all, what was sickening was the way that Ashley's mother fawned over the reporter, praised him and he just sat there, sucking it up with that stupid grin on his face. Ashley thought she may truly become ill. If she had ever felt any kind of attraction toward the man before, and she hadn't, it was definitely gone now. Any man that her mother approved of had to be the devil incarnate.

"Ashley," Dan looked at her now, "I was hoping you could meet me tomorrow night at my office, around seven? I've got the names and pictures of all the women that were the victims of the midnight stalker, I thought you might want to take a look," he said, then added, "Just to put your mind at ease that Susan Bishop isn't one of them."

Not on your life, buddy, is what Ashley was thinking. "I'm sorry I really can't. My mother's in town and I should really spend some time with her," is what she said.

"Nonsense," Loretta interjected, rising and picking up the empty plates. "I'll be fine. It'll give my grandson and me some time to spend together."

Ashley looked at her mother with a grimace. "Thanks mom," she replied in a mocking tone.

"You're welcome, dear," her mother said back with the same tone.

"Good, it's all set then. Tomorrow at seven." Dan stood and put his napkin on the table, looked at Loretta and said, "Mrs. Malone, Dinner was wonderful. Thank you."

Vacant Spaces

Loretta blushed. Her mother actually blushed. "Call me Loretta, Ashley you should walk Dan downstairs."

Dan turned and smiled at her. "Yes Ashley, you should."

Ashley began to mumble under her breath, "Condesending son of a—"

"What's that dear?" Her mother asked.

Ashley smiled and cocked her head. "I said I'd love to."

As the two of them left the apartment Dan looked at her and said, "Condescending, huh?"

Ashley stood outside the doors of the brownstone, on the bottom step of the porch. She watched as Dan Phillips drove away. Knowing that the reporter was only trying to do what was best for her by telling her about her past did little to ease the animosity that Ashley felt toward him. Still, he did save her life, didn't that count for something?

"Hello, Ashley." A deep voice said from behind her.

She turned to see Thomas Robinson standing in the doorway of the brownstone. Had he seen her with Dan? If he did would he be jealous? Ashley thought she would like that, a man being jealous over her. "Hi," she said back, sheepishly.

Thomas walked down the steps, came to stand beside her. They both gazed out past the street at the city lights that peeped through the trees and beyond the houses.

"I heard about what happened, I do hope you are all right." Still he did not look at her.

So he had heard about the supposed suicide attempt. That was to be expected. She knew how fast word got around in the brownstone. "I'm fine. A little embarrassed, but fine."

Thomas turned to her now, swooped her hand up in his own and gazed into her eyes. A gaze so intent Ashley was sure she would melt. "Don't ever be embarrassed around me," he said to her. "I only wish I could have been there for you, to help you. That you could have talked to me."

She looked down, so he cared, she thought, and then, but so does Dan.

"Can I take you out tomorrow night, to dinner, get your mind off things?"

Ashley's heart leapt, she wanted to scream yes, yes of course you can, but instead said, "I'm sorry, I've got plans, and my mother is in town."

"Oh," Thomas replied, not hiding his disappointment. "The weekend then, if you want to I mean. Maybe I'm being presumptuous."

"No, no, not at all. I do want to."

He smiled at that and said, "Good. Let's say Saturday evening then, about six. I'll meet you at your apartment."

"Sounds good," Ashley smiled and began walking up the steps. She turned when she realized he wasn't following. "Are you coming?" she asked him.

"No, you go ahead, it's such a beautiful night I thought I might go for a walk."

"Oh, okay," she said. "Goodnight."

"Goodnight." He replied.

Ashley went inside the brownstone, door squeaking at her entering. She hoped she had not upset him. She shivered as she past the door to the basement and walked faster, taking the stairs two at a time.

Sunken in deep and comfortable in her own bed felt good. Her mother had insisted in sleeping on the sofa. Having her so close again gave Ashley a sense of security. A safety she had needed since her arrival here. It helped to know too that if any more strange happenings occurred she would have a witness, someone other than Austin, some one who could speak up. As her eyelids became heavy and started to droop, Ashley became aware of a soft whistling. A tune she hadn't heard since she was a child. 'Hey diddle, diddle, the cat and the fiddle, the cow jumped over the moon.' The whistling seemed to drift up from outside the brownstone, carried by the wind, up to her window. She was tempted to just drift off to sleep but the tune sent strange chills down her spine. She was filled with a sudden and terrible fright and she wasn't sure why. Ashley rose from her bed and strode quickly and quietly over to the window. She squinted. The moonless sky provided no illumination to the mysterious whistler, but as her eyes scanned the darkness she saw a dark figure enter the dim circle of a streetlight not far down. It was a tall lanky man, dressed all in black. His head was bald except for patches of hair on either side and in back. The man stopped and so did the whistling. He stood just at the edge of the circle of light and turned. His face was hidden in shadows but he seemed to be staring up at Ashley. Her room was dark and he was a little distance away so she was sure he couldn't see her. Then she noticed he wore a white collar. He was a priest. Was that Father Jerod? The priest turned and began his stride once again, picking up his tune were he had left off. The whistling faded away as he trailed out of sight, and the shivers faded away too as they trailed down Ashley's spine.

An hour later, on a lonely street in a bad part of the town, a young girl steps out of the doorway of a tavern. She is a regular there. She goes there when she's lonely, or broke and needs a drink. There's always some sucker who's had a few too many willing to dish out drinks for her if they think she might dish out for them later. Usually she just waits for them to get so wasted that they pass out and then she leaves, although, she has gotten into some sticky situations before. Some blokes just refuse to pass out no matter how much they've had to drink. They're like a freakin' camel or something. They refuse to take no for an answer too, but she's always managed. She's good at taking care of herself; like this joker who was back at the tavern tonight. He bought her five vodka tonics and only had expensive wine himself, then expected her to just go home with him. For five vodka tonics! What did he think, she was cheap or something? Ten maybe, but not five.

As she walked, she thought about the dump she was going back to, the rat and roach infested slum that she had to shell out a hundred and ten bucks a week for. God how she hated this city, this life. Sometimes she wished she were dead. It was then she realized that someone was close behind her. Before she could even turn to look someone grabbed her. She tried to scream but heavy hands clasped over her mouth. She

Vacant Spaces

was being dragged into a dark alley. Kicking and flailing her free arm, she bit down hard on the hand that clamped her lips. It didn't budge. As she was dragged off into the shadows she heard the bastard laughing softly to himself and smelled the expensive wine on his breath.

CHAPTER EIGHTEEN

Dan Phillips plopped two Alka-Seltzers in a glass and watched the fizz rise to the top. His stomach had been turning ever since he had written the story and turned it in. 'The Midnight Stalkers Latest Victim.' A young girl abducted late last night. Sexually assaulted, rope marks burned into her hands and feet, throat sliced open like fruit. Last seen leaving Mick's Tavern. And of course none of the junkies in the place saw anything, God forbid they help the cops catch a lowlife piece of scum like themselves. And the girl was only twenty-one too. What a waste. Still, at least the police had something to go on this time. Seems the girl was a fighter. She bit the son of a bitch. Forensics found blood and skin in her mouth that didn't match her own. They had the bastard's DNA to match him with when they did finally catch him. Dan swigged down the clear liquid, knowing it wouldn't help ease the pain of the ulcer that kept nagging him. He looked at his watch, almost time for Ashley to meet him here. He had better add this last victims name to the list before she arrived.

"I shouldn't be gone very long mom, but here's the number to Dan's office and cell just in case something happens." Ashley handed Loretta a tiny scrap of paper with the number scribbled on it. She didn't like the thought of leaving the two of them alone here, not after

Vacant Spaces

what she'd experienced at this place. She still wasn't convinced it was safe. "You have your cell phone in case you need me, right?"

Loretta Malone rolled her eyes as she held up the phone for her daughter to see for the umpteenth time. "Really, Ashley, I wish you would get one of these things yourself, they're so convenient. Now stop worrying, Austin and I will be fine," her mother said, pushing her toward the door and opening it. "You and Dan have a good time. I do wish you would change into something else though."

Ashley sighed and looked at her mother with dismay. "Mom, I told you, this is not a date." Loretta had been pestering her to change outfits all night, she was worse than Mrs. Winthrop when it came to match making.

"Well if you keep dressing like that it'll never be."

"Bye, mom. Love you." She pecked the woman on the cheek and rushed off. She knew that it was no use trying to argue. You couldn't win an argument with her mother, it was impossible. The woman wasn't dealing with reality. How could you win with someone like that? Then, she thought to herself, everybody is saying I'm not dealing in reality either. God she was becoming her mother.

"Oh by the way," her mother called after her as she reached the stairway. "The toilet's still stopped up, I may have to call on the buildings handyman to fix it."

"No!" Ashley almost yelled and then calmed herself. "I'll fix it later, or I'll call a plumber tomorrow, just don't worry about it, mom." She heard her mother rambling under her breath as she went back inside and shut the door. "I don't know how your not suppose to worry about a stopped up toilet," she was saying. Ashley waited until she heard the lock turn and went down the stairs.

Just as she was just about to walk out of the brownstone, the door to apartment A1 swung open. "Going out on a hot date, dear?" Mrs. Winthrop's smiling face asked, auburn hair blazing, green eyes shining.

Ashley was turning into her mother and her mom was turning into Mrs. Butterworth-er-Whinthrop. "Just meeting a friend," Ashley replied. "My mother is watching Austin for the night."

Mrs. Winthrop clasped her hands together. "Such a friendly woman, that mother of yours." There was that tone in her voice again. The one were you couldn't be sure if she was being sincere or sarcastic. "I do hope you're feeling better, after the little incident, I mean."

God how Ashley wished people would quit hoping she was feeling better. She was feeling fine. "I'm good, thanks for asking," she said to the old woman.

"Good, good. You better run along then, don't want to be late." She winked at Ashley, then quietly closed her door.

Ashley hadn't really expected anyone to be at the New York Times' building this late in the evening, but there was still a handful of people scurrying about like ants, always looking as if they were in a rush and running late. A chubby, African American security guard smiled at her and nodded his head as she entered. So this is when the nice people of the city come out. Two more African American women were mopping the floors at the other side of the large entryway of the building.

"Tasha, get your black ass over here and give me a bite of that," the larger of the two women said. She was quite large actually; her hair had blue extensions springing out of random places. Definitely a home job, Ashley thought.

The other girl was mopping with one hand and eating a large chocolate covered doughnut with the other. "NO, Chandlin, you done already ate yours, leave mine alone." She yelled back, her hair braided and decorated with colored beads.

The big one dropped her mop now, "Oh I see how it is, uhuh," she placed her plump hands on her plump hips and nodded her head. "You think you're all that, way over there, but just wait till you get closer, I'll eat you to get to that doughnut if I have too."

Ashley quickly ran for the open elevator, holding her breath, waiting anxiously for the doors to close, holding her purse with both hands in front of her. When they did finally shut, she let her breath go and relaxed. Okay, maybe this was the time when all the crazy people were out, like those janitors, no, custodial engineers, that was the politically correct term for it now. And like the midnight stalker, the thought leapt into her mind and she closed her eyes while the elevator made her stomach do flip-flops. The doors open with a ding on the third floor and Ashley headed for Dan's office. She was happy to see that Greg was not there, she really couldn't deal with people like that after spending an entire day with her mother. The door to Dan's office was open and there was light spilling out so Ashley went on back. Dan was sitting at his desk, staring intently at his computer screen as his hands typed a hundred words a minute. He was even more attractive here, like this, Ashley thought. Sitting at his job, intent on his work, so deep in concentration that nothing else could get his attention. She bet he made love to a woman the same way and then wondered where the thought had come from. She tapped on the open door lightly; he looked up and smiled when he saw her.

"Come on in," he said, standing up. "I was just finishing a follow-up."

"To the latest attack?" Ashley asked, leaning on his desk and reading what he had wrote on the computer's screen.

"You've heard?"

She nodded, "Picked up the paper today, read your article. That poor girl."

Dan picked up a folder and walked around the desk to stand beside her. These damn mysterious folders that kept popping up in her life were becoming irritating.

He held this one up and shook it. "No surprises this time," he stated as though he had just read her mind. "It's the name of all the victims, some photos too but there kind of graphic, that okay?"

Ashley nodded and he handed her a picture of the latest victim, he wasn't kidding when he said graphic. Ashley felt sick looking at the pale face of the girl, her eyes closed, throat open. She quickly handed the photo back to Dan.

"Her name was Carrie Dawson, twenty one years old, address and family unknown."

Vacant Spaces

"The police don't know her address?" Ashley quizzed.

Dan shook his head still looking at the list of names he held. "Nope. All of the girls are found naked. No I.D. Usually somebody at the last place they were seen can give the name of the victim, but rarely an address. The coroner determines the age. Some of the girls families have come to report them missing then we get an address, find out more about their lives, but out of the nine victims so far, four are still no addresses, only names, this one included."

"But none are named Susan Bishop?" Ashley asked.

"None so far," he replied and immediately regretted the way it sounded.

"How can the police be sure that they have the right names for the ones who haven't been identified by family?"

"They can't," Dan said, matter-of-factly. "They could have used fake names at the places they were last seen. Most of them were bars where you wouldn't want anyone to know your real name. Or the scums that gave the police the name could have just made it up, to get the cops off their backs. That's why I brought the pictures too, so you can be sure."

Ashley nodded, tried to mentally prepare herself. "Okay," she said, lets have the next picture."

Dan handed it to her. He was impressed, most women that had been through what Ashley had been through would have crumbled, leastwise be standing here beside him looking at pictures of mutilated corpses, trying to find out what happened to her friend. Susan Bishop was one lucky lady, wherever she was.

"Tracy Bellows, twenty-nine," Dan went on. Ashley shook her head and handed the picture back to him. He could smell the sweet scent of her perfume and moved closer handing her the next picture.

Ashley studied it. Brenda was the only name they had for this one. Twenty-eight. It wasn't Susan, although the hair color was the same. It had been ten years since Ashley last saw her friend but she was sure she would recognize her even if she was…dead.

"Okay, last one," Dan said holding out the glossy photo, the overhead fluorescent reflecting off its shiny surface. "Another one-namer." Ashley took the picture out of his hand and looked at the young woman just as Dan said her name. "Abigail."

CHAPTER NINETEEN

"What did you say?" she asked, the photograph had began to shake as her hand trembled, first starting at her fingertips and now, slowly inching throughout her entire body.

"Abigail," Dan repeated. "That's the only name we have for this one. Found like the others, naked, raped, neck sliced open. Her body was discovered on the east side, thrown in a dumpster.

Ashley forced herself to look at the picture of the young woman. She was about Ashley's age, long dark hair. Black stitches lined the skin of her pale neck were the wound had been sewn up.

Dan moved closer to her and saw that she was breathing heavily. "Hey, what's wrong?" He brought his hand up, laid it lightly on her shoulder, felt her trembling.

Ashley dropped the picture on the desk and looked at him. "In the drain of the bath tub at Susan's apartment I found a small gold cross, on the back the name 'Abigail' was inscribed."

Dan thought about this for a second. "Could be a coincidence," he said finally, taking the photos and placing them back in their envelope.

"Or it could not be," she said. "Abigail could have been a friend of Susan's. She could have been scared and stayed at Susan's apartment, and that's how the midnight stalker could have…could have…"

"Killed your friend," Dan finished her words for her. Suddenly tears were welling up in the girl's eyes and he thought what an ass he was for saying such a thing.

"Hey, c'mon," he said and he went to her. She needed no second invitation as she buried her face in his shoulder, the tears absorbing into the cotton of his thin, white button down. "We don't know anything for sure. Susan wasn't one of the girls in the pictures, that's a good sign. Right?"

Ashley raised her head, wiped tears away with the back of her hand. He was staring at her, their faces close. She laughed a nervous laugh. "What? Do I look that bad?"

Her eyes darted away from his as she asked the question.

Dan shook his head, "No, I think you're beautiful."

Beautiful? Had she heard him right? He had said beautiful hadn't he?

Suddenly and without hesitation his lips locked over hers, she wasn't quiet sure what to do she was so stunned. Then he put a hand on her back, pulled her closer and she was kissing him back, full and deep and warm. He stopped, looked at her, saw the longing in her eyes and kissed her again. She really was beautiful, he thought, and strong even if she didn't know it herself. She was trembling again in his arms and she was thinking to herself, what am I doing, what about Thomas, but she didn't stop. She never wanted to stop kissing Dan Phillips, the man who had hurt her, the man who had helped her, the man who she insisted to herself that she was not attracted to…who was now

Vacant Spaces

igniting a passion inside her that was flaring up and spreading like wildfire.

He stopped again, then looked at her and said, "You hungry?"

The pizza parlor was full of college kids at this time a night. Dan and Ashley found a small table near the back, away from most of the noise. They ordered, a large pizza with all the toppings and two cokes to drink. So what if she gained fifty pounds overnight? Her mother's meatloaf was still weighing on her like a ton of bricks anyway.

"Have you checked were Susan worked at?" Dan asked her as she sipped her coke through a straw.

She shook her head, swallowed. "No. The last time we saw each other I was still…ill, and well, when I got better and found out I was pregnant I moved and we lost each other." She sipped more soda. The college students in the front of the restaurant were raising tall glasses of dark beer, toasting nothing and everything. She smiled. "Makes you wish you could go back and do things over again, doesn't it?"

Dan followed her eyes to the loud kids. "Nah," he said, reaching across the table and taking her hand. "I hated college, everyone always thought I was a nerd."

She smiled at him. "I don't see you being the nerdy type. More like the party animal."

Dan laughed out loud, threw his head back. "I see my reputation proceeds me."

Ashley looked down; her expression had grown serious now. "Thanks for not telling them at the hospital."

"About what?" he asked.

Ashley wouldn't make eye contact with him as she said, "About my past, about the…possession. They probably would never have let me out of that place."

Dan squeezed her hand, leaned closer over the table. "Look, I can't say I believe that it wasn't some mental breakdown or something, I'm not a religious person. But the fact is that you were…assaulted," God he almost said raped. "You needed to know that. And you need to seek counseling for it."

Ashley began to shake her head no but he wasn't finished.

"Your mind swept all these dirty little secrets under the rug because it couldn't deal with them, well now they're out, and if you just try to forget them then your doing yourself more harm than good."

She knew he was right, of course he was. But she didn't want to face the fact that Austin was a product of rape. She didn't want to think that her mother and her father, a man that she adored and idolized, had hidden this from her, lied to her. She fought back tears, she wouldn't cry, not here.

"Hey," Dan said, squeezing her hand until her eyes met his. "I don't care about your past, Ashley. I only care about your future."

Out of the corner of her eye she saw someone approaching the table, she assumed it was the waiter, she didn't want to tear her gaze away to look, and then a deep familiar voice said, "Hello Ashley."

She jerked her hands from Dan's out of sheer reflex, looked and saw the looming figure of Thomas Robinson standing at their table.

Ashley was flustered, tried to speak and stumbled on her own words. T-Thomas, oh, hey."

Vacant Spaces

Thomas looked from her to Dan as if demanding either an introduction or an explanation. Ashley couldn't be sure which. She shook her head as though she were just coming out of a daze, and in fact, to be totally honest she was. "Thomas, this is my friend, Dan. Dan this is—uh—my other friend Thomas."

"Pleased to meet you, Dan," Thomas said the name like it was venom as he extended his hand. Dan took it and Thomas squeezed. It was all Dan could do not to flinch. Suddenly furious Dan squeezed back, even harder, saw the man grimace.

"The pleasure's all mine, Thompson."

"That's Thomas," the older of the men corrected. Dan simply smiled.

Ashley could see were this was going and interjected. "What brings you out to a place like this, Thomas?" Ooh. That was bad, she thought after the words had left her mouth. It sounded like a crack on his age. But if the man thought so he didn't show it, he only smiled at her with that gorgeous, confident smile and said, "I come to these kind of places to get inspiration for my books."

"Oh, Dan is a writer too." Maybe their love of writing would smooth things over.

"Really, anything published?" Thomas asked the man, looking down at him with a kind of loathing jealousy.

"Sure, everyday in the New York Times," Dan replied, winked at Ashley.

Oh, I see, A journalist, how…nice." His words dripped with sarcasm as he turned his attention back to Ashley. His features softened, his voice gentle now. "Well, I'll let you two get back to whatever it was you were doing. Ashley," he said and took her hand leaning over, "I do hope we are still on for this weekend." And without waiting for a reply he kissed the back of her hand softly and was gone.

My God, she thought, her face was a burning fire, he kissed my hand, he actually kissed my hand. Things like that only happen in the movies or in romance novels, certainly not to somebody like her. She looked back at Dan and tried to still her beating heart.

"I take it you two know each other?" he said as the waiter arrived with their pizza.

Loretta Malone kissed Austin on the forehead as he tried in vain to keep his eyes open. She smiled down at her grandson, leaned in close to him and whispered softly in his ear, "Don't fight it, go to sleep." She kissed him again and his eyes shut. He really was a beautiful child. His dark brown locks of hair falling in loose curls, those beautiful dark eyes. Loretta loved him, loved him so much that it hurt sometimes. She didn't care now how he was conceived, he was here, and he was as much a part of her as Ashley was. She left the room, closing the door quietly behind her she let out a sigh, back to the task at hand. With that she entered the bathroom and dawned the big, yellow rubber gloves and picked up the plunger. She was determined to get that damned toilet unclogged even if it killed her.

Dan and Ashley walked arm in arm down the streets of New York. The rain from the previous night left huge puddles that people skipped around in a kind

Vacant Spaces

of dance, in order not to get their feet soaked. The street's hard surface, still wet, reflected the city lights like a dark mirror, an upside down world, distorted and out of focus. That's what her life felt like lately, Ashley thought to herself as she clung tighter to the reporter, an upside down world. The ringing of Dan's cell phone coming from his inside jacket pocket interrupted her thoughts. The man reached in and answered. Ashley listened as he argued with the person on the other end.

"C'mon, you've got to be kidding, can't Paula handle that? All right...okay, I'll call Greg and be right there." He hung up the phone and looked at her.

"You've got to go," she asked, still walking, slower now because she didn't want this to end.

He nodded.

"A story. Seems some congress man may have been caught with his pants down with someone other than his wife."

"Nice that his wife will get to read about it on the front page in the morning, it's so much more personal than coming from a human being," she replied sarcastically.

Dan shrugged his shoulders, "I just do what the big boss tells me," he replied, then stopped and turned to her. "I really enjoyed tonight—I mean not the looking at dead people, but the rest of it."

Ashley smiled and that made him smile too. He was just leaning in for a kiss when the inside of his jacket began to ring again. He pulled back, answered and then handed the phone out to her, "I think it's your mom," he said.

Ashley snatched the phone; my God did something happen to Austin? "Mom," she spoke into the tiny receiver. "Is everything okay?" Her voice was on the verge of panic, oh she should have never went out, she should have never left the two of them alone in that apartment.

"Calm down Ashley, everything is fine," her mother's tiny voice sounded as though it were coming from a tunnel. "I just called to tell you we won't be needing that plumber after all, your old mom did it."

"Did what, mom?"

"Unclogged the toilet," the woman replied with an air of accomplishment about her.

Ashley rolled her eyes as Dan mouthed silently 'Is everything all right?' Ashley nodded yes to him as her mother began to bellow from the tunnel again.

"I'm sorry to bother you on your date dear, I just thought you would like to know where your cross went."

Ashley was about to say that it wasn't a date, but to be perfectly honest she wasn't sure herself. "What cross?" she asked instead.

"The little gold one, how in the world did it get in the toilet?"

Surely it wasn't Abigail's cross her mother was referring to, that was impossible, Mrs. Winthrop said she put it somewhere safe for her.

"Ashley, are you still there?" the tiny voice crackled with static and cut out for a moment, Ashley moved for better reception.

"Mom," she spoke louder, "I want you to turn the cross over, does it say anything on the back?"

Vacant Spaces

"Let me see, dear. I don't have my reading glasses on but it looks like it says...Abigail."

Ashley felt her heart skip a beat and it seemed as if the city had stopped around her. She wasn't aware of the noise of the passersby or the cars that splashed along on the street, only that name, Abigail. Had Mrs. Winthrop lied to her, flushed the necklace down the toilet? But why? And then Ashley remembered the strange look on the old woman's face the night she saw Ashley wearing the cross, how she had insisted, almost demanded that Ashley take it off and wear something else. She regained her senses now, the city started to move again. "Mom, listen to me. I want you to take Austin and go to a motel room tonight."

"What," Loretta asked confused. Then, "Oh Ashley you're not letting Dan spend the night are you, remember what I told you about how no one will buy the cow if they can get the milk for free?"

What the hell was her mother talking about now, a cow? "No mom, Dan's not spending the night," She saw Dan's eyebrows rise in surprise and wonderment. "Just do as I say. Take Austin to a motel room, I have to take care of something."

Loretta started to protest but Ashley cut her off with a sternness in her voice now that said she wasn't kidding. "Look, don't argue, just do it. I'll call you on your cell phone in the morning, now go," she said.

"Fine," Loretta replied but added, "I think it's silly to wake a boy up in the middle of the night though. Goodbye, dear, and remember what I told you,"

Ashley shook her head, "About the cow, yea mom got it, bye," she thumbed the off button and handed the phone back to Dan.

"Hey is everything okay?" he asked, with genuine concern in his voice.

Ashley nodded and told him everything was fine and not to worry.

That didn't satisfy him though. "Why the hotel room then?"

She sighed. She didn't feel like going into it. She didn't want him to think she was being paranoid again or crazy or whatever it was he thought of her.

"Just for my own piece of mind. There are some things I have to get straightened out and I will just feel better if I don't have to worry about the two of them."

He stepped closer now, rubbed her cheek. "You sure?"

She smiled, nodded and said, "Now go, you'll miss your story."

"Can I see you tomorrow night, just dinner not any of this mystery and mayhem stuff?" he asked her.

Ashley nodded. "I'd like that. What time?"

He sighed, thought for a moment and said, "Might be kind of late actually, around eight-thirty, nine?" He hoped she wouldn't say that was too late.

"Okay, pick me up?" She wasn't sure if she could stomach another bad smelling taxi.

"You must be learning to trust me, letting me drive and all,"

She smiled. This time she kissed him and he returned the kiss.

"See you tomorrow," he said and turned, immersed himself into the crowd of people and became one of them. Then he was gone.

Ashley then turned her thoughts to Mrs. Winthrop. The more she thought about the cross the more furious

Vacant Spaces

she became. Why? What was going on at that brownstone? What did that old lady have to hide? There were just too many things that didn't add up here. And Ashley was tired of playing this cat and mouse game and feeling like she was always the mouse. She was going to find out what secrets lay buried at 311 Beech Street once and for all, and she was going to find out tonight.

Loretta held Austin's wrist with one hand and made sure she locked the door with the other. Austin was still in his pajamas and rubbed his eyes sleepily with the back of his fingers. Loretta thought that this was silly, leaving in the middle of the night to get a hotel. What was Ashley thinking? She knew her daughter was worried because of Susan disappearing here and all, but it all seemed perfectly safe to her. She was about to head down the hall when she heard something coming from the attic stairway, it sounded like whispering but she couldn't make out the words.

"Hello, is anybody there?" she called out; her voice sounded odd in the stillness of the narrow hall, bouncing off the hardwood floors and plaster walls. She dropped Austin's wrist and walked closer, trying to see around the corner of the shadowy entrance. Still the whispering continued. Behind her Austin stood as still as death, his eyes large ovals of vacant spaces, then his head began to shake, as if saying 'no', slowly at first then faster and faster. Loretta placed a hand on the wall, let it glide her along and walked slower, closer, and as she reached the dark entrance to the stairwell she heard what the voice was whispering…

"Here piggy piggy piggy…"

Mark Andrew Ware

PART THREE

REVELATION

Mark Andrew Ware

CHAPTER TWENTY

It was after nine when Ashley returned to the brownstone and the foyer doors were locked, she fumbled on through her key chain until she found the small silver key that Mrs. Winthrop had given her, unlocked the heavy door and slid inside. The brownstone was quiet, so still that it was almost odd, as if no life existed inside its walls at all. Ashley walked noisily to apartment A1 and knocked. No answer at first, she raised her fist to knock again when the door was swung open and Ashley's closed knuckles came down on air.

"Hello dear," Mrs. Winthrop's smiling face beamed at her. The woman was dressed in a purple, floor length nightgown and held a book in her hands. This made Ashley wonder if the mountains of books had returned to the old woman's living room or were they still in hiding.

"Sorry to bother you so late Mrs. Winthrop, but I need to talk to you," She was trying her best to stay stern even in the face of the woman's charming and friendly demeanor.

"It's never too late for you Ashley, come on in, dear," she opened the door wider and Ashley entered the apartment. Nope the tons of books were still nowhere in sight. "What do you need to see me about, it isn't Topples is it? He has specific instructions never to set foot back in this building." Mrs. Winthrop waved her finger in the air as she stated this, as though she were demanding her authority be followed or else.

"No," Ashley shook her head and nervously looked about the apartment. "It's not Topples."

"Then what dear, is everything okay?"

She looked at the old woman now, built up her courage and said, "No, Mrs. Winthrop everything is not okay. I want to know why you lied to me."

The old woman put a hand to her chest, backed up a step. "Why Ashley, what do you mean? I would never lie to you."

Ashley stepped closer to the woman, she had to come at her with guns firing, just say it, just say what's on your mind. "Then why was Abigail's cross found flushed down my toilet, Mrs. Winthrop? You were the last one to have it and then it disappeared, and then Cross' cell phone shows up under Austin's bed and you were the last one to see her alive. Now I want to know what's going on around here and I want to know now," her voice was loud, getting louder, out of control. She had to remind herself to stay calm. She couldn't loose it.

Mrs. Winthrop was left pale at the words; she stood there clutching the front of her nightgown, the material fisted up in a ball and the book in the other hand, hanging down limply at her side. She just stood there staring at Ashley with this wide eyed, pale faced stare not saying anything to these accusations. Well, Ashley certainly wasn't going to give her time to think of an excuse and so she began battering her with words again.

"Mrs. Winthrop talk to me!" she demanded stepping even closer to the woman. "I know

Vacant Spaces

something funny is going on around here and I want to know what right now! From the moment I walked into this Godforsaken building I've been attacked, drugged and made to feel like I was loosing my mind, and every time you have some witty excuse to help that feeling along, but not this time, do you hear me! You're going to tell me what's happening around here or…" She stopped then, saw that the old woman was trembling. Something wasn't right. Mrs. Winthrop was no longer clutching at her nightgown, she was now clutching at her heart. Her knees buckled and Ashley caught her as she began to fall to the hardwood floors.

"My heart," the old woman gasped in a wheezing breath, "My heart."

It was all Ashley could do to hold the woman up; she was heavier than she looked, stouter. She eased Mrs. Winthrop to the floor and ran to the phone frantically dialing 911 as the old woman lay on the floor jerking, still clutching at her heart.

Ashley sat in the hospital waiting room for what seemed like an eternity, but the clock on the wall told her that only a couple of hours had passed. My God, what had she done? Pounded an old woman with dire accusations until her heart gave out on her? She knew how sensitive Mrs. Winthrop was, how easily upset she could get, and here Ashley had come knocking on her door in the middle of the night yelling and ranting like a mad woman. Why did it all ways come down to her looking like the crazy person? She sighed a long and weary sigh, because maybe she was.

She looked up as she saw Thomas coming down the white hospital corridor, his hard sole shoes clicking loudly on the tiled floors and echoing off the sanitized walls. Ashley hated hospitals, they were so impersonal, even more so than motel rooms.

"How is she?" she asked, rising as he came to her. Ashley had ran up to get him before the ambulance arrived, she told him what had happened, he probably hated her as much as Mrs. Winthrop did right now.

"She's going to be fine, Ashley. The doctors want to keep her overnight just to make sure, she wants to see you," he added, almost as an afterthought.

Ashley shook her head no. "I couldn't Thomas, I just couldn't, not after the things that I said to her."

He took her by the shoulders then, gave her a light hug. "It's okay Ashley, Harriet is very forgiving." He looked her in the eyes with a light smile and motioned with his head for her to go on back. Ashley nodded silently, obeyed.

The room smelled of sanitary cleaner and was dim. A small heart monitor made a bleeping noise every time Mrs. Winthrop's heart would beat. The old woman lay in the bed; a tube ran up her nose for oxygen. She looked so frail lying there like that, not at all like the woman Ashley remembered bustling up the stairs of the brownstone so full of energy that Ashley couldn't even keep up. And she had caused this poor old woman to loose strength like this; she was a monster, a horrible, horrible monster.

"Come on in dear," The woman's voice sounded as fragile as she looked. She motioned for Ashley to sit close to her.

Vacant Spaces

"Mrs. Winthrop, I am so sorry, for what I said to you, for all of this," she raised a hand at the heart monitor and felt tears stinging her cheeks.

"Rubbish," the old woman said, scooting up to an almost sitting position in the bed.

"You're not the one that gave me a bad ticker. Besides, it's these crazy doctors who say that it was a heart attack, and what do they know? It could have been gas! That mother of yours sent down some meatloaf yesterday that could fuel the world for years."

Ashley smiled in spite of herself and Mrs. Winthrop leaned closer to her and whispered as if someone might hear.

"Besides, I have been keeping something from you, about the necklace and…" she paused and said even more hushed now, "about the night Cross died."

Ashley's eyes grew wide and her own heart began to beat faster, seeming to beat in unison with the bleeps on the monitor.

The old woman looked down, had her hands in her lap, fidgeting. "That night, the night Cross died you had left to go on your date with Thomas, I went to put the necklace in your jewelry box, I distinctly remember doing so. When I turned around, Austin was watching me, after that you told me that the cross was missing, but I know I put it in the jewelry box," she clenched a fist and shook it in the air, looking far away. "I know I did." she repeated.

"You think Austin took it?" Ashley asked.

Mrs. Winthrop nodded. "Oh I didn't want to think that, but now you tell me you found Cross' cell phone under his bed?"

Ashley shook her head yes; she didn't want to hear the answer to the question that she asked next. "What happened the night Cross died, Mrs. Winthrop?"

The old woman looked at Ashley, didn't speak for a moment as if she were afraid to say anything, afraid Ashley would start yelling at her again perhaps. Then she looked the girl right in the eye and said, "I went to check on Austin, he wasn't in his room, the next thing I know I heard a terrible scream, It was Cross, I pounded on her door and no one answered, when I went back to your apartment I looked out the window, and there she was, neck broken, poor thing. Then I turned," Mrs. Winthrop's hand was moving along with the story and she was no longer looking at Ashley but seemed to instead be seeing what she spoke of. "and standing there in the doorway was Austin."

Her words hit hard and Ashley wanted to tell the old woman she was crazy but it all made too much sense, after all, why would Mrs. Winthrop want to flush the cross? And Austin had disappeared on her too; she had seen him up in the attic.

The woman placed a hand on Ashley's now, said with kindness and concern, "I love Austin as though he were my very own, dear, but I think he may be more troubled than anyone knows."

"My God," Ashley said, was it true, she couldn't handle it if something were to happen to her son, if he were taken away from her.

"It's okay dear," Mrs. Winthrop tried to soothe. "We won't tell anyone, just get the boy some help."

Ashley nodded, her eyes were glassy and she was trying hard to keep herself from crying. She had to get out of here, had to call her mother and try to figure all

Vacant Spaces

of this out. "Thank you Mrs. Winthrop," she said, and, "I really am sorry for all of this."

And with that she left the room. Ashley practically ran down the hospital corridor and Thomas caught her in his arms. He saw the tears she was trying to hold back, felt her trembling. "Ashley, what's wrong?" he demanded.

She wiped a tear that escaped. "Nothing," she said. "Really, I just need to call my mother, her and Austin are at a motel and—"

"Listen," he cut her off. "It's very late. They're asleep by now as you should be. Why don't you let me call you a cab, you look exhausted."

She was exhausted too, he was right, and it was late. "All right," she said, nodding. "Are you coming too?"

"No, I'm going to stay with Harriet, make sure she doesn't kill a doctor or something."

This made her smile and he smiled back at her. "Thank you, Thomas."

He kissed her forehead then walked over to the phone.

As Ashley climbed into the taxi she was still wondering what to do about her son. His birthday was only three days away. Her mother was planning on going back to Atlanta immediately afterwards, would she stay longer, was it safe for her too? How could she not know that something was terribly wrong with Austin, how could she not know her own son? She looked up at the tall, looming hospital just before the cab pulled away. The windows of the building lit up it's shadowy front like a hundred glowing eyes, digesting what was inside. For once Ashley couldn't wait to get back to the brownstone, she really was tired, more than she had realized, and she hoped sleep would come quick and easy.

Thomas crept into Harriet Winthrop's hospital room. The old woman lay still with her eyes closed. She looked peaceful, he thought. Suddenly her eyes fluttered open, the bleeps on the heart monitor became faster as she saw his dark silhouette against the dim back light of the room.

"You startled me," she said to him.

"How do you feel?" He asked, a smirk upon his face.

She shook her head, "Weak, I haven't felt this weak in a long time."

Thomas sat at the edge of her bed, caressed her wrinkled cheek with his cold hand. The bleeps on the heart monitor were coming quickly now, as Harriet Winthrop's heart pounded in her chest. Thomas smiled, "Why Harriet, if I didn't know better I would think you were frightened of me." Then he laughed loudly, a cold, unearthly laugh.

The night had grown thick and quiet by the time Ashley stepped out of the taxi at 311 Beech Street. The insect world sang strange songs and shadows opened doorways to dark and eerie places. It was all Ashley could do to unlock the foyer doors what with the way her hands were shaking. Inside a cold shiver ran down her spine as she passed the door to the basement. The brownstone would be empty tonight except for herself and the Briar sisters, unless the priest was home, and she doubted that. Ashley wished now that she had never sent her mother and Austin away, it was going to be a long night with strange sounds and shadows at every turn, she knew that. Maybe Thomas would come home later, she was even tempted to go out and call Dan. No, she refused to play that scared woman routine; even if it were true it would only look like an act of desperation. She climbed the first set of stairs now, up into the second landing. The hardwood floors creaked as if the brownstone itself were screaming 'intruder' and Ashley guessed in a way she was an intruder, she didn't feel as if she belonged in this place. She slipped passed Thomas' door, then the priests', both dead quiet. She climbed the second set of stairs and it was as she reached the third floor landing that she let out a gasp. A figure was drifting down from the end of the hallway, draped in white and almost glowing from the light of the hall's dim bulb. At first Ashley was sure she was seeing some ghostly apparition, she was stunned into immobilization, frozen, rooted to the very spot were she was certain she would die, but, as the figure came closer she realized it was human, and old. It was Elizabeth Briar. The woman had not seen her so Ashley quickly backed back into the stairway and peeked out as the old woman quietly slipped into apartment 3A. What was that she was wearing? At first Ashley had thought it a nightgown, but upon closer inspection it looked like some kind of formal robe. Crazy old woman. And where was she coming from at that end of the hall? It had to have either been the attic or Cross' apartment. But what would she be doing in either? Ashley waited another minute, made sure that the woman didn't return, and crept from her hiding place. She skulked slowly down the hallway, careful of loose floorboards, she felt she was getting good at determining where they lay when she stepped on one and it groaned sorely under her weight. She stopped, waited, and when nothing happened crept the rest of the way to the Briar sister's door.

"Is everything prepared?" the mysterious Lilly's voice asked.

"Yes, dear sister, everything's ready, as it should be," Elizabeth replied.

What in the world were they talking about? She waited, heard nothing else and started down the hall, only, she passed her own apartment for the moment, she wanted to know what two elderly old ladies were doing 'preparing' stuff at two o'clock in the morning. She looked now, to the dark deep recesses of the attic's stairway and then to Cross' apartment, it's big brass 3C boldly, proudly marking the territory. Ashley was going to one or the other; she knew that and she had made her mind up already. She chose the apartment. It was the closest and, even though she told herself that this wasn't the reason, the less scary of the two. Walking over she tried the knob, just as she had suspected, locked. Fumbling around in her purse for a moment she produced her old Atlanta driver's license. She had done this trick twice before actually, back when she was in college and some of the girls wanted to sneak in the Dean's office for a practical joke, it worked best on old doors like this one. She shuddered as she thought; of course we got caught back in college too. Ashley slid the card hard and fast down the crevice of the door between it and the doorjamb,

Vacant Spaces

pushing at the door with her free hand. She felt it slide past the latch and the door swung open. Still got it kiddo, she thought slipping inside.

The apartment was completely bare. Apparently Cross' parents had already sent the movers to empty the place out, must have been sometime while Ashley was gone. That's when Ashley remembered the secret closet, and the now missing journal that was once in it. If Cross really was murdered, if it really was fowl play, might she try to leave a clue or something in the closet? Without hesitation she crossed over to the wall panel were she remembered the bookshelf used to sit. Kneeling down she tried to recall how Cross had opened it. Ashley ran her hands along the surface, pressed in at the corners, but nothing. Then, while sliding her hand on the outer edges of the panel's carved molding she felt the tiniest little knob and pressed it, the secret door clicked and swung open. Ashley was about to peer in when suddenly, from out in the hallway, she heard the faint sounds of footsteps treading lightly over the floors. Her heart began to pound as a loose board creaked. Was it Elizabeth returning, or someone worse? There was nowhere to hide in the tiny room, certainly not the bathroom it was too obvious. As the footsteps came to just outside of Cross' door, Ashley quickly slid into the tiny closet and pulled the door shut. God she hoped she could open it from the inside. The space was tight and cramped. It was full of dust and Ashley could feel her nose tingling. She raised a finger to it to ward off a sneeze. Cobwebs stuck to her hair and she was deathly afraid that a spider or some other hairy creepy-crawler would scurry up her arm, onto her face and into her open mouth. She quickly clamped her lips shut at the thought. Light played at the cracks around the closet door's edges and if she pressed her eye close enough she could see out into the apartment. She watched with heavy breathing as someone entered the room. A tall figure, a man, that she could tell for sure but she couldn't see his face, only his legs. Her heart pounded away in her chest as he stepped into the room. He was walking right towards her. My God did he know she was in here? Her eyes were open wide in terror as the shaft of light that played across her watching pupil caused it to dilate. The man was coming for her, almost to her now and she was just about to scream when he stopped, stood in front of the hidden closet for a moment. Ashley held her breath, waited and then he turned once, scanning the room, and walked back to the open front door. Ashley caught only a glimpse of the back of his head as he exited the room, closing the door behind him, and although she couldn't be sure, she thought for a moment that it was Thomas. But he said he was staying at the hospital with Mrs. Winthrop. Maybe he'd come home, maybe she wasn't alone in this God-awful brownstone after all. Ashley waited another moment before moving. Sure that if she left the safety of the tiny hidden space that the door would swing back open, that a knife wielding intruder would grab her and slice her throat open like a melon. She shook the horrible thoughts from her mind. She had to get out of here, out of this apartment, out of the whole damn brownstone. Something just wasn't right here and she could feel that.

She moved slightly, her left foot tingled with thousands of pins and needles pricking it. Her hand brushed up against something heavy and solid on the dusty floor. She felt for it, picked it up and held it in the shaft of light. A book. Not the journal, no this was thicker, heavier. Ashley was sure it wasn't here before, that the closet had been empty when Cross had taken out the journal. Quickly now Ashley felt along the edges of the closet's door, found another knob and the door swung open. She stood up from the cramped quarters, body aching and stiff, and walked to the front door, clutching the heavy book to her chest. Cautiously she unlocked it, turned the knob and creviced the door open only the slightest little bit. Her eye peered out into the empty hallway and she thought about how she probably looked liked Lilly Briar with her peering eye. Ashley tried to peer into the dark shadows of the attic stairwell but the blackness was thick there and if it held a waiting intruder then it hid them well. Without another seconds thought she quickly moved from the room and with cat like motion slipped past the clutching night claws of the attic opening and to the safety of her apartment door. It wasn't locked. Was her mother still here after all? Surely she would have the sense to lock the door behind her. Ashley took a deep breath, clutched the book tighter to her chest and swung the door open. The apartment appeared still, undisturbed. The table light burned beside the couch, the room looked warm and inviting, but in its shadows and under the comfortable facade, Ashley knew evil secrets lay. She checked the kitchen first, then her and Austin's bedrooms and closets, all the while expecting hands to come out from behind the rows of clothes and grab at her waiting neck. Nothing though. By the time she reached the bathroom she was trembling, not only from fear but also from the bundle of nerves that had knotted up her muscles and tensed her posture. She really was a nervous wreck. Her heart hadn't stopped pounding since she saw Elizabeth's ghostly stroll down the hallway. Her head was light and she felt unsteady on her feet. Ashley clicked on the bathroom light, her own reflection in the mirror made her jump. On the sink was the tiny gold cross her mother had fished out of the toilet, Abigail's cross. The one Mrs. Winthrop claimed Austin must have taken and flushed. In Ashley's mind, images of the dead girl in the pictures Dan had showed her flashed. Was it the same Abigail; was she a friend of Susan's? And how would Ashley find out? Then it dawned on her. Susan's phone bill, she had never gotten a chance to look at it, Cross' cell phone had started ringing and she left it lying on the sofa. Book still in hand she raced for the living room. Unless Abigail lived out of town and Susan called her, her number wouldn't be listed on the phone bill, but somebody's would. Ashley lay the heavy book on the coffee table and began searching in the cushions of the sofa. Nothing. Her mother had slept here; perhaps she had found it and placed the mail somewhere. Ashley began checking around the room, on the fireplace mantle, in drawers and on tables but found nothing. Missing, just like the journal. But she still had this book. She picked the thick paged book up and ran her hand over its black cover. There were no markings on the front or back and only a bookstore's i.d. number sticker on the spine. Ashley bent over and replaced the couch cushions, her back still aching from being crouched down in the tiny space of the closet. She

Vacant Spaces

flopped down onto the sofa with the book. "Now," she said out loud, "Let's see what was so important about you that Cross needed to hide you." She opened the cover of the book and her eyes grew wide as she read the title of the first page. The brownstone's evil and dark secrets were finally seeping out into the light.

CHAPTER TWENTY-ONE

She wanted to tell herself that it couldn't be true, that what she was seeing wasn't real, but here it was right in front of her, on paper and in black and white. In undeniable and bold print the first page of the book read: Love for Lucifer. "How to Worship Satan in the Twenty First Century" by Thomas Robinson. Ashley could only stare at those black words on white paper. The title itself was so utterly ridiculous that Ashley thought maybe it was a joke, but as she scanned the books inner pages she realized with devastating horror that there was nothing funny about this man. The book talked of dark rights of passage and human sacrifice, of bringing Satan as the head of a new world order and that those solely responsible for paving his rebirth on earth would be rewarded with power and eternal youth. It was disgusting and sick. How could this be the same Thomas that she knew, so soft and gentle-spoken? It was at this thought that she turned to an entire chapter devoted to the demon, Azreal. A photograph showed the same statue that sat in Thomas' curio cabinet. No, there was no mistake, Ashley knew this now, and suspicion that he may have been the one to lure Cross and herself here to the brownstone began to dawn upon her. She checked the index of the book and found a chapter on possession and quickly flipped to it. Of course, it was all making some horrible sense that Ashley couldn't quiet comprehend yet. He wanted her

Vacant Spaces

here because she had been possessed at one time and so had Cross. Her thoughts were broken by a noise coming from the back of the apartment. Ashley jumped and listened as she heard it again, coming from Austin's room, but she had checked there, she had checked everywhere in the apartment. Not behind the shower curtain, her mind told her, not under the beds. Slowly Ashley closed the thick covers of the book and laid it on the sofa as she rose from the couch and looked down the hallway. The sound had stopped now but she had to check, had to be sure she was alone. Walking down the hall, her shadow stretched out enormously large in front of her, like a dark decoy of no substance, one who could not be hurt by the thing or things that were creeping around the brownstone tonight unlike herself, who was only made up of flesh and blood. God how she wished she hadn't thought of the word blood right now. As she approached Austin's bedroom she saw that the door was still open a crack, a sliver of light framing the darkness, piercing her shadow decoy, so it could be hurt after all, she thought. Ashley peered inside the tiny crevice of an opening, saw nothing and swung the door open all the way. From inside the room and behind the door hands came at her suddenly, striking her with a closed fist between the eyes. Ashley saw a brilliant flash of light and nothing else as another heavy and closed fist pounded at the base of her skull. A deep and agonizing pain shot first through her head and then her body as she fell to the cold floor and slipped into unconsciousness.

CHAPTER TWENTY-TWO

In the darkness Ashley could hear heavy breathing, the sound of a drill, the snap of a pad lock. She heard footsteps and then slipped from agonizing present to terrifying past. She was in her parent's house, in her old bed. She was laughing and clawing at Susan's face, she was speaking in a language that was foreign to her and Susan was slapping her over and over screaming for her to snap out of it. Then came the voice, speaking directly to her friend, in English, a voice that was old and sounded like the rustling of autumn leaves caught in a wind, or the crisp pages of an old book being shuffled, it said, "Get on your knees and worship me, I am the beginning of the end, the break in a cycle of centuries of rule by your weak god. Bow to me now and I shall let you live when my time for rebirth is at hand, bow to me now and your parents shall be spared their suffering and have eternal bliss at my side."

She could see Susan shaking her head, backing away from the bed and crying, Ashley could see her out of eyes that were her own but somehow foreign. "You worship a false prophet," the voice continued and behind it was the faint sound of a thousand screams. "Jesus was only a man, Mary was never a virgin, it was all a lie."

Susan crossed herself and kissed her rosary, screamed for Ashley to stop as the voice began to bellow and laugh, "I am Azreal, I am the beginning and the end. We are many for we are legion. Praise Daemonicus Praise Daemonicus Praise Daemonicus." And the laughter, that horrible evil laughter that dripped with rot and all that was unholy ring in the air like bells, spewed from out of the demon's mouth, out of her mouth, and Ashley woke up and realized she was laughing now, in the brownstone. Quickly the grin left her though, as the scrutinizing pain sent sharp waves of agony jolting throughout her body. The room was pitch black and for the longest time she just lay there, not sure if her eyes were open or if she was still unconscious. Finally she tried to rise, the pain in her head was too much though and she dropped back to the floor. It was Thomas. He was behind all of this, he was crazy, believed that he could use her to get to the demon Azreal because she was once possessed by him. At least that was the conclusion she had came to as she lay there in pain. And as her mind began to slip out of consciousness again, she was comforted only by the shadows and the fact that she knew her mother and Austin were safe.

Loretta Malone had screamed and screamed until her throat was raw and bloody. The blood had all rushed to her head hours and hours ago and veins were bulging out and her eyes were swollen and red. She was hanging upside down in a dank and mildewed room. Her ankles bound so tight that the rope cut into her and broke the skin. Loretta's arms had gone numb a long time ago from dangling in this position. Someone had hit her, beat her over and over again and then she woke here. A dim bulb hanging on a wire was her only source of light. She opened her mouth, tried to scream again, coughed and choked on blood. She heard footsteps then and she began to panic. Loretta knew it wasn't help coming, she could tell it was the man who grabbed her, she could tell because he was whispering to her now, from the other side of the door. "Little pig, little pig, let me in," he whispered in that God-awful voice of his. The door open and a hand snaked in and hit the light switch casting the room into darkness. Loretta could see his silhouette as he stood in the doorway, his front shadowed by the light from behind him. She saw a large knife in his left hand and felt tears running from her eyes and up her forehead, getting caught in the tangles of her hair. The dark man came to her, gave her naked body a push and she swung from side to side. Her fake fingernails scraped against the cold concrete floor. He leaned down low to her ear and whispered, "Don't cry little piggy, it won't hurt…much." She heard scraping and her eyes rolled up far in her head so she could see the floor swaying under her, he had slid a silver saucer under her. She had seen and heard horrors that were demonic and not of this world before, and she knew now that that evil had come back for her, for her daughter. The voice whispered again and it stunk of dried blood. "Do you know why you're hanging upside down?" it asked, hot and wet in her ear. "Because it makes all the blood drain to your head." And with that he slid the blade of his knife across her throat and Loretta felt a sudden cold sensation at her neck as blood met air. She clawed and swayed and gurgled there for two minutes trying to catch her escaping breath, as blood ran from her open throat to her chin, in her eyes, soaking her hair. The man laughed over and over as Loretta Malone's life drained out and dripped into the tiny silver saucer below. Drip…Drip…Drip…

CHAPTER TWENTY-THREE

One singular beam of sunlight streamed in from the thin part in the curtains, a bright ray of light that cut through the darkness as though it were a solid thing and came to rest across Ashley Malone's eyes, as though heaven itself were calling for her to wake. Her eyes fluttered open and her hand shot up shielding her face from the blinding light. It was morning, or probably late afternoon, she thought, judging from the position of the sun outside. She rose slowly, cautious of the pain that still throbbed at the base of her skull. She was sure that she had a concussion. The blows had come down hard and her vision was still a little blurred, still she could stand now and she did so shakily, feeling as though her knees could give way at any moment. Ashley leaned against the wall, taking a moment to try and regain her strength as well as her senses. Someone really pounded her good. Thomas, she was sure of it. The man was crazy, devil worship, human sacrifice. Poor Mrs. Winthrop, she was so taken with the man, she was even more duped than Ashley herself had been. And Ashley had blamed the old lady, suspected her of all of this, when in actuality, Thomas was more than likely responsible for Cross' death. Ashley raised a hand to her head, it hurt to think and her eyes were growing heavy, she couldn't pass out though, she had to get out of here, she had to warn Mrs. Winthrop, and the others. Slowly, swaying

Vacant Spaces

a little and with her hand pressed against the wall for support Ashley moved to the door. She jerked on the knob. Nothing. She tried again, pulling harder and causing the throbbing in her skull to intensify and still the door wouldn't budge. From the recesses of her mind she vaguely recalled the drilling noises and her heart began to race as she realized that she had been locked in. Quickly now, the pain replaced with a panic that was beginning to crescendo into fear, Ashley went to the window unlatching it she pulled upward. Damn it all to hell, she thought as she saw that it was nailed shut. She was three stories up and this side of the brownstone faced nothing but the garden below, no street, no neighbors, she was trapped. Her eyes darted about the room. She needed a weapon. There were only two reasons to lock her up here, one, to keep her from telling anyone what she'd found out, and two, to kill her. The thought stuck in her mind as a lump formed in the back of her throat, someone would find her. Her mother would be worried when she didn't call this morning and…come to the brownstone to find her. Ashley flung herself at the door again. She had to get out of this God forsaken room. She pulled and pounded until the pain filled her head and tears streamed down her face. She slumped against the door sobbing, slid down to the floor and buried her face in her hands. How could she have been so stupid as to come out to this place, to be fooled so easily? Her whole life, since she was nineteen, had been ruled over by that dark and evil secret that her mind had repressed and it was still haunting her, after all this time, had even brought her here, in the midst of this crazed mad man. How had he known about the possession, and

Cross'? Probably the same way Dan found out, she thought. Dan. Kind, sweet Dan. He's the one she should have trusted all along. She stared now, for a long time at the walls, past the walls, thinking about Austin and her mother, Dan, her life. Outside the sun stayed on a steady course, sinking farther down and losing it's luster as it went. The wood polish on the dark paneled walls was so thick that Ashley could sit and stare and watch her own blurred reflection, a darker version of herself. Then a thought struck her, how had Austin gotten into the attic that night when the front door was locked and how had an intruder hidden from her when she had checked every room in the apartment? Unless. She was crawling across the floor on her knees now, going to the closest wall panel. She let her hands glide over it's edges, nothing. She went to the next one. If there was a secret closet in Cross' apartment then there just might be…her heart raced as she felt a familiar tiny knob. She turned it and the panel made a clicking sound and slowly swung outward. Ashley almost laughed out loud as she looked into the small doorway. Inside was a narrow space, just tall enough for a person to stand, and a set of old rickety stairs leading up to darkness…to the attic. So I'm not crazy, Ashley thought to herself. This is how Austin got up to the attic that night. Then a shiver ran down her spine as she recalled the missing journal. My God, someone could have been coming and going into her apartment anytime they liked, while they slept, they could have killed her, and her son. Poor Susan, she thought, and realized now that her friend probably was dead, and that Thomas had been the one who killed her.

Vacant Spaces

Without hesitation Ashley crawled into the opening and stood. The smell of mildew and rot met her nostrils but she didn't mind, it smelled good for once, it smelled like freedom. Her only fear was that the attic door may still be pad locked, still, there was a chance, and there may even be more secret ways out. She closed the tiny, hidden door behind her and moved for the stairs. They looked ancient and as though they may give way at any moment but they held steady under her weight, not even a creak, she thanked God for that. The darkness was so total and complete that she had to take it slow, feet being sure not to stumble on the steep incline, testing every board for support. How many times had Austin sneaked out through this passage? Mrs. Winthrop still thought that he was the one that had been involved in Cross' death, just wait until she found out it was Thomas instead. Holding her hand out in front of her now she felt a solid barrier fumbled and found a knob, a regular door, that was a relief. Cautiously she turned the metal knob, it gave a small squeak and she inched the door open only a little. She could see the portal windows pouring in the last of the day's light but nothing else. She listened, hearing nothing she opened the door the rest of the way and stepped into the attic. Ashley's jaw dropped at what she saw before her.

The clutter that she had fallen into in the darkness was gone now, replaced by a long black altar covered in black satin, candles unlit, decorated it, along with seven large silver goblets. The statue of Azreal that had once sat in Thomas' apartment now sat in the center of the altar, in front of it was a silver saucer. Ashley took two cautious steps closer and saw that it was filled with what looked like blood. Over her head the sound of thunder quaked as if giving her an omen to leave but she couldn't, she was glued to the scene. To the left of the altar was a table, bare wood and a large silver dagger with intricate designs lay atop of it. Human sacrifice, Ashley gulped. But, dominating the room, in it's very center was a single, simple wooded chair. A large pentagram, unlike one that Ashley had ever seen before was drawn around it, strange symbols and objects placed neatly and painstakingly at certain points, and the chair at its very center. That chair was the most horrific sight that Ashley had ever seen and filled her with terror and she didn't know why. She wanted to move, to get out of this room of the damned but she felt as though a force greater than herself was holding her here, immobilizing her, rooting her to the spot of her destruction. The statue of the demon seemed to be staring at her, Ashley's eyes were locked to it, it seemed to waiver, to pulsate with life as though it were breathing. It must be my head, she thought, the concussion. Then a smell filled her nostrils, acrid and familiar, the smell of sulfur and brimstone, an image flashed in her mind, her face in a mirror, tied to a bed, a priest on top of her, Susan crying and again she was in the past. Susan was standing before the bed, head in hands, sobbing for Ashley to snap out of it. Suddenly the rope that had been binding her hands loosened of it's own accord, her hand was free, Ashley, the demon placed it on Susan's head, stroked her hair, Susan gasped, looked up into the face of Azreal.

A clap of thunder brought Ashley back to the present. Rain had begun to beat at the slate roof and there was water dripping into the attic, landing just in

Vacant Spaces

front of the pentagram drawn on the floor. Ashley moved now, quickly, the floor groaning and buckling a little under her weight and she realized that it wasn't very sturdy, she would have to be careful, and she laughed to herself. Her life, her soul was in mortal danger and she was worried about the floor. Ashley went to the table, snatched up the dagger and clutched it tightly in her sweaty and clammy fist. She moved to the door, stepping around the large puddle of water that was beginning to form. Ashley gave the door a hard push, expecting it not to budge but, to her surprise, it opened with ease. She stepped out of the room, glad to see the attic stairwell for once. More thunder roared over her head, causing her to jump and look back. Lightening flashed through the portal windows, filling the attic with an electric blue hue, casting the alter, chair and pentagram in an unearthly, pulsating glow. Ashley shuddered, left the attic without closing the door behind her.

The hallways seemed to be closing in on her, mocking her and watching with secret eyes, she made it to the stairway and descended to the second floor's hallway. From here she could see Thomas' door. But surely Mrs. Winthrop was home from the hospital, she was supposed to be released this morning and it was already dark outside. Thomas wouldn't dare try anything with other people around…unless, he had already went off the deep end, that unholy set up in the attic told Ashley that something was about to go down, and all she knew was that she had to warn Mrs. Winthrop and then get to her own mother and son and get the hell out of this city.

Ashley took a deep breath and began walking in great strides, ready to run at the first sign of an attack. She didn't care that her shoes were making noise on the floorboards; she simply clutched the shiny silver dagger firmer, held it in front of her. She passed the priest's door. Shouldn't she warn him, and the Briar sisters? No, better to get to Mrs. Winthrop's, use the phone and call the police. Ashley slowed now as she reached Thomas' door, facing it, her back to the wall and using the knife as a shield, she slid past and darted for the stairway. Her heart was pounding faster now, she had made it, she kept thinking as she clambered down the stairs and went to apartment A1. She rapped on it loudly, so hard that her knuckles hurt and the door came open slightly. Oh no, she thought, this wasn't good, she had seen this sort of thing in the movies and it was never good. She pushed the door open the rest of the way, knife darting to the right, the left. The living room seemed to be in order. Ashley stuck her head in, "Mrs. Winthrop," she called and only silence answered. Outside the front entrance rain was battering the ground, the storm had grown more fierce. Please be all right, Mrs. Winthrop, please, Ashley kept thinking as she stepped into the living room, crossed over to the kitchen and flipped on the light. The room was calm. Ashley moved on to the hallway. She knew she should use the telephone and call the police, every fiber in her body told her this but she had to make sure, she owed it to Harriet Winthrop to see that the old woman wasn't tied up and being tortured. The hallway had three doors, the first of which Ashley knew was the bathroom, she cautiously opened it's door, empty. So far so good, she tried to

Vacant Spaces

calm herself, took deep and slow, deliberate breaths. The dagger trembled in her hands and images of the past began to flash in her mind. The demon's voice, the headaches, Susan crying out for Ashley, for her parents. Ashley closed her eyes, gripped them shut tightly. Not now, she told herself, not now. The memories her mind had repressed were trying to come back in full force and they didn't care when or how. She stood there a moment longer, the throbbing pain at the base of her skull seemed to be spreading, like icy cold fingers gripping her head and squeezing, but the memories had seemed to pass for the moment and Ashley moved toward the next door.

With her hand on the knob she had a sudden and horrible feeling of foreboding, as if whatever were on the other side of this door could be nothing but death and evil. She took a deep breath, readied herself, and readied the dagger she carried, pushed the door open, and was greeted by a hundred books.

CHAPTER TWENTY-FOUR

The books were stacked high, in spiraling mountains of pages, covering the small office space, covering tabletops and floor. The missing books from the living room, Ashley thought to herself. She really had just tidied up. Along the far wall of the room was a desk that was not covered with the books, only papers…and a telephone. Do it now, something told her, don't wait. Call the police. She crossed quickly over to the desk, lay the dagger down and was about to pick up the receiver when she saw a typed note lying on the desk's top. It read: Harriet, all the preparations have been made, meet me upstairs. Thomas. Ashley stared at the note, saw something familiar, he typed it on his type writer, only, all the 'A's' had there tops cut off, like the brown manila envelope Ashley had received back in Atlanta, the damned envelope that had brought her to this house of evil in the first place. It really was true, Thomas had tricked her here, he had been the one who sent the fake article on Susan. There was no time to wait, Ashley picked up the phone, punched in 911 and held the receiver to her ear, her breathing was heavy, she could hear her own heart thumping rapidly in her chest as she waited for the ring on the other end of the line. Her eyes scanned the desk, darted nervously and paused at a drawer that was partially open. Inside she saw something beaded. Pulling the drawer open further she reached inside and pulled out her rosary. Her missing rosary, it had been here all along, in Mrs. Winthrop's apartment. Did the old lady know that it was hers, or that it was even missing? Ashley remembered then the first day she and Austin had come here, Mrs. Winthrop had commented on it, why had she not given it back to Ashley when she'd found it, unless...she had been the one who took it. And then something else in the drawer, Ashley shook her head in disbelief...the missing journal and the phone bill, it was all here, in Mrs. Winthrop's office drawer, like a bizarre lost and found containing only things that belonged to her. But why the phone bill, so she couldn't trace any of Susan's calls? It was then that Ashley realized the phone's receiver was still held up to her ear and that it was never going to ring, the line was dead. She slammed her finger down on the button, trying to get a dial tone to no avail. A sinking feeling was forming in the bottom of her stomach, it felt as though her intestines were tied in knots. She had a feeling she had made a horrible mistake coming to apartment A1, trusting Harriet Winthrop, and as she thought this she began to read the titles of the books that lay about her, surrounding her. 'The Science of Evil', 'Worship of the Dark Forces', 'Satan's New Army', 'Dark Circle'. They went on and on, funny titles for romance novels, Ashley thought to herself and was amazed at how calm she was now, how she was able to make a joke at a time like this. Perhaps it was the concussion, or maybe it was that she had already accepted the fact that she wasn't going to get out of this brownstone alive.

Quickly taking the phone bill from the drawer Ashley saw that it had all ready been opened, she took out the bill, unfolded it and stared wide eyed at what she saw. Susan Bishop's name wasn't at the head of the bill, nowhere on the bill for that matter. No, apartment 3B's phone bill was made out to Abigail Reynolds.

"I guess there's no secrets to keep anymore, is there dear?"

Ashley spun on her heels and saw Mrs. Winthrop stepping into the room. Behind her a six foot four mammoth filled the doorway, weighing all of three hundred and fifty pounds and Ashley's mind remembered the dark figure that had loomed above her the first time she had went into the attic. Mrs. Winthrop smiled, like the demon who had just ate the canary. She beamed at Ashley then looked over her shoulder at the hulking giant eclipsing the hall's light. "I don't think you two have met, Ashley, this is Topples, say hello Topples."

The human mass only grunted and Ashley's throat went suddenly dry as she said, "Susan Bishop never lived here at all, did she? It was just all a lie to get me here."

Harriet Winthrop just rolled her eyes, "Boy, can't pull one over on you, can we?" The sarcasm ran thick in her voice. "No, Susan never lived here; you really don't remember anything do you? At first we all thought this playing dumb, repressed memories thing was an act, but you really are in the dark aren't you dear? And that mother of yours, lying to you all those years, she was more help to us than she could ever know."

Vacant Spaces

The old woman's voice was no longer sweet and friendly, it was tainted with mockery and disgust for the young woman that stood before her.

"I thought you were our friend," Ashley remarked. The calmness was beginning to be replaced with fear now and she was looking for an escape route but the only exit was being blocked by Topples' hulking figure.

Mrs. Winthrop smiled as she came a little closer, looking a little more like the sweet old lady that had rented Ashley the place. "To answer your questions, no, Susan Bishop never lived in this place. The apartment you live in was occupied by a woman named Abigail Reynolds, a real bitch, hateful to everyone,"

So that was why Cross had said Ashley's friend was a bitch, she was talking about Abigail, not Susan.

"Still, she had been chosen by the demon Azreal as a host at one time in her life and the rules of the coven go that anyone possessed by him must be offered initiation into our group, just like Cross and the Briar sisters and Father Jerod. Only poor Abigail and Cross were not interested apparently, so they were disposed of before they could expose us. You should have seen the look on poor Cross' face—" Mrs. Winthrop said, pausing for a moment to smile, then, "When I threw her out the third floor window!"

Ashley was trembling now, they were all a part of it, every one of them, she had moved her and her son into a cult and didn't even know it. "Even the priest?" she spit the words at the old woman and got a chuckle back.

"My dear, you really must get your memory back, you've met our dear Father Jerod once before, when you were privileged to be host to the all mighty Azreal." The old woman laughed even harder at the dumbfounded look on Ashley's face.

The movie reel of the past rolled in Ashley's mind again and she looked through foreign eyes as the priest raped her and then climbed off, whistling that silly tune, 'hey diddle diddle, the cat and the fiddle, the cow jumped over the moon,' and he dressed in his black suit, white collar. Then the movie reel sped up, flashed forward and Susan was in the room and the demon was telling her to bow down and save her parents. That was when Susan came over to the bed and started slapping the demon, Slapping Ashley, calling for her friend to come back, calling for Ashley as she dropped in exhaustion beside the bed, buried her face in the mattress and Ashley remembers her hand, free from the bed post, as if the ropes had untied themselves, and her hand stroking Susan's hair, and Susan looking up, shocked, into the eyes of her lifelong friend, into the eyes of the demon Azreal.

"Oh, look Topples, she's starting to remember, isn't that cute?" The old woman's voice broke the memories and the past shattered like glass revealing the present. Ashley was shaking her head, looking at the two evil fiends that stood before her.

The old woman's eyes shifted to the antique rosary that now lay on the desk's top.

"Oh I see you found my rosary," she smiled and enjoyed the look of bewilderment on Ashley's face. "It belonged to a nun, the first human sacrifice I had ever made. When your father joined our cult we desecrated it with blood and unholy spells, making it an object of great power...evil power."

Her father, had she said her father?

As if the old woman had read her mind she said, "Yes dear, your father was one of us. He craved wealth and power and you were his sacrifice to Azreal, a vessel to host the demon. The moment he gave you the rosary you were initiated, being prepared to receive Azreal inside of you. It was your Father who talked your Mother into allowing Father Jerod into your house, to perform a supposed exorcism. Instead he fathered your son. Your poor Mother never knew anything, she wouldn't have understood, she wasn't devil worship material, if you will." Harriet Winthrop's smile grew wider as she spoke, as she saw the blood drain from Ashley's face and leave a ghostly after image in it's wake. "Your poor Mother had no idea that her husband worshipped the dark Gods. But he did it all for her, and you. It was through him we found out everything we needed to know about Susan Bishop. And it was through him we kept track of you all of these years, watching you, waiting for exactly the right moment, the right time when the seeds of our efforts would be ready to bear fruit. Your Father would have had everything he'd dreamed of had he lived long enough to see this great moment, he would have had life eternal, all because of you."

"You're lying," Ashley cried and wiped a tear from her cheek.

"No Ashley, I'm not. Your father was a great man, he loved you very much. He wanted you to join us one day. When he gave you that rosary it was his way of showing that he loved you, that we all loved you.

What your father gave you was a great gift, and it's not too late to accept it."

"I won't join your cult, I won't!" She screamed at them. "My body is my own now! I won't be your-your vessel for demonic possession." And even as the words came out of her mouth they sounded ridiculous.

Harriet Winthrop laughed and laughed, then she actually had to wipe tears from her eyes she was laughing so hard. Whatever she had found comical stopped as quickly as it had began and she gave Ashley such a cold glare that the young woman felt a shiver. "You still don't get it do you?" The old woman snarled, "it's not you that we want, it's the boy!"

Ashley backed away, felt as if the words had struck her physically. The room seemed to be spinning, closing in on her. She just kept shaking her head no. No, they couldn't have her son, not Austin!

Mrs. Winthrop went on talking, inching closer and closer to Ashley. "He has no soul, he was born of demon and man, to be the permanent host for Azreal, reborn in flesh to rule the earth as the antichrist, to bring about the destruction of God's power." Then a smirk. "You are only a sacrifice."

It was Ashley who laughed now and said, "Your too late, Austin isn't even here, I sent him and my mother away, you'll never find them."

Harriet Winthrop shook her head sadly, as if the sight she saw before her was pitiful, pathetic even. "Oh, I'm sorry to have to tell you this dear, but your mother never made it out...alive, and we have the boy already, preparing him for the ritual."

No, it wasn't true. This old bitch was lying. Her mother and son were safe and faraway from here, her

Vacant Spaces

mother was alive, she was. Ashley tried to back away from the old woman who was so close that she could smell her. She bumped into the desk, hands behind her for support and felt her fingers brush across the cold metal handle of the dagger. Grabbing it in a sweaty palm, a flash of anger came over her and she screamed, raising the dagger in the air and lurching at Harriet Winthrop with the last of her strength. The old woman's eyes grew wide at the surprise attack and she brought her hands up to protect herself but it was too late, Ashley had buried the dagger deep into Harriet Winthrop's left shoulder, missing her expected target of the old lady's neck.

Mrs. Winthrop screamed out in pain, a horrid wail that sounded more like an animal caught in a trap than a human. She pulled the dagger out as Ashley stepped back, feeling as though she had just made a grave mistake. The look on the woman's face spoke of murder as she curled her lips in a snarl. "Topples, take her upstairs!" She demanded producing the hidden handkerchief from her sleeve to stop the profuse bleeding that flowed freely now from the pulsing wound. Topples moved to Ashley, grabbed her hard by the arm and when the young woman fought him and screamed he smacked her hard across the face. A flash of blinding pain filled Ashley's eyes and a ringing in her ears pursued as the side of her face where the blow had landed throbbed and stung. Suddenly she was losing consciousness, being thrust into darkness and was sure she would never wake up again, at least not in this world. And as she slipped away she prayed, "Please God, save my son from these monsters," only she must have been praying out loud because the last thing she heard was Mrs. Winthrop's evil laughter ringing in the air.

CHAPTER TWENTY-FIVE

The rain had lessened from huge, battering bullet sized drops to a fine mist of drizzle by the time Dan Phillips finished the last sentence of his article. He glanced at his watch, damn it was nine now, Ashley would think he stood her up. He hit the send button and e-mailed the article to his editor's computer and, with a swift cat like motion, bounced from the chair and grabbed his jacket from the back of it at the same time, tunneling first one arm through a sleeve and then another. He had to hurry, he didn't want to blow this chance with the woman, he really cared for her, more than he realized at first, he felt as if she needed protected from something…life…a real live killer? He didn't know for sure, all he did know was that he wanted to be the one to shield her from harms way. He clicked off the lights as he left the office, glancing out the window one last time to see the weather, it was going to be hell getting there, traffic was always grid locked after a storm like the one that had just passed. He bolted out of the outer office and into the harsh fluorescent light of the building's hallway. The elevator's doors were just closing and he made a last minute dash to stop them but was too late. Damn, it's going to be one of those nights were nothing goes right, he thought as he fingered the ground floor button impatiently over and over.

Ashley Malone woke at the very moment she felt rope burn into her wrists. Opening her eyes she stared in horror as Mrs. Winthrop and Topples stood on either side of her, binding her wrist to the bare table that she had seen in the attic. Slowly her senses came around and she realized that she was indeed in the attic, and atop the sacrificing table! They tightened the ropes, Topples' side much tighter than the old woman's, so tight in fact that it was cutting off Ashley's circulation to her right hand, the hand swelling red with the blood trapped in the veins. The two moved away from her and Ashley's eyes grew wide in horror at what she saw. All the candles on the altar had been lit. The Briar sisters were there, one in a wheelchair, apparently the mysterious Lillian, both were dressed in black robes, as were Mrs. Winthrop and Topples. They were forming a half circle around the strange looking pentagram, around the wooden chair that sat in its center, and they were praying in a language that Ashley didn't understand but she knew they were evil prayers, prayers for dark things that people thought only existed in children's shadows, but Ashley knew they were real, she had been one of the dark things once. Her view of the chair was blocked by the black robed backs of the worshippers she had lived among until Topples swayed and she saw...saw with unbelieving horror at what they were praying for...praying to...it was Austin. He sat in the chair in the center of the devil's mark and stared at the four people as if he were in a trance.

"NO!" Ashley began to scream over and over again. "Austin," she pleaded with the boy, "Run, baby. Get out of here!"

Still, if he heard her he made no notice, just stared straight ahead, arms dangling loosely at his sides. Instead it was Mrs. Winthrop who came over to the young girl.

"You won't be screaming for much longer," she mused and pulled the dagger from underneath the folds of her robe, placing it carefully on the edge of the table, near Ashley's throat. "You should be honored really," Harriet Winthrop said, as she tucked strands of hair behind Ashley's ears, almost lovingly. The girl jerked her head away, not wanting this monster to touch her. "Remember the story I told you about the family who use to live here, in the brownstone? The one whose daughter was the original host of the devil child? Well that girl was me. I lost the baby and the only way I could prove my worth to Azreal was by sacrificing my parents. So you see, it is the utmost honor that was bestowed upon you."

Ashley snarled at the woman. "You're all sick, you need help."

Mrs. Winthrop giggled at that, as if she were a jeering schoolgirl. "With all due respect dear," she replied, walking around the table. "It looks like you're the one who needs help. I mean it is you who's tied to a table."

Ashley looked now at her son. He looked so pale, so helpless.

"We've been preparing him," the old lady told her. "Every time you left him in my care we have showed him the dark ways, getting his soulless vessel ready for his host."

"He's not soulless!" Ashley screamed at her, twisting her wrists in the ropes, trying in desperation to get free, twisting so hard that the stiff and course ropes burned deeper into her, breaking the skin and drawing blood. Mrs. Winthrop saw the crimson liqiud at the edges of the ropes, the candle's low glow reflecting off of it. Ashley watched in horror as the old woman licked her lips, then she screamed in sheer terror as Harriet Winthrop dived down and began licking the blood off, sucking at the Ashley's injury. Tears stung at Ashley's eyes as she shut them tightly and shook her head from side to side. No, this isn't happening, she cried softly as she felt the old woman's tongue snake across her skin, her wrinkled lips suckling at the life force that was seeping from Ashley's opened flesh, lapping up the blood as if it were milk. When she had finished, Mrs. Winthrop rose, smiled down at the girl, blood rested at the corners of her red lips. "Tastes sweet," she said.

Suddenly there were footsteps on the stairs leading to the attic. At first Ashley thought that it may be help coming, that maybe someone was coming to save her, to save Austin, but her hopes were dashed quickly as a black robe with white collar came into vision, and then a face. A familiar face of an unholy priest that she had seen in her nightmares a thousand times.

The man smiled at her, came close and leaned in to her face. He inhaled deeply through his nostrils taking in the scent of her and then he spoke, "I've missed you so much since the last time we saw one another." His voice was rough but somehow soothing and his breath smelled of dried blood; she had smelled his breath on her before. The night he raped an innocent teenage girl possessed by an evil not of this world. Then there was another voice in the room, coming from the doorway

Vacant Spaces

of the attic, a hoarsely whispered voice that dripped wet with evil.

"Little pig, little pig, let me in," the voice whispered.

Ashley's heart beat even faster and she thought she was about to hyperventilate, but she caught her breath and held it as the priest moved and her vision was unobscured. Thomas Robinson stood in the doorway of the attic...with murder on his mind.

Dan sat in traffic, drumming his fingers on the steering wheel. He had been right; traffic was at a stand still. He glanced at his watch for the fifth time in ten minutes. Maybe he should just forget about it, go home, it was too late to do anything tonight. He released the pressure from the brake peddle as traffic inched forward a bit. The Buick in front of him flared it's blood red brake lights again and Dan stomped at his own brakes bringing the car to a stop with a jerk. Damn, pay attention, he thought and looked at his watch. It was late, but still, he didn't want to stand Ashley up, he felt the need to be the one person in her life that didn't disappoint her or let her down. That's what he kept telling himself anyway, but the whole truth was he had this nagging feeling in his gut all night that something just wasn't right. He couldn't quiet put his finger on it, just that Ashley may need him. He chuckled to himself as traffic crawled forward again, he was being silly, Ashley was probably safe and sound in the brownstone right now, surrounded by family and neighbors.

"You should feel very honored, Ashley." Thomas was smiling down at her, his eyes sparkled from the light of the candles that were now ablaze at the altar surrounding the statue of Azreal. That smile, and those eyes that she had once found so charming and comforting had lost all of their kindness. There was coldness behind them now, a hollowed out indifferance for human suffering, an evil that she hadn't recognized before, but now it blazed in her mind like the hot yellow glow of the candles wick and she would never forget it. Thomas touched her cheek and she turned her head, saw Austin sitting trance-like in the chair in the center of the strange pentagram, saw the others all dressed in their black flowing robes circling him, saw the silver goblet of blood being readied. What had she gotten them in to, what had her Father gotten them into?

Thomas picked up the dagger, ran a finger along the edge of its long silver blade.

"Let me explain to you what's going to happen." He waited for Ashley to look at him and when she didn't he circled the table and knelt down to face her. He was so close she could smell toothpaste on his breath. My God, she thought, they take the time to brush their teeth before they call forth demons!

Thomas smiled again and spoke softly. "When the ceremony begins we will call forth the demon Azreal, the moment he appears to us we will kill you, offering your soul to his world in exchange for his presence here. You see there must be a sacrifice made at that precise moment, otherwise the demon will leave and, well, let's just say he will be pissed, and we would be punished with the most vile deaths. But I digress,

Vacant Spaces

anyway he will then possess the boy's body and the reign of the antichrist will begin. And all of us shall be rewarded with wealth and power and life eternal. It's what your father always wanted, always craved. Could he have lived just a few more years he would never have had to worry about death or illness, we all will be immortal, like Gods," then he chuckled and added, "or devils." The bastard was still smiling, as though he were talking about everyday events.

"You're crazy!" Ashley screamed at him causing the others to look. "You're all crazy, you actually believe this is going to work don't you? Don't you!" She yelled looking at each of them. They looked bewildered, as though she spoke a foreign language. Then she turned her icy cold glare back at Thomas and in a low and calm voice said to him, "You're all going to burn in hell for this."

At that the man chuckled, "Now you're beginning to come around to our way of thinking."

Ashley spit at the man but missed and the spittle just rolled down her own chin instead. Her head was throbbing again, she could feel the blood rushing through it and was sure she could hear it too, the sound like the rushing of water filled her ears and a numbing pain pounded at her temples. Her concussion threatened to snuff her into unconsciousness and she thought that that might be better than all of this. Maybe she would wake up in a better place than this world, and then she looked at Austin and thought no, she had to stay awake.

Thomas stood now and laying the dagger down close to Ashley's head clapped his hands. "It's time to begin the ceremony."

Ashley could see Austin past the shuffling figures in black robes and tears welled up in her eyes. "Wake up baby, please." She said lowly and then closed her eyes as the tears caressed her cheeks with warm, salty comfort, mingling with the spit still on her chin. "Please, please, please God…"

CHAPTER TWENTY-SIX

Chanting filled the old plank walls of the attic, bounced around and amplified by the acoustics of the room. The strange, monotonous words filled Ashley's throbbing head with gibberish as Thomas stood above her, head tilted up, eyes closed and the dagger raised above his head, steadied and ready to plunge into Ashley's blood soaked heart.

She had lost sight of Austin. After the group had passed the silver goblet around drinking from it, they swore their soul to Azreal with lips colored in blood. They then formed a circle around the boy and the chants had begun. Now the strange words pounded away at Ashley's skull, mingled with the throbbing pain, causing her vision to blur. The concussion she knew she had was more serious than she'd thought, not that it mattered now. As Thomas' chants grew louder, Ashley twisted her wrist, tugging at it, trying to free it from the ropes on the side Harriet had tied, they were much looser than Topples knots and she thought she may be able to free herself. Latin and Hebrew were spoken like poetry as blood seeped from her rope burned flesh. Ashley gritted her teeth to keep from crying out in pain. The blood was acting as a lubricant and she could feel her hand slide a little, just a little, but just not enough.

Suddenly the gibberish turned to English.

"Azreal we call upon you to show yourself and take possession of this pure and untainted vessel. We offer you this sacrifice. We spill our blood and praise all that is dark." Thomas shouted now, then more gibberish.

Darkness was creeping in at the edges of Ashley's vision. No, not now, she told herself. I can't pass out now, and she tugged harder at her wrist. Was it just her or had the room grown suddenly cold? Freezing cold actually. The temperature must have dropped at least thirty degrees in a matter of seconds. Ashley could see her breath coming out in fogged gasps in front of her face.

"We summon you now, Azreal, to this realm!" Thomas yelled as the others chanted. Ashley's head jerked as the candles' flames shot up in a blaze ridiculously high. She blinked her eyes, tried to clear her vision. The small stone statue of the demon seemed to be pulsating, almost as though it were breathing. A wavy haze was beginning to form in front of it, like heat rising from hot pavement. Thomas was yelling chants now and the others were moving in the circle, eyes closed, around and around. At every break in the bodies Ashley could see Austin. He was looking at her, yes, like the autistic trance he was in was broken. With a new found strength she pulled at her wrist, all the time keeping an eye on Austin and the strange haze that had now turned into a swirling mist.

"Appear to us, we beseech you, take your sacrifice and your place upon the world." Thomas yelled and raised the dagger higher.

The mist grew thicker as an image seemed to appear in it's swirling center. My God, this was really happening, she thought in terror. These fools were really doing it.

"Appear to us!"

Ashley could see a huge torso and broad shoulders through the fog. Huge outlines of wings spread out from the figure's arched back.

"Show yourself to us!"

She could make out a dusting of course fur and a neckline.

"We command you in the name of Satan!"

Two heavy thuds and Ashley saw cloven hooves the size of her head hit the weak hardwood floors that groaned under the new weight.

"Come to us now Azreal!!!"

And then out of the mist she saw two red, glowing eyes and a face...the face of an evil so indescribable that it burned itself into her mind like a permanent after image!

Ashley screamed at the grotesque thing in the swirling mist and she pulled her hand so hard she felt a ripping pain as flesh tore away, caught in the ropes as her bloody hand slid free.

"Oh great Azreal we offer this humble sacrifice to you now!'

And then Ashley saw it, as if in slow motion, as she struggled to get her other hand free the dagger was coming down at her. Quickly, with one hand still tied, she rolled off the table and the dagger buried itself into splintered wood. Ashley cried out in pain as she hit the floor and her arm twisted behind her still bound at the wrist.

Thomas opened his eyes in confusion and a look of horror came across his face as he looked into the mist and then to Ashley. "You will die tonight!" He cried and pulled the blade from the tabletop. Desperately Ashley twisted and fumbled at the knots in the ropes with her free hand. Thomas was standing above her once again, the dagger raised over his head taking aim like a horrible instant replay. So this was it, she thought, this is how she would die. It would end here in an old attic among these insane, sadistic people.

Then a stranger's voice cried out, "MOMMY!"

Ashley turned in disbelief and saw Austin fling himself from the wooden chair, it toppled over and hit the altar, upsetting the candles, causing them to roll to the floor. The boy broke through the circle of startled black robed figures and thrust his body into Thomas' midsection. The man let out a groan and both he and Austin tumbled to the floor. The dagger slid across the hardwood stopping to rest just at Ashley's side. She watched, as the image in the mist seemed to fade a bit and let out a wail.

Then another scream filled the attic as one of the fallen candles' flame caught on Lillian Briars black robe. The old fabric ignited into flames as though it were doused with gasoline and the woman's wheelchair began to roll across the uneven attic floor as if it had a mind of it's own. Ashley watched in horror at the flaming chair of death. Lillian's screams filled the small attic space like the smoke from the fire, she sounded like a dying animal caught in a trap. Suddenly Elizabeth threw herself at the flaming chair, desperately trying to put out the flames that were already out of control and save her sister.

But the fire was hungry and soon she too was going up in flames. The smell of burnt flesh was filling the room as fast as the smoke was and Ashley turned her head away as she saw Elizabeth's hair begin to melt. Desperately she tried for the dagger but it was just out of reach, her fingers dangled, barely touching the cold blade of the knife. Then Thomas was on his feet. He watched the two flaming women flailing and crying for mercy and then saw the demon in the mist let out a howl of pain as it faded away, the mist mingling with the smoke until there was nothing left of the unearthly creature. Thomas turned to Ashley, his face red and crazed and the look in his eyes was almost as terrifying as the monsters.

"You did this!" He screamed at her and then he was on top of her, his big hands fixed around her neck, squeezing with all his strength. Ashley couldn't breathe, her bloody hand clawed at the man's face but he persisted in his efforts. She could feel the trapped blood in her head swell up in her veins until she felt like a balloon that was about to burst. Darkness crept in around her vision until Thomas' face was all she could see. It was filled with so much hate, so much anger. Then there was silence as the sounds of the attic, the crackling fire, the agonizing screams, all died away, replaced with the sounds of her own rapid heartbeat. Then it to began to slow and fade. She felt detached from the situation. She could see her hands flailing in front of her, clawing at the man with both her hands, the other hand was free now too, although she didn't know how. Then as Thomas' face melded into the darkness and the sound of her heart beat stilled the pressure was released, Thomas' face and all the sounds of the attic came rushing back at her as she gasped in air. Her lungs ached as they filled and she saw that Thomas had the strangest look on his face. That was when she noticed the long silver blade of the dagger protruding out the front of his throat. Blood gushed from a pierced vein and squirted into her eyes. Thomas' hands fell away from her and his limp body slid off of the blade and slumped across Ashley. She pushed him away, his blood covering her and she saw Austin. He was just standing there, still holding the dagger with both hands looking at Thomas' body. Staring down at the man he had just killed.

"Oh baby, come here." Ashley said in a hoarse voice and grabbed the boy, hugged him, heard the dagger fall to the floor and then felt her son's arms around her. "I love you Austin." She cried into his shoulder. Suddenly she was aware of their surroundings. Most of the attic was up in flames now and the smoke was rolling out in thick clouds of gray. We have to get out of here, she thought, but flames blocked the door. Her mind raced, the veil of fogginess lifting and she remembered the secret closet that led to her apartment, that side of the attic was clear. Ashley stood quickly and had to hold the wooden sacrifice table as her head swam and the room began to spin. Smoke filled her lungs and she coughed uncontrollably, trying desperately not to breathe in. Out of the thick, gray-black clouds of smoke someone emerged, coming at Ashley with incredible speed. Before Ashley could react, Harriet Winthrop pounced on her, knocking her to the floor. The old woman clawed at her eyes and neck. Ashley saw quick flashes of fake fingernails and large jeweled knuckles as the woman kept up the attack, finally slapping Ashley hard across the face, causing her ears to ring. "You did

Vacant Spaces

this!" The old woman kept screaming at her over and over. Ashley tried to shield herself from more blows as the crazed woman kept striking at her. Fingernails ripped into the flesh at Ashley's neck. Finally, regaining her senses, Ashley grabbed at the woman's shoulders, struggling to gain control. With incredible strength Harriet stood, picking Ashley up off the floor and throwing the younger woman hard against the far wall of the attic. Ashley could not regain her balance as she hurdled backward toward one of the large, round portal windows. She felt her head hit hard against the sill of the window and then her back hit the old waved glass. Ashley could hear a crack form in it like thin ice on a frozen pond. She reached out quickly trying to grab hold of the window's sill so that she wouldn't be thrown through the glass and out the window to the ground four stories below. The image of Cross' crumpled and twisted body raced through her mind as she grabbed with bloody hands and steadied herself. Her head had hit the sill hard and Ashley was sure she was about to pass out. Putting her hand out for support she stood in front of the cracked glass on wobbly legs. If she could only break the glass she could cry for help. The entire attic was ablaze now, the smoke so thick it was hard to see and Ashley couldn't breathe without inhaling a lung full of the deadly black clouds. She had to break the window with something, but what? Then, against a backdrop of smoldering flames, Ashley watched in horror as Harriet Winthrop emerged, running at her, determined to finish what they had started.

By the time Dan Phillips pulled his car to the curb in front of 311 Beech Street the rain had died down to a thin drizzle of mist. As he hopped from his car he stretched out his cramped muscles, what a drive. He hoped Ashley wouldn't be too upset. He began to walk up the concrete walkway towards the porch when he sniffed. Was something burning? Just then the sound of shattering glass mingled with the last of the distant thunder and as Dan looked up he had just enough time to shield his face with his arms as a hailstorm of deadly shards of glass rained down on him.

Watching in disbelief, his jaw dropped open as a body fell from the fourth story window of the brownstone. The person's arms flailed about, trying to catch air in what appeared to be a feeble and failed attempt at flying. And then it was as if time had sped up in fast motion as the falling body landed with a dull thud in front of his feet. Dan's first thought was Ashley, but then he saw the auburn hair and the wrinkled face underneath the blood. The woman's head lay still on the concrete for a few seconds, then it shuddered and a stream of red liquid and gray brain matter ran from beneath it, hitting the sole of Dan's shoes. He just stood there for a moment, stunned, shocked, and then he looked up and saw the billowing smoke escaping from the attic, spiraling high into the night sky.

"Ashley!" He screamed and then he flew past the body and up the steps of the majestic burning building. Dan pulled hard at the knobs on the heavy wooden doors and cursed when he found them locked.

Vacant Spaces

Stepping back a few paces he steadied himself and then rammed his shoulder into the solid old wood. He heard a cracking sound but it came from his arm instead of the doors and he grabbed it in pain. Damn, damn, damn! All the windows on the first story had bars on them. Maybe the back of the house. He was off the porch before he had even finished the thought.

All the windows were covered in bars on the side and the back of the house but then Dan noticed a basement window, half above and half underground, almost hidden from view by shrubbery. The glass had been blacked out by paint from the inside and it was only a small opening but he thought he might be able to fit through. As he began to kick the glass out he dialed 911 on his cell phone. He told the operator the address and told her to send an ambulance and a fire truck then pushed the off button as the dispatcher tried to urge him to stay on the line. He had to get to Ashley. He lowered his legs into the broken window first and slid in freely until it came to his waist. He pushed and struggled cursing himself for not going on a diet like he had been planning. Finally with one good push he slid through and felt a shard of glass he had missed in the sill rip into the flesh of his stomach. He cried out in pain as he dropped to the dark attic floor five feet below. He lay there for a moment. His hand found the wound; it was bleeding and felt pretty deep. Then Dan felt something dripping onto his face, something warm. He stood, still holding his wounded side and felt for a light chain, found it and as light flooded the room Dan Phillips screamed in horror at the butchered body of Loretta Malone hanging upside down from the ceiling.

CHAPTER TWENTY-SEVEN

"My God, she's dead!" The thought kept repeating itself over and over in Ashley's mind. One minute Harriet Winthrop was coming at Ashley gripping the dagger in her hand and Ashley had, at the last minute, moved away from the window and gave Harriet Winthrop a shove and the next thing she knew the old woman had stumbled under the defensive move and fell into the glass. Ashley could still see Harriet trying in desperation for something to grab hold of and then the cracked glass was shattering and the old woman was just gone.

Her thoughts were suddenly broken by Austin's scream. Topples snatched the boy up from the floor and held him under one arm. Behind the mass of human flesh Ashley could see Father Jerod coughing and crawling about on the floor, trying in vain to dodge the flames that now lapped at the hem of his robe. Looking around Ashley saw that the fire had spread blocking even the secret door. The only way out was the window and no one could survive a jump like that, they were trapped! Topples was heading right for her now, Austin scratching and biting at the huge man's arm, but if the hulking mass felt it the boys teeth digging into his flesh he showed no signs of it, it was probably like an insect's bite to him. Topples looked as though he was in some sort of trance, his face frozen in anger. Then Ashley realized in horror what he was

Vacant Spaces

about to do, he was going to throw Austin out the window!

Without thinking she ran to the middle of the attic and leapt at the man, he smacked her hard and she went flailing to the attic's floor. In an instant she was back on her feet and clawing at the beast of a man. Water was falling on her face and she realized they were standing under the leak in the attic's roof. The three of them looked down at the same time as the attic floor groaned under the immense weight and the rotted floorboards began to give way. There was a terrible sound as though the house itself were crying out in pain and then nothing under their feet. It all happened so quickly, Ashley heard breaking crystal, felt her body hit the floor below the attic. Splintered planks of floorboarding and ceiling rained down around her as she hit the floor below with a loud thud! She lay there on her back for a moment, the wind knocked out of her, above was a huge gaping hole and pieces of flaming wood fell threateningly close. Smoke was following them down and she realized that they had fallen into her apartment. Quickly she tried to move, was able to stand but only on one foot, she was sure the other ankle was broken.

"Austin," she cried, looking about. Topples lay unmoving, blood was splattered across his face and body, fragments of the chandelier covered him in glittering crystal, sparkling like diamonds, reflecting the fire that ravaged the house on the floor above them. Then past the large man she saw Austin's arm. Ashley stepped over Topples and touched her son's back. He lay unmoving but she felt the steady rhythmic motion of his breathing. Thank God the large tub of lard had not landed on her son, he would have been crushed. Ashley tried to wake her son but he didn't budge. Already the room was filling with smoke and the burning wood that had followed them down was igniting a new fire. Unsteadily she picked up her son, he felt so thin and fragile. With great effort she limped past Topples and toward the door. What was left of the ceiling above them was groaning and sagging precariously. Ashley fumbled for the door's latch and swung it open to the fresh air in the hallway. Groaning came from behind her but this time it was human, she turned in terror to see Topples large mass rising, shaking off glass crystal that clinked to the floor. He was dazed and confused but when he regained his senses she would never be able to out run him, not carrying Austin and with a broken ankle. She limped out into the hallway just as Topples made eye contact with her, he grinned a rotten toothed grin and then, looked up in confusion as the ceiling came falling down on him, burying him in mounds of flames and lumber. Ashley limped for the stairs as fast as she could, Topples screams dying in the background. She was almost to the landing, but how would she ever make it down two flights of stairs?

"Ashley?" A voice was calling from below, Dan's voice.

"Dan, we're up here!" She cried as she held her son close to her body. Thank God, she thought, As Dan came rushing up into the hallway. Outside, the wails of sirens became louder. Dan took the stairs two at a time, came to her, hugged her and the boy, holding

Vacant Spaces

them close. Ashley saw the blood on his face and stomach.

"You're hurt."

He smiled weakly at her, "I'm okay, can you make it down the stairs?" He asked.

"I don't know."

"Here," he held out his arms to take Austin. For a moment she hesitated, she had almost lost her son once to people she trusted, but then she nodded and let the man take the boy. Austin opened his eyes then.

"Mommy," he said weakly.

She hadn't imagined it, he had spoken, he had, and it was the most beautiful sound Ashley Malone had ever heard.

The three of them left the brownstone that night, the top of the house eaten up in flames. As men in uniforms helped them out and off the front porch strange sounds were heard amidst the crackling and popping of the burning embers, but Ashley never looked back. Nor did she look at the sheet-covered body that lay on the concrete walkway, blood already staining through its crisp hospital whiteness as they walked passed. Even when she heard the flapping of huge wings above and the gasps from the shocked firemen as they exclaimed they thought they saw something in the smoke fly from the attic, even then she didn't look back. She was so tired of looking back. From now on Ashley Malone was only looking forward, into the future…

Mark Andrew Ware

EPILOGUE

Flight 247 from New York to California left the runway at 8:14 on a clear and crisp Saturday morning. Ashley and Dan sat nearest the aisle, holding hands tightly. Austin had the window seat and was watching as the plane lifted and the ground began to drop away. He turned to look at his mother with a wide smile. Ashley smiled back. "I love you, kiddo." She said and ruffled his hair.

"I love you too, Mom." He said slowly, avoiding the stutter that attached itself to most of his words, then turned his attention back out the window. He had been going to speech therapy classes for three months now, the doctors were the ones who were speechless now. They kept trying to look for events that could have triggered this new breakthrough, but Ashley didn't care how or why, all she knew is that she had her son, talking or not she would always love him.

As the plane leveled out she eased back into her seat, her stomach was doing flip-flops already.

Dan squeezed her hand. "Hey, you okay?"

Ashley nodded.

"And you're sure your ready for this move?"

At that she laughed. "It's a little late now, we're all ready on the plane."

"It's never too late, I just want you to be sure this is what you want. That this is what's best for you and Austin."

She gave his hand a squeeze back and smiled. "I am sure. You are what's best for us."

And with that she leaned in and gave him a kiss. After her mother's funeral and all the police questions were satisfied, she and Dan had begun to date seriously. After his breaking story of the identity of the midnight killer he was offered a job on network television as their star reporter in California. He told Ashley he was going to accept the offer on one condition, that she and Austin would go with him and after they were settled she would marry him. Ashley thought about this proposal for about a whole second before she threw her arms around his neck, smothered him with kisses and said yes.

Now life was perfect. Almost. She still had nightmares at night about the brownstone. About Mrs. Winthrop and the priest, about the possession and the events that had transpired in the attic of that God forsaken house. And about Thomas Robinson. The police identified Thomas as the midnight killer. His DNA matched that found in the mouth of his last victim, well the last victim other than her…mother.

They estimate that he and the other residents of the brownstone were responsible for about twenty known murders in the past decade, and who knows how many unknown murders. They had found bones in a secret room in the basement that had yet to be identified. Once all the remains had been recovered what was left of the burnt and blistered old brownstone had been torn down.

Dan being the down to earth one in their relationship listened in quiet horror to the events that had taken place in the attic that night. Throughout the

Vacant Spaces

whole horrifying spill he did not say a word, but when Ashley had finished he tried to explain away the supernatural events with earthly reason. Oh he believed every word, that the residents of the brownstone had been a devilish cult, worshipping demons, he knew all to well of their deadly intent. But the pulsating statue, the demonic force that had materialized in that attic room, all of that he said, were probably hallucinations caused by the severe concussion she had suffered. Ashley noted that he said 'probably'. Maybe there was a little superstition in him after all.

Ashley still had flashes of her possession too, horrible images and memories that she was trying to work through. She closed her eyes as the past shuffled like pages from an old picture book through her mind. Dark images of the priest on top of her, and the cold and calculating voice of the demon that used her mouth to throat it's evil commands. Just thinking about them brought the memories back in quick, surreal flashes.

Dan was squeezing her hand again. She looked at him and forced a smile.

"I know you don't like to discuss the brownstone in front of Austin," he said in a hushed voice. "But I just wanted to let you know I'm sorry we never found out what happened to Susan. The police still have the remains they found in the basement, though. A lot of them have yet to be identified."

The words hit Ashley hard and she had to close her eyes as memories invaded her. Again the movie reel of her diabolical past began to play in her mind. "Bow down to me and I will be merciful to your parents in hell." The demon was saying to Susan. Then Susan was slapping her hard across the face over and over. Ashley's hands were bound to the bedpost and the demon laughed. Susan dropped to the side of the bed, crying she buried her face in her arms. "Snap out of it Ashley, please," she was sobbing. And suddenly Ashley's hands were free and Susan looked up as she felt Ashley caress her hair.

Susan Bishop looked up, her eyes brimming with tears like two oval pools. She had such beautiful eyes, and they stared now, not at Ashley, but into the eyes of Azreal.

"It's okay," the demon soothed her, cooed her like a crying child using Ashley's voice. "Everything's okay now." Then the demon had Ashley's hands around Susan's throat, squeezing. Susan looked at her friend confused for a moment, and as the air was cut off from her lungs she began struggling and clawing at Ashley's hands. The demon just smiled, looking out through Ashley's eyes as Susan Bishop's life faded away like a vapor mist burned up by the morning sun. Azreal felt the energy leave the mass of flesh and bone and blood and pretty blonde hair until the only thing that was left was just dead weight and it let the body slump to the floor, lifeless.

Then the memories fast forwarded to her father entering the room, rolling Susan's body in a sheet in the dead of night and dragging it out, the whole time he kept repeating: "Praise Azreal…Praise Azreal…Praise Azreal…"

Ashley opened her eyes, back in the present, back on flight 247, tears were streaming down her cheeks as the turbulence bounced her around.

Vacant Spaces

"Hey," Dan said, undoing his seatbelt and turning toward her. "It's okay, Ash." That's the nickname he had given her after the fire. "We can keep looking, Susan could still be alive, it's possible."

Ashley just shook her head. She had never told anyone about the fact that Mrs. Winthrop had admitted Susan never lived at the brownstone, or that her father was part of the cult, or about these memories of Susan's death, Susan's murder.

"No," she said looking at him, forcing a smile. "The past is dead and buried, let's leave it that way." And with that she leaned back in her seat, closed her eyes with her father's voice still ringing in her ears..." Praise Azreal...Praise Azreal...Praise Azreal..."

Mark Andrew Ware

ABOUT THE AUTHOR

Mark Ware was born in the small southern town of Dalton, Georgia where, as a child, he developed a love for things that lurked in the dark. Now residing in Chattanooga, Tennessee, he implements southern folklore and urban legends into the deep-rooted religious beliefs of the region to create unique tales of the supernatural.

Printed in the United States
822400001B